ANNA NEMZER

PRISONER

TRANSLATED BY RONAN QUINN

AD VERBUM

Published with the support of the Institute
for Literary Translation, Russia

PRISONER

by Anna Nemzer

Translated by Ronan Quinn

Book created by Max Mendor

Plen (Prisoner), originally published in Russian by AST, Moscow, Elena Shubina imprint, as *"Плен"* in 2013.

Glagoslav Publications Ltd
88-90 Hatton Garden
EC1N 8PN London
United Kingdom

www.glagoslav.com

ISBN: 978-1-78437-974-2

Contents

PART ONE

Order no 227

On Tuesday they were to execute an Uzbek deserter but the soldiers refused to shoot. In truth, they had refused so that nobody else would, but each one was hoping that he would be the last to shoot, and that no one would notice his simulation. And the same for all eighteen people. The order and then silence. The Divisional Commander pretended that nothing had happened! Once more the order! And again silence. (In actual fact, such things happen. Strange but there was nothing too odd.) They would all stand at twenty paces and watch. But this unhappy Uzbek began by burying his head in some birch tree, begging God and the birch tree, he didn't find any other tree. But when no one shot the second time, he rushed off and escaped. Then some bolt turns in the soldier's head, and if he hasn't already shot at close range, he stops the fugitive, the traitor. At any price! Catch and disarm! Therefore when the Uzbek ran off, the shots themselves began to thunder without an order. And the Divisional Commander again reacted as if nothing had happened. Well the same for the others.

This was on Tuesday, but on Wednesday a telegram arrived for Gelik, which woke him at sunrise: 'Come quickly, Father is very ill. Alexandra.'

And a load off his mind. What fine fellows, how good!

He ran at once to the headquarters, without washing, or brushing his hair, nothing. He put on his belt, while running as the sweet phrases of the rapport were going around in his head: 'Due to . . . allow me to submit . . .' only he didn't know there, what to attribute it to finally, since he hadn't been home for two years, from the very start. And he decided for the time being not to write, not to rely heavy on pity, but simply to explain the situation in the most business-like tone.

He wrote it. Handed it in.

'Smooth your hair! Good! Lieutenant, cunt . . . Gaer!'

He stood to attention: 'Yes, sir!'

'Go fuck yourself!'

This one was from the intelligentsia, he swore with emphasis and with the polite 'you.'

Returning is also like flying. The morning is so murky and dreary, it's only six o'clock, but you can't lie down and finish sleeping any more, although you have a chill from lack of sleep and aching gums (due to the wisdom tooth cutting painfully for the fifth day), and as if all of this wasn't tough and murky enough, like the tooth ache, through a milky curtain the wretched sunshine breaks, and only worse it's blinding. But! The telegram warms.

The whole of the previous half year with Alka went more or less regularly, although it was a painful correspondence indeed. She didn't understand an-yth-ing! and Father didn't understand. But Gelik quietly carried on. Finally, something would suddenly begin to get through to them, but then, they would also get another anecdote. He was not able to tell them the exact place of his sojourn, but simply by way of an experiment, in order to train them, he wrote: 'Now I'm? . . . Do you remember these books, that I left you on my table before my departure? Work it out by the name of the author.' He left a little collection of the poems of Bely and the 'Little Housewife of the Big House.' So they didn't seem to know about the existence of the little town of Bely and in total seriousness, the saintly people, they decided that he had been sent on a secret mission to London.

Later, out of the blue, Alya wrote: 'These days brought me unpleasantness. Now I'm about to make a big decision. I can't write in detail, but try to understand: they are proposing to work with Nadya, Katya, Vera and Dora . . .'

He jumped up suddenly, can you imagine, what an intelligent girl! And only a moment later he was taken aback, oh the poor girl! What would she do? But after a couple of letters, the phrase flashed up: 'Vera and Dora are not worried at the moment.' Relief.

But he himself wrote every time: asking after Father, whether he is ill? I worry about you, about you, about you.

And there they understood, good people. Like three days ago still a cheerful, a shockingly cheerful letter arrived from father, with a little parcel and a postscript: 'My sunshine, acned Gelios! I wanted to send you chocolate, but Varvara Erofeeyevna said that you're well fed so instead I'm sending you tarragon.' They made themselves powerfully ill with laughter. 'Eat well!' and he himself laughed, but he was already irritated: well what are they there generally, do they think straight? 'I feel decent, as long as you, my sunshine, are healthy.'

In six months his efforts are killed by one phrase. Honesty, her mother.

But here suddenly a precious telegram.

. . . He had only just stretched out on the bed, he had fallen into a blissful dream, a short dream, contemplating every minute of his illegality and short life span and that is why he felt shamefully sweet. And they were already shouting over his ear, a violent, clumsy foul language: Polevoy!

He jumped! Present! Yes sir!

'I will kill you some day. You found time to snooze! Blockhead!'

Something happened either in our section or in theirs, but it was impossible to understand anything.

'Quickly! I will wait for him here!'

And they rushed to their section.

Running Gelik was finding out the details from Polevoy. Something was strange. Like the Divisional Commander Baev had drunk himself to hell. A mad Lieutenant just rushed in and, hiccuping, said that the Divisional Commander had locked himself in in his place and fired from foolishness without hitting anything. People! They started to force their way towards him, as he watched, suddenly opened the door and bang! Panchenko grabbed him. He shot him in the leg, the calf, the bone was not hurt, but what is it, Mummy?!! Panchenko was in the infirmary, the surgeon looked at him and took him by the head; but Baev dug himself in, three fighters gathered under the little window, the ones he could get hold of and he was allowed to shout orders from the little window. And what do you order the fighters to do? The fighters, the cretins, obey, and he cursed benevolently some nonsense of the sea-ding dong: surveying compass! Protractor! And if someone isn't listening to him, he fires straight at that person, the bitch! And he shouts: 'squadron, shoot! Bottoms up!'

(But here are brackets, because the artillery team . . . I know from childhood, what an artillery team is. I know in particular that there is no such thing as 'squadron, shoot!'

Before the weapon produces a shot, shells should be enclosed in it, hence the team should be given the option of a shell; next there should be some fire: active, the platoon or of the whole battery, continuous or with intervals, and then most important is how the barrel of the weapon should be inclined towards the horizon (such as a protractor) and how the barrel should be turned relatively to the sides of the light (such as a compass).

Around this time, while Gelik found himself near Bely, another friend of Grandmother's, Seryozha O, was fighting in the Ukraine. The heaviest operation took place, and from out of nowhere journalists from 'Pravda' appeared.

'Coverage from the scene of the action, comrade Senior Lieutenant,' exclaimed one of them, loyally looking Seryozha in the eye. 'Literally from the thick of it, comrade Senior Lieutenant!'

It brought them difficulties. But not just that.

'This is what we wanted to ask you, comrade Senior Lieutenant! Today is a holiday, the birthday of our great writer, Maxim Gorky! We couldn't, well, dedicate the operation to him?'

'What?'

'Well, I mean this, comrade Senior Lieutenant! You in the detachment should mark this important date for all of us! Something like: 'Forward! For our Gorky! Well, something like that, comrade Senior Lieutenant! So that our fighters are inspired in heroic deeds in the name of our great writer!'

He touched his temple with his finger and said: lads come out of there.

And they kind of went.

After a couple of days he suddenly noticed that the older officers were looking at him strangely somehow, looking and laughing. He put up with it for a while, but then he couldn't contain himself and went to find out what the problem was.

'How about it,' one of them answered laughing. 'We read about you in 'Pravda.' 'Battles on the front lines!' The fearless Senior Lieutenant O, breaking his voice, shouted at his soldiers:

'With the riff-raff brothers! For our Gorky! For the heart of Danko! For your mother and your motherland, shoot!' Well there is still more there too . . .'

And Seryozha remembered this little article for a long time, it was worth his while to play his part, the officers began to laugh: 'But Senior lieutenant O! This is for our Gorky!'

Well then. But Baev, entrenched at a pleasant distance, shouted something exactly in this manner, if it's not for Gorky, then it's certainly for the motherland, for Stalin, the squadron, fire, and such nonsensical, craziest co-ordinates; but these nitwits, under his window, in trousers of course, dutifully, like gophers, carry out all this nonsense: the gun fire settles for the second hour through the whole settlement, and the Divisional Commander does not come on the airwaves.

That is what Polevoy told Gelik, while they were running. Somewhere in the distance a chaffinch went into hysterics and the shots were heard throughout.

There were already a lot of people at the headquarters, all the top brass; and Polevoy played his part, of course: 'And there, sirs, is indeed our operation, from our fantastic efforts I would say,' the old regime scum bag. Gelik did not move an inch, he was at the apparatus at once and kept ringing.

And here he is lucky, the telephone operator pressed on the buzzer endlessly, and then something got through, visibly, and he picked up the receiver for Baev. The firing abated. There was interference down the line, then suddenly the fresh and sober voice of Baev bellowed:

'Well?!'

'Comrade Commander,' suddenly almost stuttering, Gelik began 'on the airwaves the on-duty watchman . . .'

'Oh its you, prick!' Baev handed Gelik the phone softly and with hatred. 'I need you. That's what, my chicken. And well tell your bosses there, that I will all of them, everyone of them, personally, do we understand, yes? Per-sona-lly! I will shake the sperm on the nose. Everyone. Have you written it? That's all, adieu, you little prick!' and he hurled the receiver, not at the arm but past it, and right there again is a mad howl: 'Forward, lads! For the motherland! For saintly patriotism! Don't piss around! Our whole management pisses around; the deserter scum!' And again shots ring out.

Gelik carefully put down the receiver. They were looking at him from all sides.

'Ehhhh . . . Well he's completely drunk,' he said carefully. 'And . . . Well yes. That. He has binged. Drunk.'

'We don't need your diagnosis,' the Chief-of-Staff gloomily announced. 'Tell us what he said.'

'He says . . .' Slowly hoping sharply, that the ceiling would collapse or something similar. 'He curses a lot . . . and this, personally.'

'Listen. Lieutenant!' Lavretsky let out a roar.

'Report accurately,' said Polevoy. 'What is at the start, what next . . .'

'At first . . . at first . . .' and understanding that he had nothing to lose, that's how he chatted with all the stupid girls: 'First he called me a prick!'

The officers neighed like stallions, and right here the second round of laughter struck like an echo under the window: there, the lads, it seems, were listening in.

And they could go to hell with all their Baevs! It was useless to even find out about the rapport, he only strained, waved his hands: what are you, he said, like one possessed, do you see what is happening in the world? We have a Divisional Commander in a white fever, the fighters are excited, up to you now? Well deal with it when there is time. Your Dad won't die, jeez.'

Such bastards. And the gums hurt even more from illness.

They announced that Baev had shot a pig in the yard, he injured Levchenko and Esenin and at lunch ran to the forest.

'I didn't want to worry you,' wrote Alya even earlier, 'but our affairs are not good. Dad is severely ill. If only you could come! As you see, I didn't annoy you at other times, but now the situation is very bad, and I hope that your top brass understands our extreme circumstances. My dear little one, ask, beg, insist. Despite everything I'm quiet, nothing but silence, do you remember? I'm on the move all the time and all the time there is 'silence' here and still the island of Madagascar . . . Oh what a terrible time, my little one.' She wrote theatrically and pompously, she just warned of course, she calculated completely correctly in this, but all the same he winced while re-reading, because where is this from? My dear little one, she had never called him that in her life, it was never the custom.

Sheets of paper lay around on the crumpled bunk, he began to write but discarded it. There were always a lot of drafts. When enough of them were gathered it was possible to collect them in a poetic collage. He composed such a poem, even before the war, and he became quite angry at Erlikh, who gave him a ticking off about non-coordination and sketchiness. Gelik noted the sketchiness from the threshold, it was not generally necessary to have an ear in order to blabber. All right, a variance, let it even be sloppiness, but there was such feeling in it, in these drafts, that there was sketchiness.

And there now again the start.

'I returned home upset,

I threw my hat and walking stick on the bed.'

And

'I go along stone marshlands.

It's dark. Nothing is fucking visible.'

Started and discarded. That somehow stretched desperately to prose, uncontrollably, and he feverishly wrote a wonderful passage, the intonation of a fairy novel with high Germanic notes, with Gothic traits and wonder, with a Hoffman-like little silver coffee pot and then a mystical awe should have erupted with thunder; there it was: Pani Angelina, a consumptive blush, a sudden and fantastical disease; a pale chrisolyte sky, the nectar of dog rose, mercury balls, he was hassled, she was a pani or a Frau and suddenly he cooled it all together.

And now again he looked with a heavy glance. There is no strength to compose, the gums are annoying him, all his passion had gone.

He collapsed on his bunk.

Perhaps he never wanted the dear doctor from the infirmary. There were none too few chicks around then, well as in war understanding of course, none too few, seven in the officer compound and the doctor the eighth. But she was, firstly, a lot older, thirty two, a joke perhaps! He knew well then that after thirty nothing more interests them. Secondly, the medic was decisive and capable, her terrifying hands were white, strong, had no fear of scalpel or needles, how could she manage it all? And more importantly she could do everything: pull a tooth, an injection, apply a plaster cast, cut out appendicitis just twice here; and everything so special from her doctor's spirit, a little carbolic acid and sea salt. He was afraid of doctors, like a little boy. It was understood that the doctor for him was a sexual object.

In the infirmary he ambled along because of the same damned gums. He decided firmly that to cut it would not be the answer, it needed an ointment or a mouthwash; if the doctor herself, known for her sudden temper, begins to get restive, he will complain about her to Polevoy.

He entered the office, an overpowering medical smell, a shameful fear, the inescapable, childish, good Lieutenant. He got up by the wall, behind the half see-through screen Inka fastened her belt, straightened her skirt and pulled on her boots. The doctor sat at the table and detachedly looked at some papers. Inka came out from behind the screen, so clumsily inept, dishevelled in a creased skirt, but in this case, yes, Gelik saw there was in it a certain chilly charm.

'I'm fed up with you, my girl,' the doctor said faintly, 'how fed up I am with you. With such a delay, as you have, indeed you're simply a cunt, that's what. You don't care about anything, you're considered lazy, I'm lazy to look after you. Eh, that's what. . . What are you looking at me for? What are you all looking at me for?' In truth she looked somewhat strange, smiling foolishly. 'How many times have I told you, it's all to no avail. On the whole, that is it, Inna. This is the last time, and after this do as you like.'

But this one still smiled her idiotic smile and did not leave and it would have been all right for her to dress in front of him, to fasten her skirt, that was at once so clear, what they did with her now and what they were yet to do, neither shame nor a conscience, not to show the gums to her or to gossip with her, that they don't permit them to be cut. Alka's recent Madagascar beat in the ears, it latched itself on to her but didn't keep up.

The doctor got up with difficulty, exited from behind the chair and stood up at the window, holding herself by the waist, and he somehow suddenly shot her a glance and at once understood that she was pregnant and in quite an advanced stage, but not as he had thought before, she was putting on weight. Everything left his head, that is what, the war all around, but there would only be the one thing for them.

'What did you want?' she asked in the same dull voice.

Either the wind raised up the curtain, or the frame slammed, or a vulgar detail came out, Gelik had already forgotten, but I can't get on without her, because - something should have foreseen Baev's appearance.

With a revolver but not drunk. In this there was also a fear that he was not drunk. There was no smell of fumes, his stride was even, his hand was firm and a firm sober madness in his eyes. Gelik suddenly remembered his own conversation of that morning, of a prick, the happy laughter of the lads, he recalled and screwed up his eyes, having remembered something suddenly and moved to the door, but it was already too late.

First Gelik tied Ina's hands. Then the doctor tied his hand. Baev didn't let the doctor go, but continued to keep one hand behind his shoulder. All this was indeed in the utmost silence, there were only four different intakes of breath: Inka's was private, greedy, the doctor's seemed as if suppressed, Baev's sniffling was like his, Gelik's, personal and normal, every gasp had a tinkling sound in his temples. The terror was outrageously unpleasant, shameful; the good Lieutenant who was taken hostage, and oh, shit, no.

'Baev, what do you want? A tribunal?' The doctor asked quietly.

'Silence,' Baev just as quietly and dryly called out. 'Better that you do it yourself . . . but you know that . . .'

And that was the worst, his sobriety. Also. He was more outrageous, disgusted and certain that none of them had made an effort. But it would seem, that he takes the chick by the shoulder, but what was Gelik himself to do with her? To rush forward, to scream, take the door by the shoulder, and let him do what he likes to this chick, even shoot, or kill. No. There was no opportunity of any kind to move.

'I will tell you, Tamar, what I want. I can tell you. I have to take leave due to a health condition but with limits. With that as with me, by and large it's not allowed to give weapons into the hand, because I say that I shot the leg off one female ass hole, did you hear? Well then. And the guys today eat to be healthy, I recommended to them that they have a little fun to make our Perm citizen cry, do you know our Perm man? Our dear Lieutenant, who tried all of you. 'Comraaaaade Divisional Commander!' Here Baev's face contorted terribly. 'You confuse!' Here Baev screamed wildly but then suddenly he stopped howling and began to guffaw. 'I got confused, did you hear? Nooo, little chicken! I don't fucking get mixed up! I'm for my homeland, I don't fucking confuse it with Stalin.' Here he stopped behaving like an idiot and again spoke quietly and carefully: 'I, Tamara, am for my homeland, for Stalin, whoever I want I can kill now because I'm dying to go into battle and not a single deserting scum stops me. Order or no order, it's all the same to us Tatars, it's single battle preparedness, but if I don't always dwell on this, but here I am suddenly, if you please, a storm warning, but I'm not fucking wanked off and the bullet isn't shelled, put simply I have shat, then what am I? A traitor to the homeland. So I will not wait for an order, I will fight do you know, like Pestel said: only ass holes and cowards want to write an encyclopaedia first and then to go into battle. I will fight not by word but by deed; but if I inadvertently finished someone in this case, then, so first there is no need to distract by pushing and secondly I placed him on the altar of the homeland. And Tamar, while we are on the subject, we have more internal enemies somewhere than foreign ones and if this twit of yours with the brush of command does not give battle; he is the worst bitch udder for me, worse than any Fritz, because he has sold himself to the Fritzes. For Martel. Which, I saw myself, he feasts in the morning with a chii . . . Well stop!' he shouted frantically.

Gelik moved and froze. The devil! How he only sees, indeed as if enthusiastically carrying on with his nonsense! But it meant only . . . only one movement . . . and right here he noticed, right here! But right here a wave, a shameless terror. Ohh, cu-nt.

'Bear in mind, you little bitch,' Baev pronounced with an even voice, swallowing, and in it most terrible of all were these momentary passages from the full likes of madness towards calmness and discretion. 'Don't make me nervous. I don't only shake the brain of this chick. I'm this minute, you don't manage to fart, I'll shoot you in the spine. And immediately in your little body. Then to you again, by the dotted line along the spine. Caviar, swept with fire by the dotted line, this is very unpleasant, you can believe me, you can ask your sidekick. I did this intricately from this morning, simply intricately. I won't perform on your spine any worse, but the spine by the dotted line, this, little chicken, is a bad story. Then only pray that you die straight away. So I say to you kindly, well you have understood. Well there, what did we stop at? I say, eat like animals in the mornings Martel with boar. And I, Tamar, so hate this deserting scum bag, that the hatred is boiling inside me,' here he suddenly winced, he made a laughable little face of a grieving old woman. 'and periodically flowing out, well there like today. Therefore you see yourself, the person's heavy situation, poisoned by war.'

The doctor somehow clumsily got going under his arm and he asked with care: what? She, wincing, answered: don't press on the stomach.

He of course did not remove the pistol, but he shifted his arm, grabbed, 'so are you comfortable? Yes.'

Inka didn't howl yet, she only whined from time to time complainingly and nastily and monstrously annoyed, because it was as if she translated on the surface the same sound, which itched in his very insides. And still Mad-agas-car, having pestered from the morning, but now he was already angry at him and, on the contrary, attempted to tune into the waves of Madagascar and not to the hysterical sobbing. But how the frenzied chaffinch of yesterday, ey-ey.

But Alka, Alka! Suddenly he thought with a terrifying despair, a terrible, unbearable one, that it's impossible to live. How is it possible that I will not see her any more? They, the poor fools, sent a telegram and perhaps they would have let him go to them, but he would have read poetry to them. To Alka and Dad, everything that he managed to write to them, this is it, 'soon whether the heart adds soundtracks with songs,' and a prosaic fragment about pani Margarita, so he couldn't decide, a frau or a pani, it would have had to be a frau, but somehow pani sounded better, and how she swallows the silvery balls of mercury. But now he is sitting on the floor in the white room, on the left is a sink, on the right a screen, and behind it the armchair on which was everything, whether you want an abortion or tooth decay; in the middle of the table, doughnuts were scattered from the bag; and there Baev holds the auntie in a white dressing gown, by the shoulders, the pregnant auntie, who always made him shiver with fear, but now he doesn't know any more what he's afraid of, afraid of Mad-agas-car, the island Mad-agas-car, but Baev with his free hand rakes the doughnuts and breaks and hurls a piece into his mouth. And there this doughnut finishes, to fall thus because of some kind of doughnut, and tango! Ooonce! Aaaaand once! Kum-pars-ita! Dou-ghn-ut pam pam pam! Literally he had already gone out of his mind. And he really wanted to sleep.

And when under the window a clatter had been heard and a multi-voiced agitated muttering, Baev smiled greedily, and in one go he fastened all the buttons, with a powerful gulp he swallowed the doughnut and with a fresh voice he shouted from the window:

'Well, listen to my command!'

They piped down.

'I have here three hostages!' (And kill me if you want,' he was clearly taking pleasure in the situation, no other way could you explain his full and satisfied physiognomy.) 'I will perhaps release some of them . . . I will also shoot someone for the hell of it perhaps, but this we will have to decide. Therefore,' and his mug simply oozes with honey, ey-ey-ey, 'the conditions are these: I will have two standard fighters for hostages, munitions, meals, and I will go to the forest as a partisan. And everything is according to rank.'

Downstairs a disturbing whisper, and a minute and a half later Lavretsky (it seemed to be Lavretsky, but Gelik generally could not distinguish voices), shouted:

'But are you not afraid of a tribunal? Here is a corpse for you, two injured . . .'

'There is no corpse for me, you're lying now!' Baev momentarily answered. 'But generally I don't like how you talk. I feel that today I will be forced to shoot again . . . but I'm sorry for the lad . . .' and so he was talking calmly, seemingly posing, but yet when he discharged a volley from his female fool, no one was expecting it, and Gelik, having nearly choked, listened, how his inner chaffinch walked its feet off with a wild shout and broke somewhere on the peak of something . . . on ultrasound. Inka shouted and crashed onto the ground. Blood . . .?

'Baev. Have you been fucking around?!!!' They howled underneath the window.

'Of the two of you, aha? And the ammunition. And all following rank,' exceeding a howl, clearly and distinctly. Inka stopped, she lost consciousness.

And there had been a pause for three minutes. Then the whisper underneath the window resumed. The accordion played. Some kind of nightmare. Kanavella.

Dad, Dad, when the war started Dad cried for two days, copious tears, without ceasing, he sat at the table, the tears dripped a dark stain on the table cloth, and Kapitosha ruefully said: oy, what is to be done, there isn't a thing to eat; you didn't even kill yourself so, when you buried Mum. But he, Gelik, having despaired had already left here, wrote rapport after rapport and finally couldn't contain himself and when he awaited a precious telegram, he lied, in vain that he was about to take himself in hand, and lied again totally monstrously, Godlessly, supposedly, Father is ill and he has the same diagnosis as Mum had, dying in 1941, not managing to say goodbye. But Mum actually died in 1938, and the diagnosis that she had was uncertain, she had never been ill from anything, she felt good, and the unpredictable blood clot, and all that happened suddenly. This is already not talking about Dad being generally healthy, but Gelik already felt so sick, not superstitiously, that he didn't care about anything and wrote that tearful rapport. To puke once.

Dad would have been in a state of terror. Yes, earlier. But now he himself sent that telegram. Generally, he would certainly have understood him better now, his unlucky boy, his ideal boy, with such a disposition and such great talent! And to write poetry and songs, although, well yes, he is clumsy of course, he can't master himself and he tries to do too much, not a single engagement either along the way . . . but the talent is good, this you don't take away. And Dad always believed in him. Although he argued sometimes and he didn't understand Gelik's attraction to the effective garish word.

You should understand which is more important to you, the meaning of the statement or its sound: there it's for me, my dear, you know that nevertheless the meaning is more important . . . but Severyanin?! But Bely?! And there you know my dear . . . only don't get angry! But it seems to me, that they have a meaning, a different business and it's not always possible for us to twig. . . but if it's already directly not . . . yes, I believe that it can, and not at all, 'but then my dear, it's necessary to build this very sound, in order that nobody has any questions. But if there are questions about it, my dear . . .??'

'Ay, yes Kanavella,' said the dude on the accordion.

And here the doctor let out a wild scream.

And there he sits, let us say, on a train, he catches amfibrachs in the clatter of the wheels, he who jumps, he who dashes by in a hazy wind, nothing else is thought up, he smacks his lips, because the gums are twitching anyway. . .it's better that he goes to the doctor. But that is all for later, later, later. When he arrives, he comes tearing along straight from the station, when Dad and Alka finally believe with their own eyes, look at him, say ah, how he has grown; Dad of course will cry, the poor thing. Postponing the doctor on the very first day and also on the second; everything later, later. Yes. And now the most important.

It was as if his opinion then had improved. The excerpt about pani Katarina, of course, turned out not to be prose, why would it, he had never written prose. This was freestyle verse, he had already broken it in lines and rhythmed it gently. It was not necessary to finish there at all, the freestyle verse sat very well in this poem, which he had thought about even before the war. This will be a gallery of female forms and this Katarina encompassed different parts of his heroine, and Katya Vorms (probably because of the name) and Ivisti, because of the exterior, because of well-bred parts; the thin bones of the nose, the high cheekbones, the wearisomely beautiful narrow eyes. Of course, he noticed what Dad still says, which was embarrassing and obviously restraining: but my dear, the collection of portraits without a story, without a plot suggests a unique life experience or some improbable present, but are you certain ?. . .

Now the experience enhanced him, and Dad will not deny it. Yes and that story (as she was not crazy) that she told him gave him two female forms, the doctor and Inna. In truth he didn't understand what to do with Inna, he liked her, everything in her contradicted his idea about what genuine beauty should be. Inka was not, oh, Akhmatova. That is why he was a little ashamed of his passion. And how to describe this chubby-lipped body beauty, he didn't know. But then the doctor . . .

When she started to shout so terribly and hit his hands and strike herself by the lower part and break him, poor Baev, the trustful one, he decided that she had problems. But a woman with problems can do anything: to take his hand behind, so that he screamed, and from his broken arm he pulled a pistol, to toss it to the side, to tie tassels with the belt of the dressing gown; and he himself went blue from the pain, because with a shove at him is completely natural (she later, putting a plaster cast on the forearm, will shake her head, well excuse me, she didn't reckon on it). But the doors didn't creak any more, one fold opened with a roar, the other hung on a loop, they tumbled, shouted. But the doctor with some age-old tiredness sighed: take him away from here! And, having sat on the floor, she strongly unfurled Ina, lying face down, and she had already broken a vial with ammonium chloride and slapped it on the cheeks; well, well, come on, girl, nothing terrible.

They called her Tamara. Baev called her that.

Two months later she later gave birth to a son. Or a daughter. Gelik doesn't remember now, he talks from general imaginings, a son because people like her usually give birth to sons. But this happened later, and all will be good there.

'We'll give you eight days,' Lavretsky said gloomily, signing papers. 'thank the Divisional Commander. Ho-st-age . . .' This was around a week after Baev's story. Gelik was standing, gloomily and not breathing. Fathers, Mothers, Grannies, Aunties (he already knew this), they were all heavily ill, they all scribbled rapports, they were all urgently summoned by telegrams, to succeed, to find, to bid farewell. And they didn't let anyone go, because there was a situation.

And then with jumping hands preparing documents in the artillery board, he suddenly asked about Baev, he asked with a rattling and also somewhat agitated voice. They sent the Divisional Commander home, Lavretsky answered. On discharge. And generally, with limits, because with such like him according to the bigger picture, to give arms into the hand isn't allowed. And let them already decide about him there and then.

After a number of years, Seryozha O, the same 'Senior Lieutenant O, for our Gorky,' playing, was rolling in the palms a cut glass, in the glass was one part pomegranate juice and two parts spirits. He loved this strange pungent cocktail from war times. Then they sent Gianni Bekyana this phenomenal parcel; forty pieces of huge pomegranates. They squeezed them with their hands, they strained through a cloth, they poured the spirit and they haven't known anything sweeter since. But Gelik of course drank cognac.

'He did everything correctly, this Baev of yours. He knew everything. All, his simulation was reckoned on from the beginning to the end.'

'I implore you! What was it possible to reckon on? Who knew that they are scrutinising him so?'

'They are scrutinising or not, all this isn't important, Gel. It fitted any scenario for him. He had all the cards in his hands. When they were shooting an Uzbek the day before, he cut everything then. Order 227 then stood in front of his eyes, he read it as he had to. He understood everything then. He was able to do anything, because he was not a deserter.'

Straight from the train station. There were no trams at all, therefore he rushed on foot, swallowing the warm October dust. The sound rocked the flat, and he counted to himself 'one-two-three-four' while they were not opening; having not even succeeded at being scared, that suddenly there was nobody at home; at nine Alka opened the door and began to cry right there at the entrance. He had never, even in childhood, seen her cry, after all she was older and always reserved, a little ironic. He knew that she cried over his chrysanthemums, which he had left her in September, leaving for the recruiting station and not waiting for her from work. But this 'she cried over chrysanthemums' was a phrase from her letter, and such poetry, that reading it, he valued the transcription and only. And here she would cry like a little girl, totally small, she was always of small stature, but now, hugging her and kissing her tears, he managed to be amazed that he indeed, it seems, is towering above her.

The flat circled around him with a mad happiness, the kitchen, the lamp, our lounge, our pictures on the wall, all torn at the sides the same, dear books, books, books.

As for Dad himself they missed him by ten minutes! He only just left, to the doctors.

Probably, his face moved and changed , because she waved her hands:

'No, no everything is all right, what are you! Dad isn't ill! And not for a day has he been ill! It's all lies, Gel. Everything is ok.'

The Afghan captive

Every morning she talked to the maniac, and today also; it's good that it was today also, because if he had not called just today, she would have suspected that he knew something in particular about that day; that it was her birthday and this would have been completely unpleasant – if he had even some information about her, apart from that unfortunate telephone number. He always called at eight o'clock in the morning. She tried to hang up the receiver and not go near it, he continued to ring with a maniacal (what else) perseverance, one time it lasted forty minutes, and she nearly went out of her mind, going about the flat with the mad ringing, and finally nevertheless giving in. She didn't feel like unplugging the telephone. For what length of time to unplug it? Only for the morning? Experience showed that he then, furious, would ring later, growl, rage: but in general, she should avoid the telephone . . . she somehow didn't like that they rang her a lot, she herself rang a lot. To go over completely to her mobile? Well, it's expensive first of all, and, more importantly, she categorically did not wish to adjust to this madman, getting it into her head, that she is either his life or his death. Well, what is this – she panicked and unplugged the telephone and all the time, sitting, burying her head in feathers from a pillow. No already, let everything go as it's going. And he continued to ring at eight in the morning.

At eight in the morning he was completely mad, but he kept it short. To be more exact, not straight away, of course, he began with a high note, with tears, he Nikitin, he the translator, he the bookbinder, she the scum bag, the scum bag, for what he is, that for poor Nestratov, she had broken everything, everything, EVERYTHING!

At first it was necessary to reply. And she replied very quietly, forcing him to listen, very quietly, without petty emotions, this was important. There were neither affection nor threats in her voice, he replied to the condescension with a howl, the terror with a satanic laughter. Towards the end of this critical month she groped only for true intonation and now she automatically started with it. He gradually calmed down. It seemed to her that she was extinguishing a fire here; that here and there the alarm of the flames, that everything was quieter, quieter . . . for forty minutes he would mutter, that she could already begin to go about her own affairs, but also with care, listening to the chirr on the other end of the line. She washed, brushed her hair, put on the coffee, but it was not permitted to turn on the television, he grew fierce at once, he was ready to put up with the sound of water or the roar of the coffee grinder, but another human voice took him out of himself. Music, if without words, soothed him. He put the phone down, pacified. But the next day, he rang again.

It was necessary to be intelligent, to become a free doctor for a madman, with balsam on his bloody wounds. But there was no definite way out. When he first rang a month ago, she was very scared, to hysterics, she was numb from terror and all day she didn't know what to do, recalling his mad tenor combining with troubled nausea, she touched on two hundred variations, who it's, from where, why, who gave him her number, she was terribly ill all that day. Towards evening, she forced herself to sit and recall his delusional text from beginning to end. Yes, bit by bit, with a cigarette, overcoming throat spasms, what he said, how he said it there . . .

And she found it. Nestrukhin Oleg Viktorovich, he called himself that once, amongst the Nikitins. Nestratovs, Nechaevs, Maximov Leonidovich and so on. A translator, removal man, bookbinder . . . Yes. Yes.

A few years ago Seryozha needed a bookbinder. She accidentally asked in her publishing house, they gave her some telephone number, they called him the very same Nestrukhin. A few days later, Seryozha absolutely in the middle of things, between two cups of coffee, said 'Oy, Nad, that bookbinder of yours is a psycho, it seems!" She noted, that he was as much mine, as yours, and what strictly speaking is it about?'

'Well, yes. A total schizoid! He asked for two thousand dollars for the binding of eighty pages.' Yes, yes, this is how Seryozha then just defended his degree. "But the main thing is, you understand, he is ill, one can hear, he squeals and screams. . . Well, fuck him."

She agreed, that unquestionably he could go fuck himself and the sooner the better. They found a different bookbinder.

But Nadya's home number had been displayed on the mysterious Nestrukhin's mobile display. And here, so many years later, one morning a terrible unfortunate croak from the receiver woke her. Don't touch it, don't touch it, don't TOUCH IT!

She felt a little better, when she figured him out, not knowing why. The following day, he rang again. She again jerked, in truth not as badly as the previous day, when he only screeched and crackled, and she in a sleepy fear screamed to him, tearing voice: 'Dima, is that you? Has something happened? Bad? Terrible? With Alyona? With the children?

You killed them?' And in every one of his answers she heard 'Yes! Yes! Yes!'

She buried everyone in those few minutes. Then she still understood, that someone strange, a thought flashed, that they were playing tricks, but here it became clear, that – no, that as such they were not playing tricks, such animalistic madness you don't play at and not for anything.

The howling grew into words, and he introduced his own, about her being a scum bag, a scum bag, it had to be, it had to be, it had to be, AT ONCE!!

She fell with her face on the pillow and cried, choking, biting the pillow case. The receiver rattled beside her and fifteen minutes later fell silent. She then rang everybody everybody but couldn't talk, but simply listened that they approached the telephone, angrily shouting: we can't hear you! Thank God they are alive.

The second time she already didn't cry that badly, but oh, this wave of nauseating horror . . . waiting a minutes pause, she asked, 'what do you want?'

He wanted her to now, THIS VERY MINUTE, swear, to leave him alone and not ring any more!

Now she understood, that she should have calmly and very quietly said, I promise you, give you my honest word, that I will never ring you for any reason. This would not have changed his next phone calls, but calmed him that minute. But then she still didn't understand anything and shouted offensively and helplessly: it's YOU who are ringing me, but what the hell, something to the police . . .

The police . . . Oh, here she is only to blame herself.

If it's the fourth or the fifth day she was in a state of complete disarray. Her first terror was already easing off a little, but now she distinctly understood, that the business was taking on the character of a news story. And just here Dima came visiting, whom she saw rarely these days, but nevertheless when they did see each other, she only got upset, he was so exhausted from work that he did not have much time for her. And this time he came unexpectedly, happy, gracious, with a greasy paper bag, fried doughnuts in machine oil, terribly seldom now, he saw that he was not able to hold on. She took hold of the old hand-held coffee machine. And they, they started to talk well, hungrily, they drank a gallon of coffee, like sperm whales throwing themselves on these hellish doughnuts . . . at that moment a somewhat blissful pause after three hours of a conversation, she, laughingly, said, but I have such a story . . .

Dima . . . Oh, if she could rewind and bite her tongue, honest to God! Dima instantly became gloomy and serious, somehow got himself together and crept, moved from the couch to the stool and started interrogating her. What quality, what did he say, how long did he speak for, if she got even a sign as to how distant the voice was, did it remind her of anyone . . . listening, that the calls had already been going on for five days, he destroyed her with an icy chill; and you all this time did not take anything. You didn't tell me? Listening to the story with the bookbinder, he bristled; Why could Sergei never do anything himself? Why must he always rope you in?

Seryozha somehow had nothing to do with this, that she merely clasped her hands. She begged him not to do anything. But Dima already didn't see or hear anything around him apart from himself. And a few days later, a cop sloped in, whether recommended by someone or whether from the area, she did not understand. The business went on tortuously. Quietly, like a tortoise, the Major listened to her story, with a smile. Then for a long time, still smiling, he was silent. Dima couldn't contain himself and inquired sharply what the police were planning to do about the business. The Major continued to smile. 'Not us, but you,' he said emphatically intoning, 'it seems that this is from some comedy, or what?' She didn't quite understand, 'not us but you . . . what can we do here? What's the fuss about? Where did a crime occur? Nobody stole anything from you, didn't beat you up . . . this telephone conversation you know . . . you here, yes, you personally! You can engage in some kind of activity . . . only again what?'

Dima scowled.

'This is intimidation, I find it amazing, that you don't recognize that mmm . . . it's telephone terrorism! Him, this psycho, it's possible to work out, appear at his place and then . . .'

'Yes,' the policeman asked happily. 'Then what?. . .'

'You can threaten him!' said Dima, losing his self-confidence 'You can frighten him. Explain that he can't make trouble for long. If he doesn't stop ringing . . .'

'Aha,' the policeman caught up happily 'you're now planning to act outside the law. In my presence. That isn't good.'

In other words everything was clear. She lowered her eyes, she had known it would be like that! Dima went sour in two minutes and lost his energy. And then with complete anguish, the policeman called Dima into the kitchen and, she could hear everything well, he asked him there: is she a relative of yours or who is she? Could she not have dreamt it all up? You know women sometimes . . .

The policeman left, Dima asked for an apology and such despair fell on her, which she got rid of with difficulty and then she stared at a series of Poirot. The psycho continued to ring.

The first call on her birthday came through to her yesterday, that is already today at one thirty at night. She thought that somebody had decided to congratulate her first, but no, Boitsova rang, that irrepressible old woman, without any kind of hello, she shouted cheerfully down the receiver:

'Nadya, we have a problem.'

They always had a problem.

'You must talk to Olga, she has a Chechen man now. She doesn't listen to anyone, she doesn't listen to me. She doesn't listen to mother, she is unscrupulous, she says nothing. I know that it's eternal love. I read it in the horoscope. Go on and I will send her to you.'

'It's starting,' Nadya said gloomily. How she hated it.

'Naad!' Boitsova changed her tone and spoke up searchingly. 'Well I'm asking you. Well have a look what is going on, she has only just enrolled in the institute, how many tears have we got, ah? They are barely barely crammed her into it. Only just . . . but she is announcing to us that they are now getting married and that she will leave with him there . . . With Irinka, I never worried like that. But this one is silly! And stubborn! What has entered her head, like everything! I'm the image of her!'

'Well fine, what can I do, Nina Petrovna?' How it all annoyed her. 'Give me peace at least for my birthday, so no, there you are, please, unfamiliar love and some such nonsense.'

'Naad. You speak to her. Well, after all you're friends. She always says, I will only listen to Nadya. And Irinka to me, so Olga has announced everything to us. Irinka said to me at once: mother, ring Nadya, there is nobody else.'

They agreed that Olga would come tomorrow, in other words today already.

Up to one o'clock she sat without a break and disgruntled, at one she couldn't contain herself and looked in the cupboard, poured a small glass of 'Hennessy' and a glass of tonic and then until 3.30 watched the 'Town of God.' But at eight in the morning, of course, he rang.

But how strangely did he speak . . . the leitmotif was such: she broke absolutely everything. Everything was about her. He is a poor deserter, one who had gone too far, one who works in a sauna, someone who changes, but she is his terrible fate. Everything is because of her. Therefore he must indeed ring every morning, so she understood. She had already comforted him here. But at this invariable stage bunches of other meanings and ideas were wound. The prickly sweet cotton winds itself so on an inedible twig, oh. If this madman would only have been blaming her and despaired about his own unhappy fate, she would have corrected him with one left hand. She had already comforted and quietened him to the nostrils in two minutes. But the sweet cotton went further, a heap of words. And it was not possible to guess him correctly. Therefore she could not simply lay the receiver on the table and quietly go about her own business, all the time she had to be alert and react somehow. There he blurted out: Eff-era-lgan! Eff-era-lgan! The federation labels, they gathered strange medicine and we are cured, although be annoyed, though agree, but it was not possible to be silent. And she inevitably listened. This would still be half the problem, she had gathered some experience of a sympathetic half deal, and as if she had already virtuously managed not to go carefully, not without reason the glory of the person strengthened for her, 'who was able to listen SO.'

But. But. Three words fell in the cotton wool of hogwash time and again, which hit her with the flow. Absolutely terrible. He knew something about her. And therefore she listened to him. How did it begin? Perhaps, somewhere on the tenth, eleventh day. He cooed something about love, a train on fire, a rain in the window, broken flowers, Jarmusch, failed escapes, this, like him, he began to be nasty, she said quietly: 'Yes, yes, I understand, but I also don't remember, its not important.' 'Lillian Gish' he triumphantly shouted. 'Lillian. You can smile so? Everything is broken, you understand, everything? Yes? Yees?' and suddenly: 'The heirs of the great! Mad descendants!'

And she shuddered.

In the evening they sat in a large group, as always. Not for the birthday, not for New Year, but simply an evening tea drinking session, how pleasant it was for them. Fifteen people, only the very closest ones. Preference. Everyone sat in the big room, puffing away. She knows this room off by heart, it's worth closing her eyes, she imagines: the table, the very beautiful table cloth with yellow stains, the shadow from the ragged, luxurious lampshade, two black dressers littered with second-hand goods. Books, books on all the walls, statuettes, vases, yellowing pictures on the walls: the room, wherever you spit, nailed with antiques, under the string. The skewed Polenev the one and only free place from books, at first it annoyed her, and she asked: can I fix the painting? But she barked at Gelik in answer: no you can't, it's heavy, its centre of gravity has been displaced, it has to be changed, but who will do that? The house is full of blokes, no one can do it, how will I turn it? I won't and I'm not giving it to you, let it hang like that, if no one has anything to do.

But later she got used to it. And every object of the interior appears in front of her eyes, as only it's possible to know your own living space. But this flat to her is indeed like someone close.

And then there there was someone, Irka or Tonya Blokhina. One of them for sure, lacking patience with herself from a descendant of the great poet symbolist Valmont, not Valmont, the devil knows . . .a certain remoteness and branchiness of the heir. That is how they did it, they endlessly and she too, brought someone into the company. The company swelled.

The descendant had had enough cognac, a couple of times joking with purpose, prompting something in preference and adapting.

'Don't worry, he is so sweet,' she carefully told Blokhina.

'My dear,' that one answered 'only in a well-mannered way, I can't. He clung like a burdock. A Shagane in Magan at midnight and he doesn't leave. What do I do with him?'

They joked, laughed and the evening went by. The descendant hovered and held sway; he scurried about the flat, admired it loudly, ran to the corridor to call, called Blokhina out to dance; thereafter he suddenly sat at the chair, encircling everyone with a radiant glance and said: 'Are you happy? Well, well, frolic, my dears. But I opened the gas in the kitchen half an hour ago.'

Everyone rushed to the kitchen, there was indeed gas from all the hobs, a dreadful smell spread. Vitka then sent the heir down the stairs. Apart from some jokes, he tossed him from the steep enough spiral stairs. And also since then she has had in front of her eyes this staircase and the foppish mournful-terrorist upside down.

It was if on her birthday the psycho decided to give her a present. He almost didn't shout and didn't cry. Very calmly, intimately, as if they had been acquaintances for a hundred years, he asked, well how?

She answered carefully, yes everything is all right.

'Yes? How well you said it!' He was amazed. 'But you know, I have a thought, one such . . .' Why didn't she run off with him? Pride! This poisonous pride of yours! Ooooh, how I spit. I spit at her, do you understand? Unicellular mercenaries! Only it would be about its own and its own. Why is it like that, answer me! Let us say, there a homeland of hero-fathers, well have you imagined it? And I will appear this pig-skinned pride of yours? But never! The world doesn't simply spin. And you yourself,' he shouted quietly and bitterly, 'you yourself are what, well?'

'I think this is weakness,' she answered with an even voice. 'This must be forgiven.'

'Forgiven?!' here he was already being sarcastic, she should have been more careful. 'Fine. He has understood it all. Forgive. Forgive the mercenary, soldier beetle, sub-febrile. But drugs? You're saying also forgive? Lessons of drugs, you see, you feel. Yes, yes, yes.'

And it started to upset her, as it would upset her later.

There was nothing to film, no plot, no style, she understands this instantly, still as far as the airport. As if she had not been in Kabul for a long time, how she waited, but there was nothing to film. Everything had already been shown and told two hundred times. And there was nothing to do here. And generally nothing changes, an entirely scorched sky, entirely burned sand. Afghan, Afghan, my country and from the sand, it tickles my throat terribly. And it's hot. There is a powerful smell of sweat everywhere. And it upsets her, upsets. 'You got fever,' says Hamid and offers her water, she moistened her head, the water in a suspicious little water bottle of an unknown origin, it it not allowed in any case. She had tested water in the bottle, but in the rucksack, and how to get at it now? Clumsily. How she waited for that business trip, and what?

'Go ahead,' commanded Hamid, the driver turns around, winks, the old 'hammer' lets out a roar, like a rally car, she doesn't manage to close the window, she swallows the cloud of sand and tires herself out from the cough. Hamid hits her on the back and laughs loudly.

'Ey, baby! Zai gesund!

Surzhik-pigeon-bastard-English-Yiddish. Great, wonderful.

The school on the mountain of Navabad, sometime there was a stone fortress here, but now it was not possible to investigate any more, that beyond the wreckage lying around in the dust, if there is any interest. Just in case she photographs the wreckage, and the stone blocks. She tries to go closer and to crack even on the school window, but Hamid savagely splutters and drags her by the elbow, sorely enough and without ceremony. Want trouble, eh? Aiaiai. Wait.

He doesn't hit her any more with the current from his touch, as it hit the first time. Now it's simply a measured fever, sub-febrile, entered into as soon as she saw him in the airport lounge, from afar. And his hand is on her shoulder or back, well what of the hand, well one more wave of heat.

Everything was not as it was then when it was terrible a couple of months after September 11, the excitement and the cool breeze runs behind the gates of permanent danger. And later him. How was it?

But these days she is making it depressingly certain, that in it she has concentrated her life. And do what you want. She exerted herself on this business trip, she had so languished beforehand, well what, all is the same? Or suddenly it let her go. A few years went by and an idiotic idea turned up: in Kabul schools they presented a new subject about the dangers of drugs. She arrived ('Nad, are you certain there is a reason? Are you certain that there is something to film?') There isn't anything to film. it's all the same to her, losing her personality completely, rhythmic madness, from which she dies.

He touches her by the sleeves. The boys left on a break, after that the lessons for girls begin, it's possible to go to talk to the teachers. He touches her by the sleeves, and the heat again pours into her eyes and stomach.

Olga flew about the flat like a hurricane and she stooped to kiss.

'Grandmother asked to convey her excuses, she didn't congratulate you yesterday!'

Nadya had been moving a hairpin and asked only: will you have coffee?

'Honestly, I want to eat.'

'There isn't anything to eat. Only potato and coffee.'

There is potato, this is said strongly. There were three grey potatoes. She was daring them instantly, she looked into the fridge and clapped her eyes, poking out from behind the doors.

'What, there is basically no more food?'

'Don't bother me with your food,' Nadya without rancour snapped. 'I'm losing weight.'

And then Olya started to talk about her love. She was an inspirational idiot.

Generally, their fate was dedicated to each other, this is an axiom. If someone needed proof, then please: literally a day before meeting him, she had bought a little book about her name, such little brochures are available about various names, and therefore she bought 'Olga' and indeed literally on the first page was written, that the most ideal pairing for Olga was Ruslan. To meet him in such a vast country as ours, you understand yourself, isn't that easy, where do you get a Ruslan in Moscow? And then on the following day she hailed a car and at the wheel . . . Nadya got distracted by the fare that was displayed at the window and she missed a big passage, the description of his appearance and the first dialogue:

To put it short, he was Ruslan.

On the handkerchief lay freshly fried seeds. The sea, magnolias, the heat, Batumi. Nadya, not rushing, obviously not rushing, as if slow filming, turned her hand on the old coffee maker. Two spoonfuls of coffee, ground and mellow powder, two of sugar and very good water. No more. Other additions simply hide the inability to boil coffee. In short, here there are no doubts, and only scandal at home, wild people, who had racial prejudices. Yesterday, as she told them, mother, with Valokordin, shouted: 'Granny got sulky and was silent, but she of course is also against it and in short, Nadya, all hopes are literally on you. You know how they spoke to me yesterday? That all Chechens, literally without exception, are drug addicts. That they teach them straight from childhood: heroine, opium, marijuana, hashish! . . .'

Following on from that Nadya was not listening any more.

'Heroine, opium, marijuana, hashish. We tell the children the harm of drugs. We set examples. The school children should now already know, what they should be aiming at,' the teacher said poorly in English.

'Do you indeed think that you're protecting them?'

Rahim looks at her without blinking.

'How can I answer you?'

'The fact that he wouldn't now answer, means the articles will be splendid,' Hamid said sweetly. 'Yes, we save our children,' said a naive and beautiful man to me in his own naivety. 'No. We don't protect anybody from anything!' said a young Afghan, wonderful in his own early wisdom.

Before feeling pain from this treacherous sting, she manages to be taken aback: he begins a phrase and speaks smoothly, without a single mistake, despite this stupid idiot!

She has been afraid of clowns since her childhood. They speak insufferably while rolling out the 'r-r-r' and hideously wriggling. Her aversion bound her with a terrible despair. When she first heard the speech of Hamid, she almost felt bad, the 'cabaret,' the master of ceremonies, Joel Gray, grease, all the same accurate clown-like foolishness.

Then she asked him:

'You finished Harvard, so how can you speak like that in English?'

'Forgot!' he smiled 'Absolutely.'

A Tadzhik Jewish boy, a true war alliance. Her interpreter, the forgotten language, turning to the side of his own country. Ehh, what is she saying? How was it? When they brought the troops and him, a very small eleven-year-old boy from Kabul, him, his parents, brothers and Grandmother the Jew, they cursed that day, that she married the Tadzhik, that day, that she gave birth to a daughter, that day when the daughter married an Afghan, that day, thatday, thatday, thatday. She also listened to the knock of the hooves, that is the wheels, that is in actual fact in this car the Kardan simply knocks. Her eyes were sticking together and in reality his eyes are sticking together, he rolls the ball somewhere for sure in the corner, in the back of a heavy goods vehicle which brings him to political asylum. And he falls asleep.

'A thief killed my language, you know.'

That was then, the first of their meetings. These days she doesn't ask any questions. She swallows the offence in silence, he is right. Speaking to Rahim about nothing in particular. Yes, the lessons of drugs, not a bad title for the article. Yes, for an hour in the day the teacher repeats certain things to the unhappy boys. The boys listen, dropping their eyes. Then they go to clean cars. 'In order to earn the school lunch, one school boy has to clean five cars.' One year in school goes by and then it's time to start, there is no time to sit around too long, one must do business, to keep the family. Let them learn small things, they can do that while they can. 'About the level of illiteracy, Afghanistan leads amongst other countries in the region.' And she at once feels unwell amongst these fine formulae, which she thinks; she bites her lips, remembering the constant journalistic presence: 'I'm going amid the rumble of gunfire.' or the imperfect 'We were going under the rumble of gunfire.'

'All right,' she says sharply, almost sharper than it was worth, 'thank you, Rahim. You were a great help.'

What was the sense in everything subsequent? It was otherwise not in her memory but in her woe, in some kind of painful happiness. They leave school and go down by crooked staircases. Hamid suddenly stops, turns to her and looking down, smiles his own impossible smile.

'Are you going with me to Jalalabad?'

My boy. My Eastern boy.

He catches my glance,

And black eyes, mocking,

And centuries pour severity.

Black eyes, mocking, I can truly not breathe, how is that, the asthma, a panic attack, a heart inadequacy, which kind of inadequacy, this is already in that case redundancy, because I have this heart, still for three if need be, for four, take the surplus from me, because I'm from him, truly, I can't breathe at all.

Let me go, let me go.

She only looks at him and she can't ask if just, if just, about permission.

And they go; he gave the permission.

At the farewell, Olya kissed her two hundred times. Nadka. Nadka, if it wasn't for you, I really wouldn't know how to live in this world. Thank you so much, so much!

Hundreds of times she heard this, the plight of a good friend. Olya with a wave, the scarf on her neck, the bag from a slaughtered crocodile on the shoulder, still kissing, a final little outburst of the aroma of perfume Angel, so off-putting. Well that's it, goodbye, goodbye, goodbye.

While she washed the part for the coffee maker and the cups, the telephone in the room became noisy. I'm not going, although you can all fail.

She isn't terrified, she is very, very happy. But doesn't understand anything.

'In the provinces of Laghman tonight they blew up the cistern with oil, I told you, the voice is indistinct. Is he really confused? Do I really see him helpless?'

This is true, still in the day time when they travelled to the school, along the road a NATO patrol met them, two wild animal bristling clumsy people: a pair of armoured cars, from all directions with soldiers pointing guns at the edge. Hamid then said to her 'they are nervous, the transport went from Jalalabad to Kabul, and in the night they were blown up . . .' Seemingly there are no casualties: she made clever eyes. But now you can at least kill her if she doesn't understand, how two things are linked: this unfortunate matter of oil, this bright little word, having stuck indeed with this bright barrel, oil, which she would flaunt in conversations, the stamp of the article, and there is her life, a pistol, pulling under her shoulder blade. It hurt apart from under the shoulder blade. How was all this connected, how?!

The man with the pistol gurgles something to Hamid, this one answers briefly and obediently. Then he translates:

'He says that we can talk quietly. What else do you want to ask? Stop laughing. This is a kidnapping.'

Outside the window, the brown dusty country and blue mountains, this is from her report, the fate of which is doubtful, oh doubtful. She is trying to understand and she is fastidious in her laughter. This Taliban, schizophrenic and unlucky person, was counting on a serious diversion, but all of it, poor person, just one intern with oil. Later he hid, sat in an ambush all night and they fell on top of him on the way and they now sit as hostages in their own car. All of this is very funny.

'Hello!'

'Nadya, my dear, happy birthday to you! Be . . .' Dima rings, well something has to be done. He remembered! He rang on that very day, yeees, a story! And she reached for the cigarettes. Dima clumsily growled some salutary words, had been humming and hawing and decided to move to the attack.

'Listen, as always I'm busy. But don't worry. Tell me, are you not celebrating today at all?'

'No,' Nadya answered caustically, predicting unkindness and rejoicing in him all the sooner.

'Liiiisten, are you not coming then to Kirovsky this evening?' We wanted to leave the dog with mum but she is going to Kirovsky. We will go there with the dog but they no longer cope . . . the dog goes psychotic, the neighbours complain, well you understand . . . but Nad? you're all the same not celebrating.'

For the sake of order she muttered, is there a conscience?

But they already laughed and agreed. At eight. Great. Wonderful.

'Hello.'

A cut and a howl. The psycho calls for the second time in a day, this happened, but rarely, something it means isn't right.

Somehow I'm afraid for him, I snorted to myself and quietly quietly murmured: yes, yes, I'm indeed listening . . .

What a great love she has indeed. An Eastern boy. Eyelashes. Smile. In that, suddenly this smile is impossible: it almost pulls at the corner of the mouth, but to her, like to a marionette, a momentary recoil: pain and withdrawal. One aim, to touch his little keys, only to touch it once, and that's all, well if you please. . . she has been thinking about this for a long time. She is indeed thinking about it now, when they are both at gunpoint. And still she recalls how she complained to Blokhina for being in a bad mood. 'A bad mood?!' she angrily interrogated that one. 'Have you got a bad mood?! Korchak was in a bad mood in the train station! None of the others dared to be in a bad mood.'

And now she speaks with bitter solemnity to herself, I'm in a VERY bad mood. I got mad at a soulless Afghan boy, I was crazy all my life, there was misery about him; I have no business and place anywhere without him, but he scarcely recalls my name; I said he scorches the life from me and there, please; in actual fact I have little life remaining to me.

This mad Taliban man with the pistol doesn't change anything generally, it's left to me to count on the clock. Yes. Yes. Might I even say something now, I'm in a VERY bad mood?!

She looks up at his eyes. His mouth twists.

Then what will be will be, yes damn him, yes damn you, I don't survive any other way, it's the instinct of self preservation, she rushed to his lips, spitting out in the way some lumps of the heart.

Then everything happened quickly.

At this moment Hamid is striking . . .

Or not?

At this moment he strikes the pistol from the hands of the terrorist.

I knocked him out, yes?

But Hamid intercepts him and . . .

But the psycho clearly hit. Why did he ring a second time?

'You were not right,' he said from the doorway. 'The healing of the wounds? Dental gratification? In vain, in vain!'

She sighed, well what was the attack for. But he didn't wait for her answer either.

'No, you listen, listen to me. You always talk nonsense. The nonsense of gladioli. But you simply listen there. I see the reason for living, well how is it, I see the aim, and I go like Tsintsinat like Tsitsianov. To follow the path of the correspondent! Then why forgive? Why pity? Toads and shit, I'm telling you! And pussy also. You have seen the aim and have gone! Without pride, without pity! Not a step backwards! Have you heard of order 227?'

And here the memory plays an infernal joke with her.

. . . In a certain little medical office. The window, smeared white up to half way. The dear sun. There are four of them, a heavily pregnant auntie in a white dressing gown, a big-eyed frightened Lieutenant, the killer and she herself. She has a definite strange weariness inside her, an over saturation. The dear sun is blinding. In the distance someone is banging out a tune on the accordion, some muck, 'The Little Apple.' Her hands and the lieutenant's are tied, the pregnant one at the killer's gunpoint.

'Let me go, let me go,' she quietly begs 'Let me go and I will never again ask for anything, I will not do so any more.'

This one, with the revolver, isn't listening to her, he talks about order 227 in stupid excitement, not a step back, about deserter bastards, about the heat of fire.

And then in a rage she throws the pipe and cries despairingly. Crying, she goes to the toilet, does her hair, then chooses her clothes, the telephone peals, but she spits at it, let it explode; crying, she changes her clothes and already calming down, smokes. On the streets, they spoke in the news, it's +17, she throws her coat, checks the keys and mobile, and slams the door after her.

In celebration of Nadya's eighty-fifth, Mum, Grandmother and I arrived late. Therefore we didn't see the most important thing, her despairing, delightful amazement, when she, thinking that she arrived to let Dima and Alena go visiting, stepped over the hearth of the room and saw a huge table at which everyone, everyone, everyone was shouting at her: 'Happy birthday!' Therefore, I can only imagine to myself, how she glowed, how she almost cried, how she looked at the huge, all-age group and gradually recognised everyone; there the nephews, Dima and Shura, the Grandchildren, Seryozha, Lenka, the grandsons of friends . . .Alena and the children and a huge black-jowled dog: the unintelligent old woman Boitsova with the family, the soldiers, people from work, from the newspaper and publishing house . . . this was truly Dima's brilliant idea, to drag her out under a pretence to Kirovsky and stage a surprise.

And there she sits at the head of the table with a small glass of cognac, a glass of tonic, and smiling, she squints at the light, and at the yellow pictures on the walls and the black chest of drawers, the tattered lampshade . . . she is a little dishevelled and for a while slightly confused and touched, but she still promptly finds the ability to be snide.

We didn't catch Gelik's toast, but I know it off by heart; he was saying that he has also known Nadya under a different name, the ridiculous full 'Nadine' (Oh Gelik, you again?!

Don't you get fed up?) you have created a stupid incorrect diminutive; that they were linked to a terrible general ordeal. He remembered how they, having lost each other after the war, accidentally met on Gogolevsky, they recognised each other, he took her to Kirovsky and since then they ring each other every day. He said that Nadya is one of the bravest and romantic people in his life. That she had to survive so much loss, so little under the power of anyone (Oh Gelik) . . . but she could only save this strength, such . . . (here he stumbles, and Nadya momentarily measures for him some effervescent causticity, a burst of laughter, a taken pathos). That Nadya is the best friend, pay attention by the way, every one always calls her by the impersonal 'you!' That she, on the one hand, is a person with an amazing reporter's view point, sharp, at the root, and although she left journalism a long time ago. . . there is an example for you, by the way, of the wonderful Nadya of the romantic uncompromising qualities; she couldn't write what she wanted and left! But on the other hand, she had the gift of a rare writing imagination and she recognised this gift and endured it all her life (well and already after everything) . . .

At that moment we interrupted with a toast with a bell, and Nadya with a little glass in her hand runs to meet us, how, there are still guests?! Great, Wonderful.

The prisoner of the Caucasus

They had of course not been dying of hunger as on the Dnepr, but all the same, all the same, all the same. Something dreamt wearily and delightful, plum lipstick and plum oil. They even had a deal, in all their make-up, not a word about food. He who ate before the war, be silent. And there a huge parcel came for Gianni Bekyana, forty pieces of huge pomegranate. They crowded round the box. Dark red bombs on a canvas cloth.

'You can't eat this,' said the skinny Gianni smiling. 'Now I will show you what to do.'

They squashed them by their hands, they strained them through cloth, added spirit and they haven't known anything sweeter since. Seryozha didn't drink anything else even after the war, the pitiful luxurious KVVK hasn't tempted him. He washed the spirit with pomegranate juice from the tubby jar, in a proportion of one to one. Even when my Grandmother defended her dissertation in the year 1960 something, and in the banquet they made a cocktail brawl and everyone was terribly poisoned by this dark swill (into it went all the spirits from the table, cucumber pickle, duchess pear and the content of three ashtrays) even when one person was left alive, Seryozha, because he drank his own pomegranate spirit.

How then they indeed drank this pomegranate spirit, twenty boys, stupid from hunger and from their own victory; twenty of the thinnest idiots. The strongest of them all turned out to be Gianni Bekyan, not for nothing was he the leanest of them.

'Volik,' Seryozha asked him then 'Why are you named so strangely?'

In 1940, Mum had given up waiting for Dad to return, he was already five years in prison, and in that summer she stopped saying to Volik 'Dad will decide this' and to Archil, the youngest, she wasn't telling fairy stories any more about the Bogatyrs and Mormishki. The boys understood that it was necessary. It was clear that the eldest was now the head of the family and he would be happy, but Mum begged him to finish school first. She of course was not taken on in work and she said in a night-time whisper to her son 'You understand, my dear, it's such a pity about the education, I'm indeed a good doctor.' The little one then, happily, didn't twig anything. It was summer, he rummaged for whole days along the Vazha Shavela with other little ones and Auntie Guria called to them from the window to come and eat jam. She called them scum, but Archil then demanded that Volik explain this to him. Thank you Auntie, even the little one ate something and the older one sat at home all the time and studied studied, in order to take the exam as an extern and become the head of the family sooner, and generally not show his nose out of the house, however at home there was not much food. Although Mum ran through the whole of Tbilisi, searching searching for work, she was not taken on anywhere. Volik and mum became thin that summer, like dogs, but Archil ate the jam with bread and gained weight.

When the chemist on Grishashvil, which was beside the bathhouses, died; Auntie Gurya pressed on all the pedals, they miraculously hired Mum. Auntie Gurya was forced to lie well and so persuaded the manager; she said that Mum and Dad were almost divorced, that their marriage wasn't a marriage but a single misunderstanding, indeed where have you seen a

Georgian living peacefully with an Armenian? So this Georgian of yours was repressive towards her, and not a husband, if you think about it. Her surname is her own personal one and not her husband's, but her children have what surname?! Do you understand what surname they have?!' shouted the manager. The Auntie-diplomat swore that the surname of the children would soon change. So Gianni Bekyan hired Tamara for a probationary period without a limit, that means until the first small offence.

Mum was at her new job, Volik taught heat, but Archil brought home three defective busts of Stalin: with a skewed nose, a smeared eye, and a sharp ear, like a faun, Achiko what is this?' asked Volik, paling.

'This is what it is!' Archil proudly answered 'They are lying around there.'

Gorging oneself on Auntie's jam, all this little gop-company climbed to the edge of the plaster factory where there was a gigantic dumpster. Here they threw out the dangerous factory spoilage. For half a century the lads hiccuped and grunted, they hunted the most terrible wierdos and played happily, apparently nobody even saw them, but everyone went only along the houses with empty hands, but little Archil, panting, pulled three busts with him, and boasted, look, Volya, what a face, a? Look, no eyes! Look, what a wierdo!!

'Shut up,' screamed Volik, understanding that everyone had died. 'you're a wierdo yourself. You mustn't! You mustn't! The little one puffed up his lips and prepared himself to bellow 'it's not allowed to sssay the word 'mug'!!!' he exhaled and almost shouts himself, to no purpose that the elder brother is the head of the family and a healthy boy. But what to do?

Mum didn't cry, she turned to stone. This was the end.

'Let's put it in the chest?' Volik asked quietly.

'They will see,' mum answered monotonously. 'They will come on a search and see it.'

'Let us go to the dumpster?'

'There the mad Giya rummages every night.'

'Let us dig?'

'The dogs will dig it up.'

Then Volik took his first terrible decision.

'Lets go to the mortar.'

Until dawn they dragged the busts in the chemist's mortar, in turns, because they were very tired. In the morning they woke the little one up and went to the passport office to change the boys' surname.

'Mum,' asked Volik at night, when very little was left to finish crushing and mum sat down to smoke. 'Why is Dad in prison?'

'They asked him: what are you, a relative? And he answered; no, we have the same surname. This Djugashvili from Dido-lilo, is a better off family, but we . . . eh, what is there to remember there . . .you aren't hungry, by the way?'

And then he started to collapse somewhere, she already happy enough, though also skinny, caught him and sat on the floor. Of course, there was no food, and she took out a huge pomegranate and with force she squeezed half a glass of juice from it; then she added spirit from a beaker and forced him to drink it to the last drop. For the first time in a long time, he felt the bliss of fullness and comfort. He didn't feel like eating at all. Only sleeping a little.

At the passport office everyone stared at them with suspicion, but Auntie Guria with an iron hand brought a present obviously, she whispered what she had to about a repressive father, about a fictitious marriage, etc. The girl at the passport office shrugged her shoulders and started to scribble.

Then suddenly she raised herself he read, such a beautiful girl, a little older than him, Nika, or what? How he dreamed about her later . . . and she said:

'And why is your older boy so strangely named?'

'I love Mozart very much,' Mum said dispassionately. 'I was young then and I called him after the composer.'

Volik was quiet, basically it was dad who chose his name. Auntie Guria started to cover the red stains.

'A strange name,' the beauty Nika wasn't calming. 'Do you know what I can propose? There is such a metal, Volfram, the basis of refractory metals and metallurgy . . . and the word is beautiful. You call him Volik?'

'You're proposing that he change his name?' asked Mum.

Auntie Guria pulled Mum by the jacket.

'How are you?' asked Mum.

The boy smiled brightly. It was nothing to him.

Still from the night he continued to sense the tart taste, he that evening smiling the same way, said to Nika. 'Well now that you're leaving, have you christened me? Come here . . .' and Nika kissed his lips with the remains of the pomegranate.

'Wait a minute, what are you actually called?' asked Seryozha, swiftly getting sober.

'Its ok, Seryog,' smiling widely, answered Giann. 'What difference is there. Drink more. Drink, my dear one, I'm telling you. Basically, one does not feel like eating, it's possible on the whole to live . . .'

Order no 270

Once upon a time there lived two old women. They were around the age of 50. They were lonely lonely, they didn't have anyone. They lived together and were preparing to die when the first war broke out. The old women were processed and went off to war out of love. From hopelessness. And what do you think? They arrived at the war zone and set themselves up with the Sisters of Mercy and there they both found love. And then the war ended. The more so it was lousy there, the revolution started, the telegraph and telephone were occupied and the old women returned home in complete despair without war. Twenty years passed and again there was war! Now the second one. Our old women came to life straight away and they started to dream. And what do you think? They joined an echelon and went again to war, as nurses. Twice they were almost helped down from a train, but they held on tightly and did not disembark. But there nobody could care less, well the old women were old women. That is how they fell a second time into war, their dream came true. They even said this: we are hiding ourselves in a war for a man which was needed. And what do you think? They found love for themselves for a second time. Such is the story.

The youngest Grandson is turning in the pram instead of falling asleep, he is too small for such a story but the older one has already listened to it a lot. 'Gel, wait, do you not see, his dummy has fallen out? Stand. There. Where are you poking it, it's not allowed from the ground!!!' The oldest one snatches away his dummy and stuffs it in his pocket, the little one groans unhappily and let out tears; he stands, confused, he doesn't know what to do, he smiles; but the older one arranges everything; instead of the dummy, the slobbered-all-over piece of biscuit, almost shaking the pram, well everything, he calmed down, they left. Gelik, are you lucky. If you want to, Ill take it. No? Well ok, lets go further.

Gelik, Gronsky bridgehead
22nd February 1945
Poem '22nd February,' that was remembered
Everybody sat in a damp cellar,
The faces were hidden in the twilight
But on the street the mines were ripping,
They lit up like candles at home,
Alongside a battle was raging, not going silent,
But the ground smiled in the spring,
In the sunshine it slowly melted
The rosy snow under the feet:
Oh Spring: You were a mistake, brought from a different life,
But for us, it turned into a smile,
Unexpected and dear . . .
And then he attached a song there: We quietly sing the song:
I trudge a lot about the earth,
Lived in the trenches, in a dugout, in the Taiga . . .
He was deliberately choosing a size, although at the beginning he thought to write an amfibrach.
There was no semi-damp cellar, there was a headquarters in Bart, it was a manor house. A mine, yes, the mine had fallen

on the house, but for now everything was intact. There were no lines of communication to the command, nor with the neighbours, no one could understand anything and everyone was a sitting duck. Then it was suddenly like a butt on the head, the tanks erupted! So, it meant the people were getting ready for death. Gelik's scent sharpened at once, and he started to wrinkle his nose greedily and expanded the smell on the building, a little cucumber, the damp country house, general dampness, wet clothes and the rain. And here Smagly said they must form a circular defence. And they went.

In the shed that evening, she, the hooligan, licked the barrel of the rifle and he nearly went out of his mind. Then he carefully stroked her on the stomach and maddened from despair and jealousy, she was not him, even if you crack up! Like she is so dutiful and gentle, but everything is elsewhere, even then! And then she thought obviously of something else, about something or someone in particular, he didn't want to know. These days the people crowded there, they snatched the rifles, bullets and grenades. They also took the rifle, the grenade in the pocket and went to the surrounding area and where they stumbled in the semi-circular trench of a half height, the most suitable for the circular defence of the place.

They sat for four hours in that trench and watched as the people were running through the field. They ran in silence, even the stamping was not heard, everything stuck in the wet earth, there was rain, only a breath, a heavy sniffle. They looked and looked . . . they became numb, they didn't move from the place. Then the field became deserted and they got mad. This was not right, not right. They would sit it out a little, even until darkness, but there would already scramble to Grona through the village . . . however, well yes, they thought, that the village was taken by the Germans. And nevertheless they would probably have hung about the little trench such, if it hadn't been for an episode.

There was still a small machine gunner there, who sat with them for the entire four hours, terribly fed up. Gelik thought all the time, kiss her? She had one cheek in the mud, but her lips were cracked, they were covered by a scab, but she was all the time intensely moving this scab, picking it until there was blood, and all the time he wanted to tell her: Stop it! But he recalled yesterday's shed and the barrel of the gun . . . and he couldn't do anything. She was, of course, brave and . . .nnnnot brave, how do you say it. Relaxed? Liberated? Everything was not like that. But where was he going with all his Moscow girls before her? But how did this machine gunner get in the way, to hell . . . he said and said, said and said. And then when it became dreadfully quiet, with a quiet hum, nobody was rushing anywhere through the field with a terrible wheeze, just here he stopped rattling, jumped on the little parapet, and raised his arms guiltily, (but then perhaps simply regained his balance) and ran off. Gelik rushed to where? But Nina took him by the hand and with force pulled him down. The machine gun lay around on the ground. There were no bullets. And there they decided to run.

They ran through the field, grasping each other by the hand, and all the time kept pace, because their boots . . . by the way, it's a different story about the boots.

. . . And having written 'I stitched,' he stretched happily. Nevertheless, you don't drink away the tongue, you must train your tongue, always, at any moment. There he couldn't remember, he wrote, 'I did,' then 'I stitched,' then he crossed it out, then he wrote 'I need to be supplied with boots,' not so. He went out, smoked, licked the sugar twice and it occurred to him: I stitched! They are stitching the boots and how! And he rushed to finish the letter 'but as the boots from home have not arrived, they gave me new ones. One delightful old man here did stitch them for me my dears . . .' he stitched with the old man and they gave good alliteration.

This was the strong old man-stump, a joker and a nice one, black fleeced, a sometime cobbler and the writer at our headquarters. He looked after all the boots, drank, joked, played the guitar, nothing was taken from him. So when Gelik met him in captivity, in the camp barracks, he was already completely grey, he simply did not recognise him. What little of it! But the white-headed one greeted him. When they all went to look after the circular defence, he said, that in the headquarters together with Smagly five people were left. We sat there, nibbled sugar, we had a head of sugar remaining, there we pierced and nibbled it. The Germans looked at us once, another, but nothing, but then they found the shed with the mutilated bodies. The bodies of Germans. With the traces of violence. They demanded that the guilty parties to the atrocity be given up. Nobody owned up. Then they were shooting us. In Bart there were no Russians remaining, apart from one captain, somehow his agile Hungarian girl hid him, although how she managed to do this, the buffoon knows.

But with the boots he of course made money on the side. Who knows anyway whether he was a cobbler at some stage, perhaps he is higher than an apprentice but he didn't rise above that ever. One boot was all right, but the second one was a little baggy, the leg moved around a bit in it. And there now . . .the boot slurped, sucked in the wet earth, constantly crooked on the leg, the sole turned up. Gelik indeed slipped one time and flew flat on his breast and his mug in the mud; he was constantly forced to stand up and shove the foot deeper, even had no strength to swear. And Nina was still pulling him by the hand and begging him to run faster, she waited while he sorted himself out in the marsh, it seemed that he bolted so now and finally they saved themselves, and here again.

And, not having screamed, she fell. The cursed boot squelched and finally stuck in the clay. He pulled the foot and it didn't resist, he stood in the same dirt, sighed, grabbed her by the ankle, somehow pulled out and ran to her, dropping barefoot. It was as if she lay across their journey and fixed herself up very comfortably, it seemed to him at the first moment: 'Put your shoes on' he looked at her and noticed wet putty, he never succeeded at anything that way. That is how a man can start to die suddenly? He doesn't lose consciousness, he thinks coldly and soberly, he is a little annoyed and knows that he is now dying. Where was she wounded? The breast, the stomach? Pushkin was injured in the stomach, these days they would have saved him, but then, they were anxious days and fateful. Chekhov said that he would have saved Pushkin, even Chekhov in his time! But now. . .only she paled in the eyes and spoke with even greater difficulty. She moved her lips wearily, trying hard to pronounce the words more clearly. She stripped her lips in the day time, so now these lips with tiny cuts tried to say something to him. But, yes, 'take the watch' she said. You don't dream up the vulgar scenes, he was all the time repeating: 'Well, what are you?' but she whispered angrily: 'Gel, take it, gather them and go quickly, well!' What was it, your back? How can it be that at once, with a single spirit, she was only just completely completely with him, and now lying and he is terribly angry at her, the last thing that she still feels, his stupidity wearies her terribly, 'Gel, take it quickly and leave, well! Well! He put the watch in his pocket, squatted and tried to lift her, but she began to mumble woefully and he quickly lowered her back, underneath her everything was wet and black. Then he covered her carefully with his own overcoat and left. He went but without feeling the cold and sharply regretting one thing, what he was self conscious about, you think about it, machine gun operator. And then they left him.

Gelik Moscow New Year, 1945

They didn't publish a newspaper that year, how to do it without Butyagin and Mitka. Everyone went about dejected, they had understood everything for a long time, they had cried for their own and were not waiting any more, but here Mitka's funeral, who had been forgotten, how it really hit them all. Kapitosha was forbidden to cry and she went about all day and sniffled; and from these hellish sniffles there was no life at all. And it's New Year.

They sat at the table, it's funny to say: Mara with Kolya, Erlikh was very proud, he wrote in two parts 'Erliani' the third on the way in, Liza Komleva with a certain girl neighbour (Lina? Lelya? Not remembering already), Vityushka, well and they: Gelya, Alya, Dad and Kapitosha. There were ten people usually at New Year, it didn't happen that there were fewer than forty people. As if it's all the same: a circular table, a washed table cloth (Kapitosha washed it, the poor thing), the shadow from the lampshade, a clumsy little spider, together with every plate was an ampule of spirit. Two black dressers with clothes, books, books on all the walls, statuettes, vases, yellowing pictures on the walls. It was indeed crooked at the first Moscow bombardment, and for some reason Dad did not allow him to fix it, he was afraid that it would generally come loose. But there were only ten people at the table at Kirovsky for New Year, who to tell it to . . .

Everyone was so tired from this alcohol. . .Worse than anyone was Vityushka, he was despairing about Mitya, but for tears a desperate scum-like little hope splashed up, but suddenly? Well suddenly?! Alka, you can consider, was a widow from Stalingrad. And from this little hope he so hated himself, but he could not pull himself together, just as before the war he couldn't either: he simply saw how she went to the glazed cafe opposite, she knocked back a glass of vodka afterwards, without nibblets, lingered over a roly, and he was lost. She didn't even look at him of course, he was tall in vain, he was a kid, the youngest in the company, he obeyed everyone, he endured tender leniency, he extended himself with all his strength, adored everyone, was simply obsessed about her after this roly. But she had a romance with Mitya, still from school. A mad love.

Everyone was so tired from this alcohol. Dad was worse than everyone: only he saw his own boy dearly, only so that he could touch him, again they sent him to the front, not understanding where to this time, to Romania, what Romania, what are you about? Romanians are a noisy crowd. My God. His hair had grown long.

Everyone was so tired from this alcohol. Worse than all . . . Alya was stupefied from despair, she could not think about anything else, other than one thing: she must give Gelik the manuscript, because she couldn't keep it at her place any longer, because she had no strength any more to worry, and Mitka Mitka, why this idiotic pre-death present, even two presents, she avoided one, this one remained, and here you didn't feel sorry for me. From yesterday's tears the centuries have swollen, the eyes themselves have been closing. How I want to sleep, oho.

From this alcohol. . .Erlikh suddenly belatedly took offence at Gelik, why from the morning he cursed the wreath of future sonnets? I'm a foo-tno-te fut-uri-st too. Even himself though when he conducted something from the beginning to the end, one outline, the singer of a stump. If only to say something in that high opinion of his in his own tone, it's disgusting. Kapitosha recalled all the dead, but she was not allowed to cry from morning time and therefore she sat, with dried-up tears, to a certain extent. Or like a bud. Mara, the poor thing, looked at Kolya greedily, with despair: for four days they did not get out of bed, their bodies clung together, then they got up and went to Kirovsky, but why?! To hell with them and with this New Year, tomorrow he has to leave, but you can sit here and die, this heavy burden of grief. Why all of this? But not to go to New Year at Kirovsky . . . it's not allowed, life is ending.

Gelik climbed on the window sill of the kitchen one dirty New Year morning and in a single go read the manuscript. And he got cold on that window sill, hunching himself up. Alya said to him coldly: take it and do what you want. I can't throw it out and I can't keep it myself. If you want, throw it out yourself.

Never in her life has she spoken so coldly to him.

. . . Before the start of the war, when Gelik left them in his room, and he ran himself to Lenka in the garden to kiss her and all of them, Pashka Butyagin, Kolya Bogdanov, Erlikh and Mityushka, sat there in his place, but Mikhdikh slept in the neighbour's intercommunicating living room, they couldn't enter and therefore drank warm vodka and nibbled on cooled soup with rice, they filled half a textbook with some dirty obscenities, that at the very end it was conscientiously reread, then Mitya on the sly began to write his own poem there, he wrote a big part and hid it at Gelik's, he couldn't at his place of course: he lived with his Father, step-mother and sister in one little room and these chicks were endlessly tidying up, they cleaned corners, where there could you hide something?

His step-mother, Varvara Erofeeyevna, the most severe chick, if she were to find it, oh, to picture it is painful. But all the same Gelik is so untidy, that nobody ever finds anything: It happened there, once Kapitosha had accidentally washed away from under the couch with the rubbish, a certain poem, either Gelik, either Erlikh, or generally a female northern adjutant day-dreamer, had washed away and thrown it out, Gelik screamed at her terribly and since then she hasn't poked her nose into his room. For three years the little textbook lived behind the stove. Then Mitya arrived and gave it to Alya. He generally wore her out on his last arrival. She said to him every minute; you mustn't! You mustn't keep your idiotic little poems, let us burn them, you mustn't mess in the institute, I'm to blame, that I threw the cards around (this is yes, she was fine, she dropped the ration book from the volume of Blok), nobody is duty bound to give them back to me (he hollered like a mad man: she lost it and who is she to kick the bucket now, perhaps, all of you be damned?!); you mustn't shout all the time, you mustn't hit the mug of your superior officer, you mustn't, don't touch me, I'm not allowed to now, don't drink so much, leave us a little alcohol . . . really he heard even something from it? Has he fulfilled anything?!

Mitka was such with the paintings; a light curly boy with light blue eyes. And in truth sometimes mad, his eyes filled with blood, he got mad in a minute, it passed just as quickly, he drank without getting drunk, he coaxed a bottle of vodka once on the roof, fucking Dolokhov, he was toying, dancing, and mainly, he had in him this male allure, how he could go up to a girl, look so . . . all girls were around him and he fucked all the girls from our school and in general he didn't treat them well. And the girls were all hand-picked, handsome, though he himself was short and thickset. To put it simply a Don Juan.

And later he fell in love, strangely, Alka herself was never a beauty: small, he didn't love that type at all, cropped hair and all the time in her books, always with a roly, very proud. And there he fell in love, and as madly, as he did everything, and didn't relax while he didn't have her.

What was going on in his head, the dear friend of my loved one, of the beautiful Mitka? How did his hand raise itself to write this? The main thing is that he never read anything properly, he couldn't answer in school about Nekrasov, he was disgraced at the blackboard, but here it occurred to him just somehow that the Nekrasov lament . . .was not that it's brutality but: 'that you died, damned one, there is no strength even to wait. It's a pity that we couldn't hang in 1918, we will do this in 1940!' Live now with this bomb in your hands. The verses are monstrous. 'There is no strength even to wait!' By the way, he could never write.

Gelik. Rohman, January February, 1945.

He wrote about his muse to Alya in the spirit of Zola: 'The girl, considering herself 'cultured' and in actual fact an ordinary cu . . .' 'The foul word is so charming, it flew easily from her mouth'. This is true, she flushed curses so militantly. Actually, what a girl, funny! She was somewhere around thirty, but she simply looked younger and she carried herself . . . she was so stately, okay, so curly, resilient. A funny one, the Muse Alfonosovna. Whoever you tell they wouldn't believe it. That an idiotic ribbon fits on the head, the pancakes all suddenly decided to bake, the gramophone started. And all the time he sang in a shrill voice. Losev, while we're on the subject, didn't stand on ceremony with her. He could bellow at anyone and he didn't make an exceptions for her. 'He has an ulcer' as if he was excusing himself, said the muse, indeed, such an ulcer, to the devil, he is simply a swine and that's all. Not all worked out on that unhappy day.

'I have never had anyone. Nor has mum. She gave birth to me at the start of the First World War. The three of us lived like that all our lives, Mum, me and my Aunt. They told me everything; nothing, there will be war! And later the war truly started. And indeed don't tell me anything, not about your own Moscow, not about the front. There was never anything like it, except in Leningrad. How do I explain to you . . .well there you are at the front . . . well I don't know . . . well you're going to battle, yes? You will fulfil your mission, yes? They can even kill you. But in Leningrad you're a louse. They make experiments on you. How long will you breathe? And what will you still think of to eat? It's funny, the louse is fighting for his life. Vo! She is eating wallpaper. And he is sitting under your jar, and laughing, and watches, how you're breathing here in this jar . . . but later Shurik again arrives, the husband of the sister of the neighbour. And on the road of life they got rid of us, eighteen people crammed in the back, afraid that the ice would give way. But later when Shurik was preparing to go back to the front, we understood, there it is, it's not allowed to let go. We crawled into the framework and are not coming out. Me, mum and Aunt. He had eyes at the back of his head, of course: what are you saying: the Aunts, they swell in number? We are sitting. He understands all and is taking us to the front.'

'What are you doing it for?

Oh, Gelik, you don't understand anything. Well, of course, he himself would not have taken us . . . simply he was *his* driver. But he already . . .he, firstly, as soon as he saw us, laughed to start with, as if he had murdered. But later he says: 'From the abnormal ones! Well okay, lets go.' Also not straight away, of course. In Sorminsk we were forced to stand, he had business there. He accommodated Mum and my Aunt in hospital, they are indeed the Sisters of Charity from the First World War. Later they conducted a revolution, they bandaged the sailors, but that they, by the way, liked less . . . and woe with me, I can't see blood, and that's it. I aam falling! I was forced by the war department to act as a cleaner. But all the same I was happy! Never had I had such happiness in all my life. At first he slept with his Aunt. She is forty two. Then with Mum, Mum is older. They were more suited to him by age, he doesn't really like the young much, it's said there isn't enough maturity. And later he had to go the front, and the question arose . . .he said, you don't understand at all, I don't take out all of your buffoonery. One must . . .mum said, take the girl. He took me.

She never called Losev, neither by name, nor by surname, nor by Colonel, everything is he, yes, he.

'How are you?'

'Well?'

'Well, what? Well?'

'Oh, be quiet, ah? I thought that you would at least understand something, but you understand nothing . . .I get nothing from you.'

He was offended. Usually they conversed well from the soul, he managed to tell her about everything everything already and she already knew everyone, as if she had seen a film about them, but what about your little sister then? But you didn't make up with Zhenyok at all? But as Lalechka left, so you don't know anything about her? They touched terribly on these diminutives of his, somehow Erlikh would have been happy: Zhenyok! But to her indeed, it would have been touching, as she entered their company, although of course, to imagine herself was also terrible.

'Well, lets work then.'

'Okay.'

But also nothing came of work for them, they both drew apart too much from this subject, yes in general they didn't feel like working and that's it. The muse pulled out the machine on the table, but she didn't even start to open it, well and then he didn't start to put out his papers. Nothing! We will sit like this. And he promised much. She drew a devil on the handkerchief, then looked at it and smiled, O! Now I'm drawing your portrait! It turned out to be such a devil, only without a face and with the honker, then she crumpled up the handkerchief and pronounced chanting, suddenly and loudly, he even winced for the surprise:

I will be silent soon! . . . But if in the day I printed
A dreamy game my strings answered;
But the youths, listening to me in silence,
They marvelled in long woes of my love:
But if you yourself, changing the emotion,
Sad verses repeated in silence
And the passionate language of my heart you loved . . .
But if I'm loved . . .allow it, o dear friend,
Allow to animate the farewell sound of the lyre,
The cherished name of the pleasant lover! . . .

He waited while she stopped, looked at her puzzedly, she teased his glance, she scorched such a terrible mug! He twisted his finger at his temple, he couldn't contain himself and laughed:

'Okay, to hell with it all! Lets dance!'

Generally, this was not the custom, they had danced earlier a couple of times, on his birthday a tango, oh, what a tango it was!, but always at parties and so that it were the two of them, never. But he would understand that he mustn't argue, she was so unhappy from the morning, on edge, he suspected that

Losev had again either hit her, or something else, but she is silent from pride and isn't complaining. Some waltz was put on, so he could never remember later what kind of a waltz it was. To dance, of course, they didn't dance, he hugged her and they were quietly swaying to the beat. She buried him in her breast and quietly sniffled. Then suddenly lifted her head and demanded: definitely make up with Zhenka, when you return!

If it were a bad vaudeville Losev should now have entered. And he entered. To hell, I don't even like her.

And a couple of days before that he got terribly wet when he walked to the headquarters through the field. The overcoat was wet through going about the rain so terribly suddenly. He somehow dried off, warmed up, even ate something, and later leapt into place: oy, oy, what is indeed happened to this poem?! It had probably even dissolved into slush! She took the wet heavy overcoat from the hook, crooked, bloody hands! He unstitched the seam with a knife and pulled out from the lining the crumpled copy book, placed it on the table and started to spread the pages. The ink, how it was not strange, blurred just a little, he was afraid that it would be worse. The terrible lines began to jump in front of his eyes: 'I have no more strength to endure . . .' 'What, you say, our Soviet glory, strength, support, stronghold? No, be quiet! . . .'

Just here it would be, by the way, correct, not to 'the bank,' but 'I keep,' well what is it, the person has no kind of feeling of rhythm! 'I keep,' but then what kind of rhymer here? Hmmm . . .' I keep the rage in my heart. Tatata . . .I know, I can't forget,' 'I can go to the bank' and there 'I keep?' . . . Suddenly there it overshadowed, that is how it must be! How to be, write this perhaps? But no, why? But nevertheless he is a good man, good man! He saw the pot boiler, once, once, and here indeed he found how to correct it and well, and . . .and there was worry.

From behind his back he heard movement, he moved, he flattened the copy book, but it was already too late. My dear one! He stood from behind and shone from happiness.

'Allow me, my dear one . . . but what have you got here? Poetry? Ooooh my dear, well, what interesting poetry. . .'

He obviously grasped something with his eye, otherwise why would he have been glowing glowing?

Everyone knew that Gelik writes poetry, he himself gossiped about this, he has even read pieces to his friend. More than that, his friend confessed that he himself isn't strange . . .do you know . . .the elegant version isn't entirely strange to him . . .and he showed also two or three of its own verse, of course a full gloom and disaster, there isn't anything to talk about. Gelik, of course, didn't begin to talk about anything directly, he explained only a few of his own compositions in a delicate form. His friend didn't agree, they argued, but this was a good argument: in any case, it was an argument with meaning, with understanding; in general, his friend, though he also wrote total nonsense, gathered himself in strange verses well and managed to read something. But Gelik missed Alya terribly during the war, or Zhenka for Erlikh, or Kolya, or somebody, with whom it would be possible to talk about literature and the second boss with the fully fully idiotic nickname . . .

'A new one? And you're not showing yourself, you're hiding, yes? What are you my dear, you don't trust me?'

'What are you, my dear, jumping from behind?

Not understanding, he understood or not.

. . . And still a couple of days later he received an order, to leave immediately for the village of Bart, the 235th Shooter's regiment, where he was duty bound to the boss of the regiment. Here he felt heartally relieved, how lucky again! It's not good, of course, to be caught with the chick boss, but let it be already, better that way and the humanist turned out to be Losev, and let him change to another regiment, the fool take him. The main thing indeed is that the friend obviously didn't strike, whether he didn't want to or he didn't manage to, God knows. Because then, it's already not a transfer to another regiment, it's already then a tribunal, my dears. No, Dad does not talk in vain, I'm doubly on my guard.

Volsk Before the war

But how he has tormented her, my God. Five years in the difference, it seems to be! The parents said, well you're an adult! She has resented it with all her being and gone against it, I'm not an adult, not at that price I'm an adult; she was eleven he was six, and he was the enemy; she had been afraid of clowns from her childhood, hated them. She has been afraid of clowns from her childhood. They spoke intolerably, rolling the rrrs and wriggling ugly. This aversion bordered on terrible despair. He pronounced his rrrs like a Frenchman from childhood, how much it didn't take him to doctors, she didn't have any sense; he is doing it on purpose. He doesn't want it: he crapped around and picked arguments, he shouted at her face 'arrrrrrrr! Arrrrrrr!,' she shouted 'stop it!' he gnashed his teeth, shone his chocolate eyes; later only a little grown up, he loved the mad circus with love, the parents said: 'Inochka, you could take him, it will be worth your while.' She stiffened on the edge of the bench, she was sitting out both parts with shut eyes, even when there was something inoffensive, acrobats, wild animals, she could not open her eyes, the clown-wierdo appeared unpredictably at any moment, performing in the passage between the rows, he laughed, shouting out his own lisping confusion, the children laughed at the tone of the clown, Gunnar went, she compressed her teeth as if they were grinding in a little bowl in the mouth. That is how it seemed to her. They returned home, he did his own plombieres on the way and the weariness began again for her; at home he depicted the clown, he depicted it with talent, the little bastard; she pressed on the waves of despair and of a certain strange excitement, she could not understand anything at that moment.

He was unusual from childhood itself, from his very own seventh-month prematurity, somehow not so, an alien, later she formed an opinion. Madly talented, in everything. He learned how to read at three years, and at six, be courteous and drive a car. His feet hardly touched the pedals, but already the Father, having drunk with his friends, was sitting him at the wheel of the departmental car and the boy went home without him. The risk was the worst, but here is interesting: Gunnar infected all the space around him with a charge of recklessness and courage. All! How could his Father do it?! She was enraged, the Father waved his hand: ahh, nothing will happen!

But Gunnar . . . he came along the edge, laughing. On the bungee he flew across the river. On a bet he climbed in winter on an icy roof of the school and danced the waltz. They almost expelled him then, but despite this, he studied so well, brilliantly; in September he was playfully reading a text book, later demanded from the teachers extra knowledge, special literature, it was all devilishly interesting to him. To get rid of such like was expensive in itself. And yes, he never annoyed anyone, never. Such an impudent one, would have been able to. But, oh this charm of his, these upper teeth of his; they submitted to everything, gave in right there. Later another one: he drew fantastically, sculpted. From a little log he cut with a penknife, Ina's head, once, once, and there to you all a caustic and witty cartoon with a potato nose, half-shut eyes and a general unhappiness in the face. The parents laughed like abnormal people, as if they would have had to punish him, but why? But how he acted! From the very earliest years, all of them, the domestics, any guest, old man postman, doorman, later classmates and the teacher, he parodied genially, he was considered a momentary mimic, the intonation, whose lip picks a quarrel, who lisps slightly, who diverts the eyes in conversation, and if you please. All die laughing, she squeezes terror from this devilishness.

The parents, a Latvian woman and a Jew, gave them strange names and he teased her endlessly (Innnnnnnnnnnna! Innnnnnnnnn!), she in retaliation thought a genuinely evil nickname for him, Guslya, she thought he would be offended, but he laughed at it, grinning, and he called himself that later and his parents were taken in by it.

She hated him almost up to the war. And then it was so. She had only just finished school, and there after graduation they played at Cossacks and robbers, Guslina had a mad idea. He set himself apart for some reason with his parents in the festive area and later stayed on. All his classmates adored him and the boys talked seriously to him, she could not understand it, but every time she listened: you have sssssssuch a brother! And there this brother had a little idea: some of these activists started to shout, that it was necessary to fight with vulgarity that, well to the devil with them, these dances, walks, meetings with the dawn! . . . and then Guslya thrust forward and shouted: lets play cossacks and robbers! Everyone shouted from excitement. They broke into teams, Guslya seemed to be a robber with them. It didn't seem to be comfortable for her to to run in a long old fashioned dress with a flounce, twice she nearly fell and cursed herself, that she didn't get anything from home to change into. Tanya put her hand into a pitcher, which was appointed a treasure, she flew off, but here from out of the house with the rough rotunda the cossacks tumbled, she was confused, she noticed, she caught her skirt and cursing everything on the planet, threw herself towards the volleyball court and suddenly there was Guslya! He pulled her by the arm, quickly there! Around the corner, there is a boarded-up lodge. Gunnar approached the blind little window, carefully and decidedly, obviously he had done this a hundred times already! He pushed the glass inside, it fell but didn't shatter. Well, quickly! He sat her down, not for nothing was he small, but strong, she again was perplexed in her own frothy silks and he jumped up to it himself.

'Well, you have dressed up, auntie! He said grudgingly, she hated this 'auntie'; if you please, even more than all the other teasings. 'Listen why don't we cut it short? It's not appropriate at all . . .'

Next he, with his own favourite penknife quickly and accurately, along the horizontal seam, ripped off the lush flounce leaving the skirt long to the knee. Until dawn they sat on in the lodge, so the others couldn't find them, well the treasure stayed with them. The cossacks admitted their own hopeless defeat.

All of the subsequent happy-happiest scholastic year they had enjoyed went by in a continuous chatter, laughter and egging on. She had practice in the factory and prepared to enter chemistry school. He read her manuals and text books and jokingly did her exercises with her and scoffed at her stupidity: what an idiot!, No, but what an idiot! She only laughed. That is how a year went by. Later she went off to war, he having infected her with his recklessness.

Moscow after the war
It's wonderful how their company was spared. Gelik,

Pashka Butyagin, Erlikh, Kolya Bogdanov, Krotik, Seryozhka all survived. Vityushka didn't go to the front because of his youth, but he worked in the rear and nearly died from tuberculosis, they took him from this world. There was only Mitka-Mityushka . . .but what to remember. The first period was terribly difficult. Mikhdikh had fallen ill, Gelik had only just come from the camp, where Zhenya was born. Gelik and Gelena got married at once, she spat at the decree and struggled to find a job, wherever she went she was the daughter of a Polish oppressor! They simply turned her down. Only Vityushka worked then, they almost died of hunger, but thanks to the lads for bringing something into the house every evening and they ate it there themselves. Well and Tolya of course. Oh, this Tolya. Nobody remembered how he appeared at their place, either Tonya Blokhina brought him or Seryozhka: only as he came to Kirovsky the first time, so here he washed the mountain of dishes in the kitchen. That's how it was ever since: softly softly with this Tolya. He befriended Gelena, if you please, more than anyone else, but perhaps because she demanded more help than the others. Tolya walked with Zhenka and later brought the pram to the second floor along the spiral staircase, and he washed the damned dishes, which were eternally building up in the sink, if it was a joke: fifteen people sat at the table every evening, but no one felt like cleaning up. He spoke for a long time with Mikhdikh and when that one went completely blind he read the papers to him. He had unfinished conversations with Gelik, o o Gelik found at last an ideal conversation partner, it was possible to talk to Tolya about anything, about the futurists and the symbolists about the drama of Bely; moreover Tolya wasn't his equal, like Erlikh (every argument about literature with Erlikh ended in a quarrel), of course he got to grips with the subject, with Vityushka for example, so you couldn't agree, he is far off from it. And they, Gelik and Tolya, talked and talked, endlessly quibbling, he trained himself endlessly in some refinements . . .this was some kind of tip-toe in their conversations, that all evening they are joking, like Kristoforovna and Nikanaorovna, either knocking on the doors, like Chichikov and Manilov, or they dream up platonic dialogues and they couldn't butt in. Tolya sat with them in the evening for preference and all the nights long. Later he ran off to work, but at six o'clock he returned, he ceremoniously brought a bottle of milk for the little one. He found a good creche alongside the house, he called the doctor for Mikhdikh, advised Gelena to go to the energy institute, he pushed furniture and books with Vitka, when the flat was suddenly inundated. Well and products of course. He took out such things from under the earth! Once from their own village, what was the village? Some Kaliteevka . . . no it's Kasheevka . . .Gusya brought it! They were all afraid of going towards it, a terrible beast, something had to be plucked there, the feathers singe, then the decrepit Kapitosha got up totally from her camp bed, giving out, divided up the goose and baked it. Everyone stuffed themselves like I don't know.

Where did you get the goose, Tolenka? He only smiled radiantly, such a bright boy with almost slanting eyes. Wonderfully enigmatic, Eh, you have unexpected facets, Tolya! Deus ex machina, yes and only, Mikhdikh raised his hands. What a terrible time it was and we survived it.

The company grew and grew, earlier it was only our school friends, but later how it transpired, whoever from work, whoever from the Institute, whoever the friends dragged in. . .and how Gelik met Nadya again, whom to tell it to! He simply went along Gogolevsky, suddenly a woman came to meet him, something took hold of him: the walk, the habit, her dishevelled hair? Ina? She didn't even look up straight away, she was weaned from her old name. 'Ina!' 'Oh, good God, Gelik?'

He brought her to Kirovsky on that very day, she was at first a little self-conscious, it's not comfortable, you were not indeed expecting guests, what guests there are, you see yourself! There are already twenty five, there are thirty people almost every evening, they have been chatting, reading poetry, playing charades, later begins the preference obsession and for the whole night, from the morning crazy at work Vitya re-counted the finished articles and exclaimed throughout the whole laboratory: without a third of it! But little Zhenka, looking at the adults from under the table, hearing the shouts about the ninefold and clumsy wretch, he chose from amongst his toys the main mischief, the rubber goose Mizeya and any game began with a scream: 'Now well catch Mizey! Leave Mizey!'

On holidays they did the newspapers, they sang, oh, how they sang: in an old repertoire they gradually infiltrated Okudzhava and Visotsky, war songs went onto a second level: 'Time for an artillery bombardment' encouraged the tears, how much it would have been easier for us to fight, if we had known: 'Do you hear, the boots rumbled!' and what is in its place? 'In my little pocket there is your card?!'

Yes, well that is for later later, and for the time being, well dance! Alya, holding a cigarette in her teeth, accompanied and . . . Krotik danced well, Yura Dolin simply very well, Vityushka, so long in vain, fantastically. But all the same, better than anyone was Kolya, Kolya with his own beauty Mara, they didn't leave at once, but later they put up with them and all would deliberately make way, freeing up the place; Mara looked from under her own brows with a glance and smiled,

Kolya made a self-conscious and snide mug; well and, oh, how they danced; any way possible, as you wish. Tango? Tango! Foxtrot? They danced the two step somehow . . .but about that later. The little glasses in the wardrobe clank, the music rattled, Alya dropped ash on the piano, Nadka regally leafed through the pages of a magazine amongst all the bedlam, they would rush to confine themselves to little Zhenka and he escaped in the arms of Erlikh: 'Don't touch my namesake, he doesn't want to sleep!': Vityushka ran onto the kitchen with the kettle. Krot bored people that they must drink more. Gelik was kissing on the stairs with his next passion (once Mikhdikh encountered them, he delicately clasped half the cape, squeezed through sideways into the flat, kind heartedly set Gelena up in the commotion: girl, wherever you look, he is indeed with you in the cold without a jacket, the month of October in the yard, there is already an autumn sky . . .), Gelik returned, happy and lost, out of place in a buttoned shirt, Alya gave him the eye: 'Gel?!', Gelena spoke upset, oh, leave him please God, let him . . . as for the food, a single potato and there was little of that, what terror, to remember it's terrifying. But happy.

Moscow, 1964

. . . In the day Nadya ran in, gloomy, and sat with them to clean the mushrooms, she had only just returned from the business trip and again squabbled with the editor, she was worn out and she must resign.

'Yes, you just wait,' Alya said judgingly, wearing out the russula 'why resign straight away? You be patient a little, look how it will turn out.'

'Maybe you could lay low for a time somehow? Maybe not take on such cutting-edge themes?' Gelena looked doomed at the huge basin of mushrooms, again Tolya, thanks to him, from somewhere he dragged them over. Work for half a day, but they sweep it away in five minutes.

'Wait? Hide? It's not the time!'

Speaking quickly, this was a useless argument. Nadka was such a rebel, with a watering can and with a block note, just try to move from that place. The fool! Basically, she is as stubborn as a mule, and nearly that, she said, not these times. This isn't that, Alya was not so certain. But to change one's minds on this, to resign oneself. Frowning and angry, Nadka made the coffee and from nastiness at the end put in the whole piece of garlic to the little coffee maker. Well what are you creating, say for sweetness, a?!

'Do you know what girls? Come to the circus with me!'

Alya dropped a knife and laughed helplessly. Well then, now the circus!

It seemed that Nadya was not going out of her mind. It seemed her younger brother from Leningrad, well what are you, did you not see the poster, perhaps?

A crowd of them went to the circus, Erlikh, Krot, Mara and Kolya, all four of them, Tonya, Liza Komleva, Katya Vorms with her sister, yet someone else, already can't remember, well and Nadya of course. When else did they see such a thing in the circus, a company of adults and not one child with them (Zhenka said, parents are you in your own mind? What circus? I'm fifteen, or what). On this, they joked along the way, they just sat down, the presentation had not started yet. Viktor, tall, stately in golden glasses, delved into the pocket of his jacket for a handkerchief and suddenly took out in the light a chicken bone, he screamed from the unexpectedness and threw it somewhere below, along the rows, she slapped a bloke in the bald crown, thank God not hard. They howled from laughter, they moaned and roared, the whole circus looked at them with terror and condemnation. Big tears danced on Alya's face. Gelik also wiped the tears, they were in the family: they almost laughed and well cry straight away. 'Who, who shoved her to me over there?! Try to excuse yourself in front of the General!' Here the light was lit, the drum shot, in such a farcical mood they began to watch the presentation.

Yes. He was good, Nadya's brother. Fantastically good. A clown practically without make-up, only his mouth and eyes were a little done up, but neither a wig nor a nose, nothing, yes, nothing was needed at all. Nadka had been explaining earlier, he has such a welcome, without personal details, without an entourage he goes out and keeps the hall for two hours. A new word in clown technique, his personal director, his children, his discovery, his circus. Generally, he didn't leave the stage. Acrobats went out, so he touched the summit of the pyramid and balanced there on one leg, juggled bottles of vodka, he crowed a duet with a cockerel and played Kamarinsky on the harmonica, and there he was dancing to Kamarinsky, with this very cockerel under his arm he flew off under the cupola and went along the wires and halting in the middle, taking the bird by the leg and chanting read: 'Such a paw I have not seen in all my born dddddays!'; succeeding the tiger from above and behind backwards, drove him on a gallop around the arena, (the cockerel went behind on skiis, catching by the beak the tiger's tail). But the tricks! What tricks there were he sat that unfortunate cockerel in a veneer little box, it spewed from its mouth a lightening bolt of fire, the little box burnt with a blue flame, they heard a crack, as if a hysterical pre-death scream and satanic laughter from the bastard illusionist; the audience was forced to ah. When the fire quietened down and only a handful of ash was left, the facetious clown pulled out the unharmed fire victim from somewhere out of his jacket and he shouted victoriously and the children in the hall screamed from happiness.

Gelena looked at him, something lit up in her eye. She laughed from inertia, but a certain thought didn't give her peace: somewhere such . . .when . . . something . . . these black eyes, shining, these light tufts, very white teeth, where, when did I see them? The clown danced the foxtrot on stilts and later, getting rid of them, suddenly rushing, laughing along the rows, a wave of children's amazed yelps rose up and stayed for a second alongside them, with Nadka, who specially sat on the end place beside the aisle. He pulled his sister along by the neck, he pulled out from behind her ear a rose coloured astra, he set the knife aside, pure Chaplin! He presented a flower, he threw a light glance at the company, comically took a bow and winked at her, Gelena, and here she felt with relief that she was losing consciousness.

Moscow 2007

In the Autumn of 2007 we all gathered to mark the anniversary of the death of Gunnar, we gathered on Kirovsky, because neither at Nadya's, nor in his small flat would we have all fitted in. Apart from that it was more convenient for the old people to reach Kirovsky than nag, shall we say, Gunnar's son Dima in his Krilatsky mansion. Gunnar died as a very old person and he lived a happy enough life: facetious and Apikoros, he would have wanted them to lament him less, but nevertheless: his death hit them all so, that they could not recover for a long time. Nadya felt worst of all, it was terrible to look at her at the funeral the previous year; she stood straight, snarled at any help, at the wake she joked with all her strength, generally it was intolerable. Gelena than suggested to her; live a little with us, where else, for nothing. Now Nadya was obviously better, she gave out as usual. 'Not very, not very,' her nephew Seryozha answered in a whisper to my dumb question. 'she is delirious. . . that's how? She is completely self reliant, she lives alone and the gas, as you understand, she doesn't leave on. . . she often leaves the house, travels a lot, minds the children, goes to exhibitions, recently to the library, rushes about for some reason to a foreign one. She doesn't confuse anything, numerals, dates, agreements, I would have such a head! But there about her last fantasy.

But today Nadya was talking about Gunnar and on the whole she didn't confuse anything, and it was obvious that it was simply better for her like that; which time, to recall and let them have heard already, but what if someone wasn't listening? In truth, every time something new flickered in these stories, I'm there, although I knew them both from childhood, I never heard, that Gunnar drove a car from the age of six.

'A dog lived with us before the war . . .when the war began, he was thirteen, I went to the front, Dad was also mobilised, but they stayed with Mum and he wanted to learn quickly and also go to the front, and Mum herself, Mum, where would she go? Everyone thought that he would become an actor or an artist but he enrolled in the faculty of chemistry. In 1944, in the summer, he proceeded straight to the chemistry school, where everyone was gathered. And later, in March 1945, everything had by now finished and suddenly they bombed our school, because it was night time they didn't kill anyone. Where were the students to go? Whoever was eighteen was moved to the front; well here he was, you understand, he couldn't remain idle: he was only seventeen, how he persuaded someone, I don't know. But they sent him to the front also and here his dreams, consider, came true. Such was the happiness, he grabbed it! He no longer thought that he would get his dues. He fought.

He lost his lungs there. He only looked for me, but I was in Moscow later, well you know that. He found me. What was it! Two days he cried and laughed, he had to finish his studies anyway. The worst worries began. Start the course with our surname! I left this idea at once, I have never meddled, I was employed as a librarian, I was tired out, while I didn't get into the paper, but that was already afterwards. But he, Guslya, he is indeed mad. How is it, to say, they wont take him? It's to say that there is something to find fault with. But if he finishes learning, there isn't anything to find fault with, let them try not to take him! I indeed say Meshugenah, crazy. He tried to enrol in the institute three years in a row, everything came to naught for him. And later how it excluded everything! I wont have anything more to do with them! I thought he was going out of his mind, where to: he's laughing! He began even earlier to earn something in children's mornings. In the winter he played Grand Father Frost and Hedre there. Later a clown, later tricks. They called him to the circus but that was already later. But later he dreamt up his own presentations, he began in Leningrad, nevertheless he moved to Moscow later, closer to me, and then they started to release. . .

. . . When he first returned from Paris, he came to me . . . With presents. . . Ink, to say (he called me that, he didn't learn) . . . Ink . . . my poster is hanging in the Champs Elysees.

Everyone sat around getting sad. Michelle hugged Nadya. They passed the time a long time ago, when they shared Gunnar, and Michelle, flaunting her Russian, strained through her teeth a little quote from the beater of the sister-in-law, but Nadya just missed hiding her jealousy and caustically ridiculed the French method of rearing children. The children had grown up long ago. They have their own children.

'What happiness . . .' says the greyest-haired woman totally quietly, but all the same the improbably good looking Michelle, with an accent that was indistinct, only hissing they come out accentuated at her, 'what happiness, that he arrived then . . .'

Gelik, Hungary 1981
A clean house in Barta.
And he said in clean Russian language: hello, Gelij Mikhailovich, do you not remember me? Veshnyakov, Sylvester Sylvesterovich, Captain, remember please. The 22nd February 1945 . . .'
Who was the captain Veshnyakov, how could I forget about him?
And then
We bow to each other
And then
Decide for the two of us:
We don't die, as together we rush,
We rush, so together we die.
We are running along a pitted field,
Crouching slightly to the ground . . .
Suddenly . . .
From fingers, compressed with the pain,
Your hands slipped,
- Nina get up!
But in the malevolent ecstasy
Death brings its scythe . . .
I threw myself to the ground in despair
And fell towards your face.

Tell me, why was the Captain there for me, the boss of the Engineers Service of the regiment? Why was he there?

So. So. Calm. The 19th February 1945. I went to the place of my appointment. 'Our new commander!' says Nina, no not Nina, but a second girl in the headquarters, a medical orderly, kill me but I don't remember her name, but what I remember exactly is: she was with Smagly, the boss of the lines. The captain presses my hand, and looking past me, pronounces somewhat strangely, without question, in the affirmative: 'you're from Lieutenant Colonel Losev? He wrote to me.' I shrink. What else did Losev write? No, he hardly wrote: 'He slept with my chick,' he is vain, he, more than anything, described simply for me how being sloppy and an impudent fellow, he gave the most basic descriptions, he wiped his legs on me, and this Captain talks tiredly to me now. At the end of the day is it important? I had just introduced myself to Nina, and there was only her in front of my eyes: she was sitting on the window ledge at the side, holding herself by the knees such a . . . such a . . . I could only look at her. Therefore the Captain, well what about the Captain, to hell with him! He immediately left, and I never saw him again. Never?

Well, wait up, lets go one more time. The second girl, I don't remember her name, she was with Smagly, and who was Nina with until I appeared? With no one? Excuse me, but during a war that doesn't happen and you know who she was with, you know and you're lying to yourself. You lied then and you're lying now.

The four of us sat in a foxhole, and when the machine gunner ran off, the three of you remained, and because of Veshnyakov you were shy to kiss her, not because of some machine gunner, you would have been shy of anyone.

Yes. Good. The three of us ran through the field, but the boot spread, and for a while I pulled it out of the clay, as one machine gun line hemmed them down. They both remained lying, but I left, I opened my overcoat for Nina and left. But just then the Germans caught me, so I fell into captivity.

Yes. Good. I cleansed him from my own memory, there was nothing for him to do there, as there was nothing for him to do in my poem.

'You remember me, I see. Obviously, I should return your work to you.'

He left the room. Gelik closed his eyes, in his ears rang the clangy 'besame mucho,' but right here in front of his eyes the stupid carousel turned pictures of the final days, too many impressions. He was t-ire-d! Was it a joke, the first from their time of the war abroad, dear concentration camp, the full sweetness, salami, rivers of wine, endless drunkenness under the fond gaze of the secret serviceman, the begged for free day, a trip to Bart, it dragged out terribly, the identification of darkness; almost nobody had changed there. Towards evening they had walked enough, were starving, the guide said; A lady friend of mine lives here, her Father fought, he was in Russia, and her husband is Russian, well also she cooks fantastic goulash (again goulash!) perhaps we'll go to her? Perhaps she will remember you, perhaps, you her, she was here during the war.

They went. No he didn't remember this dark eyed Katalina, and she didn't remember him, but she had already prepared the table, there the old man-dad entered, and of course again with a bottle! His dear wine, home made, wine Gelik hadn't drunk for so many years and from it other hops, not cognac, quicker and easier. They sat. They got drunk momentarily and completely; from this fiery meat, the most tasty, from tiredness; half an hour went by and already they sang about a bird and without a guide they freely socialised in wonderful German. But tell, tell, the already completely plaited Gelena bothered old man-dad in everything, 'How did you like it there in Russia?' 'In Russia?' Here he raised hairy eyebrows, 'Not very. I was in captivity there . . .' But here, meaningfully, the very husband of Katalina came, Veshnyakov, Sylvester Sylvesterovich, he needs such a name, a?'

'Take your copy book. You have I suppose forgiven her a long time ago. Pleasant work. All the same what have you got in your heads, unhappy decadents, I would like to have known. War is all around, people are dying, but this scribbles himself about Ivan the Terrible and Josef Stalin, to sew the overcoat yet indeed, fucking conspirator. What are you looking at me like that for? No already, you listen fully to me now.'

When they sent you from Rohman, Losev told me everything everything about you, what you wrote in actual fact there, how you tried to write it again, what they sewed in the overcoat, and how your commander affected you and there you rushed to Losev. He knew everything about you, the Lieutenant Colonel. We became friends. He told me then: Silva, he is a good lad. He is an idiot but good. It's not allowed to keep him with us, because this punk taps me for him and waits for responsive action. I will send him to you, I will find a pretext and you already somehow . . . and I took you on, bitch. But you got rid of her when she was wounded, you got rid of a girl, and she, it means, says to you: go! And he went like a darling, a?! He got cowardly like a little dog! He is obedient! She says to him, get rid of me! And he obeyed her, a? Well, scum . . .yes, there is little of it! You still placed your dear overcoat, your weird rhymes, you solved the problem, bitch. You then went about the field in your soldier's blouse . . . now I think I will shoot you in the spine, between the shoulder blades, as I have already seen, only I could not turn around comfortably, I was covered in blood, the stomach, the legs . . . you somehow thought that I had died long ago, I saw everything and how I hated you. And there you go along the field in your soldier's blouse and here how it dawned on me; I won't shoot! You went straight at the Germans you went into captivity with your own legs! O, I think, how it's better, let our Commissars work everything out with them later, it works out very well, why the last cartridge is used up on him. The last one for himself, this I got well. I heard Order 270 correctly by chance perhaps? But no, our decadents don't read orders, they don't fucking know, but in the heavens they soar, I understand. That means, that you aim directly at them, they come to you with hugs, but I rest and notice the whole picture, I'm long sighted. I don't lose any knowledge from evil, the opposite, I think very soberly. I see that the eight of them carry you off, I don't know any more, how you scared them so, with muscles, not otherwise. But one lice-ridden Sergeant remains, or however he is in their opinion. Oy, I think, Oy. A clean fart came. Will you excuse me for a minute?

He moved the chair noiselessly and left the kitchen. There was darkness: they didn't turn on the light, because everyone was sleeping: Gelena collapsed on the couch in the big guest room, where they lay her, the translator settled down just there on a crooked chaise longue, old man Dad, burdening himself to go red, started to grab shut eye still at the table and they took it away; having quickly washed the dishes, Kata left. The two of them sat down. Veshnyakov returned, his mug shone in the darkness: he had washed. He was not drunk, that was what was terrible. Where do I have it, when was it, a terrible sober madness and I'm all in its power?

'Well there. This very lowest rank of theirs was a wonder, you don't say anything. For a start he was afraid of corpses or blood, I don't know. No, corpses, corpses. Here Ninochka, you consider, covered me, she died just at the minute he approached, and so he jumped back, fucking soldier. Well go on! I think. And I roll my eyes. And I'm lying all in blood. In short, he took away my Browning and ran, he didn't even take the watch from my hand, coward. Wonders happen, a? Here I think, as there is such a going-on, while I'm not dying. Until night he lay. Later he took your little overcoat from Ninochka and crawled to the village. The next business isn't the most interesting. Katka's sister hid me in the cellar, I caught a cold there and almost died, again gangrene itself, they had to take off half the leg. But I'm alive. And do you know Gelii Mikhailovich, I hate you utterly, you can believe me. I read your verses at night and waited all the time so that I could fling them in your mug. Well I have basically thrown them, my dream came true. But next I have to say thank you to you.'

Moscow 1952

In Kirovsky there weren't even two rooms. You open the entrance door and straight away there's a kitchen. Further along you go through the kitchen, and straight away there are rooms. And what for example do you do with a winter coat, it's not understood. Besides in the kitchen Kapitosha rested on a folding bed and there was nowhere else to put her, yes she would not have agreed to move form her own place. All this was monstrously uncomfortable, and even if there were guests, anyway, in Kirovsky they didn't understand this. There was not the day that someone didn't announce themselves, towards evening a minimum of ten people sat at the table, all their friends, as guests there. And they all ambled through a potato steam, through Kapitosha's slippers and they dumped coats and overcoats on the bathroom floor. There was a terrible heat on the day of Mikhdikh's anniversary, Gelena came home from the institute worn out and sat on the floor of the kitchen, the first idiotic layout of the flat seemed to her intelligent; she couldn't see anyone. In the rooms they laughed, spoke, they called a toast, Alya bashed on the piano, and Gelena didn't see, but she definitely knew, big-nosed Mikhdikh in a velvet jacket danced the polka-moth with tiny Zhenka; Viktor sang in a base, Krot adventurously shouted, Gelik dropped his own weighty voice, what were they arguing about so . . . Ah, yes; Vitka chatted about his own eternity, shall we say, we can't understand it, but Gelik objected condescendingly; for pity's sake, we can't understand this finality, but the endlessness . . .Tolya, as always, stepped in as arbitrator-peacemaker and hummed something so disciplined.

Kapitosha went into the kitchen. Within the previous hour they had pulled her from the folding bed, forced her to go to the table to drink a glass, as she waved her arms, laughed and let out tears. Erlikh, Pashka, Kolya, all stepped down to kiss her, demanded a speech, she stiffened with a glass in her hand for three minutes, then said in a whisper: dear Mikhail Dmitrich! All were moved to laughter while Mikhdikh rushed to hug her. She sat at the table for a whole hour, it was so unusual, since she seldom got up: she remembered her dead Mum, remembered when everyone was small, laughing, she cried and very satisfied went to her space. She saw Gelena, she was alarmed; my child, what's the matter?

Nothing, nothing could she tell either to Kapitosha, or to anyone. Why, why did I go to that Energy Institute, what the hell took me there? She got hot and sick from personal high spirits, she went like a lamb, and what was she to do; for two years she couldn't find a job, they didn't hire her, they didn't hire anywhere, a daughter of the oppressed? Goodbye. Gelik was also without work, only just from the camp, who needs that? Vitushka took everything on himself, the seven of them lived a hand-to-mouth existence. Little Zhenka was ill, it's terrible to remember and here Tolya suddenly advised: 'Perhaps to the Energy Institute?' By some kind of miracle they took her on, she couldn't believe it.

She knew everything, everything, but simply hoped that somehow she would make do, that it would pass her by. And now there is this boy. How hot and bad I feel indeed!

The examiners melted from the heat, the applicants melted from the heat and she herself sat, fanning herself with a handkerchief and tensely thinking only about a glass of cold milk. There was only a half hour to endure until the end of the exam. This boy, she didn't remember his name, but somehow it was stranger, Viking like, she still thought; what is with the ridiculous parental antics and the one meaning, not leaving any doubts as to the Jewish surname. He was somehow terribly unusual. Very beautiful, very, bbbbut not only . . .clear, perhaps? There was something in it . . . well, boy, personally, because the boy, twenty-four years old according to the documents, there was something boyish in it, well, dishevelled, well, he smiles . . .Whether there is a contrast, very light hair and very black, like a jackdaw, the eyes, perhaps . . .he took the ticket, he smiled and went to get ready and she couldn't tear herself away from his gaze; carefully looking at other teachers, not tearing himself away either. A kind of wraith, honestly. She went so crazy from his appearance, that she didn't picture it even at once and then suddenly she remembered and begged to herself; only not to me, don't come to me!

As he heard, he went directly to her, quick sighted, brilliant, and he started to answer. He answered very quickly and very clearly, strongly pronouncing his rrrs in the French way; he shone his eyes and his very white teeth: he was absolutely confident with his own sparkling answer. The first question of the ticket, the second and a decided task, all irreproachably. Well all right, she said in a country accent and she gave the first dirty trick. He answered. And if so? He answered. But so? Yes, please! And if it's already so? Be a dear! She gave the task for the third course, for the fifth, he cracked them open, thinking literally for half a minute. Well that is it. She blinked desperately and unfortunately misted over a glass of milk that had indeed appeared in front of her eyes; you're not ready enough, she said in a screechy voice, I can put down for you 'satisfactory' it will be better if you come next year.

The boy looked at her closely, she let down her head here and she started to be struck carefully by something in the news; he looked at everything and she was forced to inevitably meet him eye to eye 'Why was it necessary to be so weary?' smiling he asked.

'My child, you have a fever,' Kapitosha anxiously said, 'yes, severely! Where did you catch a cold in such a heat?'

For the two weeks that Gelena lay with pneumonia, she was haunted by frozen milk waterfalls, white showers and black round-eyed jackdaws.

A conversation that never was

'Well what, let us talk. You and I seldom talk these days. It seems that you met Captain Veshnyakov in Hungary? And do you remember how you fell into captivity.'

'Well, yes.'

'Well at least say something. What will you have to drink? Cognac again? Let it be cognac, you uninteresting person.'

'You're the interesting one we have! A simple Russian, a drunkard. Go on pour.'

'Your health! Talk to me.'

'Well, he and I met. We remembered our childhood, how we fought . . .how Gronsky fell at the bridgehead . . .Then I fell into captivity and still saved him, because he pretended to be dead and then when the Germans left, he crawled away to the village, and I saved his life, it turns out.'

'So so did he thank you?'

'He thanked me! He owes me his life!'

'How good that is! But you know how it sometimes happens? One threw another wounded person in the middle of a clean field, but then the other one suddenly didn't die, but survived and saving . . .'

'Shut up, please! What do you understand? I was certain that he was dead!'

'Well yes, well yes. And that girl of yours, if you allow me, Nina! How is it, Nina, a Lermontov name! So tall, blue eyed. She also . . . Listen, but this is even terrible, why are you drinking on your own? In that case pour me one. So Nina, Nina?'

'This is what kind of cognac? KVVK?'

'My dear, I'm not coming to terms with them! I understood that you don't want to talk about Nina. Well good, my dear? That is how I named you, and it cake to my mind straight away. My dear, that I squealed on you to Losev.'

'But, what my dear? A terrible cunt, that dear one! He's insinuating friendship, some verses he thrust into my hands . . . incompetents . . . fucking symbolists!'

'Poetry? Listen, what a coincidence. It means that he himself was a poet! And despite that, he rushed to hammer at you, at the poet! Who had it, when a poet was hammering at a poet? And for what? For poetry! For, if I'm not mistaken, a poem about Stalin!

'I forbid you to talk about the 'Great Tyrant!'

'Listen, what kind of conversation have we got, here 'shut up' here 'I forbid.' Really can there not be openness between us? Mitya wrote a poem about Stalin, the bloody tyrant, destroying his own people, even before the war he wrote it and hid it in your room; before Stalingrad itself he handed it to Alya, she gave it to you at New Year, you couldn't burn it in the room, it was the last will of Mitya, interestingly did he understand even how it exposes you all? Well, it's not important. And why don't you know it by heart? Is it too long? it's not important, it's not important. And then the brilliant decision, so far as the poem is of an epic quality and the tyrant hasn't been called by name, you decide to write it again in a few places, on Ivan the Terrible . . .'

'Be quiet! I can't throw out Mitka's manuscript!'

'I agree, my dear . . .Phoo, to be lost again my dear. He struck you again . . .how did you vanish so?'

'I sewed her overcoat from the very start, and then fell under the rain . . .'

'Yes, yes, the overcoat, of course. The same one that you hid . . .'

'Silence!'

'There, again be quiet. Good. Your health! You don't want to talk about Nina, lets talk about something else. I was frankly happy, sending you to Hungary. What are you staring at me for, Foma the Unbeliever? Tell me then about captivity. Where do I go with the vodka. The vodka is mine. Let me pour it for you myself. Well?'

'What about captivity?'

'What got to me isn't that you fell into captivity there, well its the least of anything. It's something else . . .that you didn't for a second think about the consequences. You're a wonderful person. Well on the whole your commander . . .well Baev, Baev that failed schizophrenic should have taught you something! Oh fuck! They robbed indeed! Veshnyakov, by the way, in comparison with you . . .well good, we got distracted. Tell me about captivity.'

'I will tell you about captivity. But how strange you are today! Captivity . . .do you know how they amazed me? First they had organisation! The war ends, they fucked up the war and what about it? They fell apart, decomposition, despair? In one minute! Everything is clear, everyone works, everyone is even happy!'

'You don't say so! Did they interrogate you?'

'Interrogate me? No they chatted with me.'

Well how did that happen? First they ask the name, yes? You named your own.'

My dear, what am I to you and Zoya Kosmodemyanskaya, who is called Tanya? They had in their hands all my documents, name, title, number of my unit . . .'

'Next. The structure of our force. And the mood of the force.'

'Yes! And what was there to hide? You think nothing, towards the end of the war they learnt everything themselves?! And I spoke my mind about the mood; what mood could there be, if we had already beaten Germany? A good mood.'

'So. And your speciality is in the airwaves. About chemical weapons.'

'And you're knowledgeable, I see! Your health. It's good cognac but this isn't KVVK.'

'And so about the chemicals.'

'Yes! Well what, iprit, lewisite, adamsit (that is how I call adamsmith). Do you understand, what did they teach us in the academy? They all yelled at us, there was the data of our intelligence about their German chemical weapons. Or

American. And that generally in the time of the First World War . . .So they all knew, I didn't tell them anything new.'

'So you didn't say much?'

'Listen, what are you insinuating? Beating around the bush somehow? You're very suspicious of me!'

'My dear, what are you about? Foo, again, my dear one! By the way, this dear scum bag of yours sort of learnt it in Volsk, yes? Yes, definitely in Volsk! He told you about it indeed in the first of your conversations.'

'Ahhh that's what you're about! Yes, it was so. They say, where do the staff prepare the chemical troops? And here I remember at once this Volsk Chemical School!'

'And surrendered it to the Germans.'

'Listen, just there mustn't be any loud words! I could explain to you, but you're stupid and you would hardly understand. Stupid and vulgar, forgive me. Your health! You're vulgar because of the way you think. What did I surrender? But there listen, how I think. There are weeks until the end of the war. Obviously ours will come and free me. All protocols of questioning fall to the Smersh and there they find out everything, what I said in the questioning. You say that you would have been as quiet as a spineless creature? No my dear, here you're vulgar. I'm not Zoya Kosmodemyanskaya! I didn't want to be our Soviet mar . . .mart . . .martyr! The situation is the other way around: to be silent means to save your skin. This I couldn't do anyhow, I have pride and belief and a congenital dislike of lying.'

'What quirks! This means that you loved the truth?'

'Quiet!'

'No, no, I'm listening to you and very attentively. But so how interesting is our Soviet person, it's difficult to cheat without sanctions, without indulgence . . .'

'Monster! You haven't understood anything!'

'My dear, be quiet for a minute and let me say, I understood everything at once, I like a few people can understand you. Don't touch my vodka, why are you set on it! I will pour you some myself, and that again passing its target. Look, the whole table cloth is wet! You will now tell me, what this captivity was like. . .the Germans had everything clean tidy and happy. How were you all in Rohman with the sense of the approaching victory, you were nearly drunk from despair. That nowhere drank so terribly and hopelessly as in the army of the victor and in that the contrast with the cheerful army of the defeated was more terrible. What were you, how is it said? Gulp another life, o yes. Well, and next. . .because of the uselessness of your testimony your conversation on the interrogation went more on personal lines and here you stalled! You said yourself, never and nowhere were you so free as in captivity and you admired the paradox and believed in it piously. And then you approved of it yourself. . .or the indulgence, and spoke freely with seniority, with those invested with power, the power in which is over you! You spoke with them as equals. And glorying in this sensation, you told them all with happiness and about iprit, luizit and about Volsk, and I even think, whether you were not excited, remembering by accident this Volsk? How you could finally be useful to them though in something. And whether you thought then, chuckling to yourself: there, they say, tomorrow the German esquadrille will fly to bomb Volsk?

'Get lost!!'

'Oh, don't shout like that! I didn't tell you anything new, even boring. I'm leaving myself. It's long since time, by the way, and that I'm here with you like a parasite. Farewell. I don't think it's worth our while meeting.'

Gelik Moscow 1981

A week after their return from Hungary with Gelik, there happened a strange incident, which had never happened before. In the day, when there was nobody at home, he drank on his own until he lost consciousness. He got drunk very strangely: Gelena came home from work, not late, at five o'clock and found him on the floor of the kitchen, but in the dining room, where he he had been drinking, two empty bottles stood on the table, vodka and cognac. Gelik ne-ve-r! drank vodka, he couldn't even stand the smell. Meanwhile, there was a single glass and on a lonely saucer half a boiled egg. All evening and all night they stayed, Gelik was so ill, that Gelena tried to call the emergency services, but Viktor laughed: the fuck, they propose to detox you! The devil knows what that was, the man isn't young, not at all the healthiest. On the following day, almost coming to himself, he asked in a dull voice 'Tolya hasn't appeared?' 'Where does Tolya come into this?!' Gelena cried out 'you drank with him or what?' At the word 'drank' Gelik wearily winced: it thundered in his head 'besame mucho' on strange, intolerably known words 'they robbed our ten scholars . . .the rage I retain in my heart . . .' at every 'r' a pain went into the nape of the neck. 'yes, no . . .I'm on my own . . .'

The strangest thing happened to Tolya, but in the same time a completely normal story. 'You're exactly like children.' Viktor angrily said, 'so pious, ey, my God. What is strange here? Eternally this your . . .you live as if in the clouds. (this was a type of leitmotif of their mutual life: Gelik and Alya, shall we say, were sublime, all about Blok yes about Blok, and Viktor kind of close, but Gelena so earthy, you don't talk to them about literature, they either all about Zhek or about the shops).' 'But how Vitya. . .' Alya said confusedly. 'Well so many years . . .(everyone shuddered, remembering the hairy goose form Kasheevy, Kaliteevki). 'Yes, so many years! Viktor angrily answered, 'and we are all idiots. Yet, consider yourself lucky.'

And such was the affair. Four days after their return from Hungary a 'penguin' appeared as a guest at Kirovsky, a secret service man accompanied their group on the journey. He had to accept it for half an hour, this was an act of loyalty and diplomacy, in such business they always put forward Viktor and he, tall and solid in golden glasses, conducted negotiations with the housekeeper, with the cleaner, with the director of the female school . . .well and this bloke took it on himself. Gelik left to walk around Chistoprudny, Alya sat in the far room, all in clouds of cigarette smoke, and nervously leafed through a new Trifonov, Gelena brought coffee and biscuits into the dining room at the front and retired to the very same far room. Viktor took out of the sideboard the 'white stork,' time went by. 'How did you like the trip? 'The most interesting country!' 'And your ladies are satisfied?' 'The ladies are very satisfied!' All in that vein. And here Tolya appeared, all the guys usually came in the evening, but Tolya, unpredictable, ran to eat in the middle of the day, he would throw up some tickets . . .and right there would run off, for a minute, poked his nose into the room: Vit, so about chess . . .he pronounced with a swift look, the 'penguin' and Tolya, Tolya the 'penguin', Tolya, smiling radiantly, said: Oh, forgive me! I flew like a naked chick in the yard. I will not annoy you. See you soon, Vit!'

They didn't see Tolya ever again.

'We are idiots!,' raged Viktor 'We are idiots! There are fifty people in the house, the door is ajar and we make jokes! That psycho was too little for us that he opened the gas! It would have been possible, it seems, to think who to let into the flat! Well Vitya,' Alya lit one from the other, her fingers were completely yellow from nicotine. 'Agree that he is here from

1950 something, which, by the way? Does anyone remember? There! He is with us from fifty something and we don't have either his address or his place of work, nothing! We don't know anything, we don't remember anything! The likes of you're not of this world. We composed a parody of 'questions of language-knowledge' and fifty people appeared at New Year and everyone read it, Vit, we wrote a parody after 1956!' Gelik weakly defended himself 'and thank you for that!' Viktor rumbled 'we haven't completely gone out of our minds yet! And little it's possible to think, you composed up to 1956?! Pious people!!' 'I don't know, don't know,' Gelena tried to fight back 'he was such a friend to us, he helped . . .(everyone remembered Gusya again) as if he wouldn't help us!!' Viktor blew up. 'Yyyyes. We must think, he had opportunities,' Alya drew out, gradually getting used to the terrible news. 'What to do now?' Gelena was confused and asked with despair. 'I don't know what to do! I should have thought earlier! That's what's interesting, but you, it means, shouldn't have?! What indeed stopped you from being discerning?! Do you know what I say to you, my dears . . .' the momentarily silent Erlikh suddenly joined in, who also took part in the family council 'don't especially panic. He won't do anything.'

They all stared into his eyes.

'Well what, look . . .he was with us since 1950 something. He had opportunities. We gave him reason . . .ah, no, nothing. Next. Tell me, why did he construct this farce. Why, Vit, did he burst into all this chess playing? Like a naked chick in the yard, yes? Like he said himself. He what, didn't understand, what you had at the side? He what, you didn't have the day before and he didn't listen to your conversations and didn't know, who should have come to you at that time? My dears, who is he in your opinion, a negotiator? You think badly about them.'

'So what do you think?'

'I think he knew everything well. He did all of this on purpose. He, how do you say it . . .went the distance. Himself. Knowingly. He said goodbye to all of us. Why is a different question. Not to me. And lets go home already, I'm frozen from your conspiracies.'

2006 ER magazine
'Confession of the children of the century'
A series of interviews with people older than 100 years
One of the interviews, the transcript:
Podolyanskaya Evgeniya Nikolaevna 106 years old
My dears, tell me, where do I talk, because I don't see very well. But can I do it just like that? Well ok. I will tell you, I'm more overwhelmed with this progress. But do you know what? Not that it's quick. Oooh, we thought that people would be flying themselves on their own wings in the 21st century, but at the moment it's only in aeroplanes and in these. . . how do you call it? Icarus was still flying in these. So that progress isn't quick in actual fact, but what shakes me up is how convenient it is. That's the main thing. I can't read, one of my eyes doesn't see, so there? My Grandchildren bought me an invention, that it's possible to listen to books; and I have already listened to so many, to both the classics and to modern writers. I love prose a lot . . .I tell you it's such a delight.

Fine, let you yourselves ask then otherwise I will begin to blabber . . .my Grandchildren say: Granny, be quiet, how you talk a lot! Not seriously, of course, in jest. And the Great-Grandchildren. But listen, here I will ask . . .my grandson is older than sixteen, so if he has a child, I will be a Great-Great Grandmother! A record. Do they write about those things in your newspaper?

My Grandchildren, Great-Grandchildren, are not mine . . . .they are my grand-nephews. They are the real Grandchildren and Great-Grandchildren of my sister, and she has already not been around for a long time . . .Oh, how many I have buried, oy, my dear ones . . .I'm amazed at how long I'm alive. At first I so regretted that I'm not dying anyhow . . .when I buried my dear sister, when my darling niece, son-in-law . . .but then I thought: there is something in this, probably, a thought, I don't know . . .but it's forbidden to grieve, it means.

Yes, yes. Drink coffee! I drink an idiotic type, without anything. Yes, there you go. You're interested in what indeed? About the nineteenth century. But I didn't exist then. But my little sister did. Natasha. She was born in 1894. And we had a great relationship, despite the difference in age. We lived in St Petersburg, and of course I remember little, but I remember Natasha from my early years. How we loved each other and were friendly with each other. And then the war started. Natasha was already a grown-up, she was right here in Tsarskoe Selo on a course of the Sisters of Charity, Princess Gedrots taught them there, you have heard, probably? OOOH, what a severe woman she was! She cut through people. And she wrote poetry under a male name. Then a lot of girls moved to the Sisters of Charity, especially when Alexandra Fyodorovna headed the committee. And she also bandaged the soldiers herself. And what about me? I was depressed. I was younger, they didn't let me out anywhere. And as only I could, as I became fifteen, there closer to where Natasha was in the Tsarskoe Selo hospitals. Everyone was scared that I wasn't up to it, that I wouldn't last, that I was weak, but I turned out to be stronger than anyone! I bandaged the worst cases and everything that was necessary and was present at operations. Later we were sanitaries on the sanitary train of ours . . .oy, what I tell you will be funny. I only later found out that on that indeed then, in 1916, the poet Esenin was a sanitary person, but we didn't know him . . .I would have argued with him for all his future presentations, I tell you honestly! Because this 'Snegina', I will announce to you that it's so vulgar! 'He is to you' is it not anything?!

(A scream from the kitchen: Grandmother!)

Oh, you have seen it? They are controlling. Well all right, it's not important in actual fact about Esenin. Well there, it was a wonderful time. Those kinds of horizons, those kinds of people, oy! At home we saw very little of interest, they cared for us with a firm hand, they didn't let us out anywhere. But it opened up here for us . . .and we didn't stay without attention. We returned from the war, happy! Yess, as I remember, it bites directly on the nose. We returned but in the town so much was happening, that . . .oy, it's even horrible to imagine it, I flinch. I always had one question: why were they cultivating a mess all around? This is some incontinence directly: straight there, where he went, there and . . .I understand: revolution, the outrage of the masses. But the mess . . . well it's not important. And here my Natasha gave birth to a daughter, my favourite niece. Because in war life is born. This, my dears, you have to learn. If the parents were alive if there were no events, oy, if it wasn't that! And so . . .no one had any business, and thank God. I remember we arrived to register her, such a terrible chick was sitting there, with a long moustache, Commissar, how do they say, call it and who is the father? But Natasha answers so calmly: her Father is Alphonse. And what do you think? The chick Commissar drools all over the pencil and writes dearly in metrics: Alfonsovna. How we laughed . . .

And what to say to you next. . .at first we raised our girl and somehow got a little distracted by it. Around we only saw the thirties . . .and further . . .oh, how terrifying a time it was, to remember it is agonising. Natasha lived with us all and thought: if only something happened, even a war, perhaps, would start. Everything better than this. A terrible time! The further it got the worst it was, the worst . . .you know that if I blabber a lot you correct me. I have become such a chatterbox, simply terrible. My Great Grandchildren say to me: Grandmother, it's good to gab. So you leave me like that. And probably, another coffee is needed. Olechka! Be good and boil some more.

. . . This is Natasha and me in hospital. This is us sending our girl to school for the first time . . .this is her at ten years old, do you see the cake? I baked it myself! I exactly baked really well and have forgotten everything. A cake with candles. Ten years.

. . .I, coffee! Thank you! Pour some yourself. And eat 'the cow,' I beg you, otherwise I will eat it all and I'm not allowed. Olya, take it away from me . . .Well there you go. We lived gloomily enough, Natasha was saying all the time: this should end with something, there will be a war, you will see! But life is natural, such a thing couldn't happen there. She didn't talk idly, she was very intelligent. The war began. We had to get it into our heads straight away, but we were here and there . . .we were not the youngest. . .the girl in our hands, although grown up, such a dopey one . . .in general, so we got stuck in Leningrad, and we had to get to the front at any price. Oh, how we cursed everything then, why we were not at the front. Well, then, you understand yourself there was a blockade next. The devil! I frankly hate to recall it, but ok already, I tackled it. The main thing is hatred, I tell you. Such wild hatred, such black hatred under a tea spoon. For the hatred. Personal. To everyone. Since I'm not able to see, I can't hear, though I know, that it's a lie, a mental disorder. I can't tolerate either

Chancellor Kohl or Chancellor Schroeder, I just turn off straight away and that's it. And I can't, I can't . . .give me a cigarette, please . . .aha thank you. Now I . . . a couple of puffs . . .that's all. Stub it the hell out! This isn't a war at all, where everything is different. This is the torture of the entire town. A torture of the most basic type, the most insubstantial. From your stomach. Like they torture in a kind of pain, with fire, and here, well what would it be like? But it betrays your stomach. Oh. The main thing isn't to become kinder, when you become kinder it's the end. We didn't get kinder for anything. And so somehow we survived and later our salvation came. There was one Lieutenant Colonel, a compassionate person, he took us to the front. First I was with him, later Natasha, she fitted his age more, he loved mature ones. And later, when an invitation arrived for him to go to Romania and Hungary, we sent our girl with him. Natasha said, it's time she lived. And we sent her.

And when they came back from the war, we were the whole life together. They had Olya. He was a very sweet person. Very soft, though you wouldn't cope with him at once, to look at him he was a bull. When we buried Natasha, when our girl also died, she had two months to go to her eighteenth birthday, she didn't last, the poor thing, the two of us were left and that's how we lived for a time. He was a worthy but abrupt man. And later he also died and then already the children came to me. Children! What children there . . .Grandchildren and Great-Grandchildren.

No my dears, I'm not getting agitated, what is there to be agitated about? But I will tell you in all my experience . . . there are things, which are not possible without war. They simply don't exist in life, and that's all. It's difficult for you to understand because it turns out that you don't know. . .I, it happens, am depriving you of a lot now . . .but believe me you don't so often see one hundred year old old women, I think, but nevertheless, foo foo I'm in sound mind. It's simpler to believe me there. There is war but everything etc, decay, nuances, but it's necessary to spit at them, as you know, it's said in a book: you mustn't finish taking from it. I read this one novel now . . .I mean hear, that it's said there.

Next? But next there was nothing interesting.

PART TWO

They sent the regiment into campaign,
in order that you did not wait for me.

M.Y. Lermontov

Mikhail Dmitrievich, my dear!

It's of course all very touching what you write, but I'm not that type. I have a tough character, but I can't cope with everything, they all leave me from subordination. Mitya is a sliced loaf. What is going on with this person, I can't understand. In the day he is drunk. He comes in at six in the morning, he doesn't come into the room, but frankly collapses in the kitchen. Fine, I get up earlier than the neighbours, but we don't indeed invite trouble or scandal. But today, I will tell you more; I go along the corridor, I hear a commotion, I enter, someone, someone's shadow, a sudden appearance and through the dark way. Mitya, who is it? He stands with a bucket, he splashes the water. His eyes are completely glassy. 'You don't hear me, perhaps?' He's silent. I turned and went away. Later he came and said: Varvara, you can't order me around.

Ok! I can't! How many times did I tell Sergei: let's move somewhere else! How many chances were there to get a flat. No, we must live the whole life in the one little room, where her Tamochka was living, where the children were born, where she died. And so I went to her, to that room with Tamochka's shadow, she raised her children and all with Tamochka's shadow: and now I can't order them around. The evil stepmother. I say, let us move, the children have grown up, time is passing! No, it's not possible to leave these walls.

Forgive me, Mikhail Dmitrievich. This is all in vain and I'm confessing my sin. But it goes badly sometimes, it means, they see me as a severe woman? You don't tell me a word across it? But where are my rights? To sit in eighteen square metres.

I write badly. Badly, and you don't even tell me anything. I don't have any style, but a single housing question in mind. There you are, yes, you own it by the pen. I'm a country chick they say, with a cool temper and confused! I let out a lot of noise and business goes all about as it wishes. So, I have already written.

That's it! I have said it all. I will go now to wash the floor after them.

Good bye, Mikhail Dmitrievich!

Your Varvara.

Dear Varvara Erofeyevna!

You upset me with your last letter, how indeed can I help you? I don't have any kind of influence on Mitya, although sometimes I chat pretty well with him, when he is with us. I see in him as a big talent and he has started to read a lot in the last while. But I see also a short fuse and passion and free will. And I can hardly do anything here, what am I to him? No more than the Father of a friend. A relic? I swear to you, they say that.

I notice that in the last while Mitya is getting close to Alya, this can seem to be a good influence on him. She is considerably older and wiser. In any case her influence like an older sister on Gelik is invaluable, and I pin big hopes on her and in the case of Mitya too.

I have a strange feeling, of course, that their company is reckless, all the signs of brainless youth is present and this, I tell you physiologically, an ongoing stupidity from the same organism, I feel this, if it's convenient, this I remember. But in this, whether you believe it, I see in them a huge talent, if not in all of them, so in most. And this I give my word, isn't about my own children: Alya is more focused on her studies than on creativity, while Gelik's writing is still very naive and whether it will bloom is God's will. But there Igor and Kolya produce an invariably huge impression on me, there is a clear blow (I beseach you not to tell Gelik), Mara is a great poet, has a rare voice and certainly you must nurture it, Krot paints wonderfully, Mitya whom I number by authority as one of my children almost and because I can't praise him, certainly is going down the necessary path, he gives in to this way of thinking. I believe so. For the time being, he is simply not up to managing his passions, which nature has endowed and probably enquire thus a bully. But he copes, it seems to me, and implements true priorities.

Don't worry, Varvara Erofeevna, I implore you, Everything will take shape.

Always yours M.D

(Mikhdikh got this letter accidentally: the answer of Varvara Erofeevna is written on the back.)

Mikhail Dmitrievich, you're simply a fool! Forgive me that I speak like this, you know how I respect you. But how indeed this pious innocence and naivety of yours anger me!

Alya is 'significantly older' than Mitya?! Alya is three years older than Mitya! Alya and Mitya have a romance! You don't see anything around your own nose with a hump!

And I'm nothing yet, I will be happy, because Alya is a good girl, and all has improved, that Mitka was with her and didn't steer the girl with Elohovskaya and Razgulyaya. And there in your place I would be worried. Mitka also drinks and fights in the day but makes regular visits. One hope, in Alya, how do you say it? A good influence. you're killing me, ej, ej.

It's amazing how everything turns out.

I don't see a penny of talent in him, nor in Gelik, don't be offended. The poems are terrible. About the others I don't know, let us say yes. Something else worries me more, their moods. I don't have any strength to chat about everything. For the meantime, when the children were small, I had one thought; that they be healthy, At Sergei you don't shout until you're heard, you don't get help. But then somehow I managed it, at least they were not ill. But now I don't know what to think. Such idiots, they are already letting go of their hearts.

Well there, I started with an idiot, I finish with an idiot. I wont even excuse myself, you understand everything yourself. Another time I will write happier.

Varvara

(something of the letter is lost. One flooded with tea hopelessly.)

Dear Mikhail Dmitrievich.

Don't worry and don't twitch, what to do if such a fate has befallen, you and I are just one thing: Hold on and don't get ill, our help to the children could be necessary. To both Mitka and Gelik. Do you know, I thought of everything the first days, we have already survived so much, what are we doing it again for? And later it seemed to me, that this is retribution. I struggle to tell Sergei, the first days were very hard already, just as Mitka left. He snapped: for what, supposedly, is this retribution? I say, for the sins of the Fathers. He started to shout that I'm an idiot. He was drunk. It's easier for him when he drinks. Little Tamochka cried all the time in the first days, she didn't go to the institute, she didn't eat. And what was I to do? I didn't start to drink, I can't cry. There is something else, Mikhail Dmitrievich. The town is white. Sergei found out. Tomorrow, the day after tomorrow I will write more, now I have to wash the window, as September is already ending.

V

Hello, Mikhail Dmitrievich!

First things first, I will tell you about the business. Now communication has already settled down, it's possible to send a parcel. Woollen socks, a few pairs. Insoles. If there are some, boots. I have a spare at home, but they are not Gelik's size. Everyone has my big feet. If you don't find any, we will send ours, it will coil at the foot more. Don't send chocolate! They eat well there. It's necessary to send tarragon! It's good also for the teeth, and from worms. So I see that you shuddered now, as you would, such vulgarity. you're very unadaptable, Mikhail Dmitrievich. You don't survive life in a velvet jacket. Yes, what to say to you is a hundred times said.

A letter came from Mitya, this you know, because he also wrote to Alya. All, he says, is great and he is torn to battle, the little fool. Sergei is in full ecstasy. The evil in me for them isn't enough. I took it on myself to sew the shirts for the hospital, so in that the goodness didn't appear, for four nights I sewed, on the fifth day Sergei took them, he should have taken them to Serpukhov, so along the road he sat somewhere, possibly, drank, sooner than nothing. I spat, it's not in my strength. Then again I took up to sew, yes I already passed it on to a neighbour, so, to hear, there is my portrait with other lead-writers hung on the wall, 'they help people at the front.'

Your eternal Varvara

Dear Mikhail Dmitrievich, Mitya is no longer with us. I know this for sure, he is nowhere on the planet. I have no intuition, not maternal, why would I, there isn't anything still there. Only I know this, I'm not talking to Sergei, I'm not telling anyone, but I'm writing this to you.

Misha, my dear,

So I indeed see, how you shuddered: ah, the conspiracy is ruined. But I tell you, I can't do any more. Why did you drag these hypocritical morals on your shoulders for so many years? Why do you carry it now? How many years have gone by since that parental meeting, when you and I sat at one desk? In which class were the boys? You don't remember, but I do. In the sixth. But Alechka was in the eighth or the ninth. That means ten years old.

I remember everything. I have a disease of the memory. It doesn't erase anything, it retains everything. We cursed Mitka as usual, we praised Gelik as always. I sit as the fool of fools and all the time thought, there in the evening I will argue with Sergei, so that he sent me to this execution. And if he wouldn't send me? It could have been so, that we didn't meet. Not so, like that, how these meet, platonically, we would have met. And not for anything it would have bred an execution. And later we went from school together, it was the coldest November. In Archipovsky you took me by the hand and unclenched it to yourself, I would never have thought, that you with your soft habits, with your old-fashionedness, with these velvet jackets of yours, how then I couldn't wake up. As later. Never. It will break me, Misha, this . . .Sergei couldn't, not for anything.

Ten years. Two years of meeting behind the corners. Seven years, then another.

What were we thinking about then, tell me? About how it would be easy to correspond? About it being like that. Such idiots.

There can't be any 'even so.' Here either with the eye down, or this breaks, will turn out that it's not held. I don't know any more.

What kind of a wedding is that for me, I live with one widower, I go out of my mind about the other. But they remember all their own dead people and I have no strength to be jealous of dead people. I know that I'm not right I know that I'm not fair, I know that you love me. Forgive me. And in truth, I'm going out of my mind.

Yes, I wanted to add, don't worry about Gelik, Gelik will soon return. Sergei again drank for three days and on the fourth day he got up and went to work, I thought he wouldn't make it, but no he made it. He returned after a day, sober. That's it,

Varvara, he says. Beria wished to curtail the business, but that. . . And all, in general, whoever is possible, to send home. But Gelik, it's possible, he fell at the very end, they will not detain these ones for long. Shorten this business, he says, it's not elastic, it collapses.

Misha, why is it all like this? you're so educated, so intelligent, so thin, explain to me, how it's that we bury our own children, but we ourselves are so strong, strength and passion are in abundance? And I only want you, only you, but Mitka is in a grave the devil knows where, and Alya didn't put any kind of headstone up for him.

That's it, I don't have any more strength, no. I thought, I'm hardy, I endure everything, but you're so thin, so tender.

Farewell, Mikhail Dmitrievich, I kiss you.

And this letter I will burn, I'm not abnormal.

(and she burnt it).

The bookbinder

The manifesto of the order of the rascals.

An old oak, a stupid, baron boar, a knight of heavenly duty, be a chorale for me, be a ward for me, be a witness for me, be a witness for all of us. Now and ever and fresh and closely, closely grouped and obese, be a witness for us. And sonorously still.

Still I announce the manifesto. So now, the manifesto.
'Don't be a rat.'
'Live on cold foods without liquids secretly on the sly.'
'Don't piss whatever happens.'
'Don't fuck a beautiful girl before me.'
'Don't be a rat, 2'
Because it's said; forgive everything and forgive all. But a rat is a battle. And if a rascal is a rat, yes, he wanks in loneliness and forgetting.

Such was the manifesto of the scoundrel form the 2nd of November 1945. Later we changed the editorship, but the essence stayed the same: there were five, we were D'Artagnans, we were hooligans, Rastignacs and squabblers. We didn't wish to know any more.

'There were five of us. We wanted to live.'
'And they hanged us. We turned black,' as the poet said.
But turning black, we we were resurrected, rose up, called, raised, rose and ascended.

Without a parachute, that was our quality.

Alyosha, Barcelona, 2007

At first the panorama: a huge cathedral. A gigantic construction, a mockery over the norms of architecture, it's not human, wearily big. That is why the frame gets gradually closer, on the sly, on the sly it runs into one of the lancet windows in one of the highest towers. The view changes, there it is, it stands so small in a window hole. There is no glass. It looks down from a terrible height, from a terrible height. Downwards, people, people, people, it doesn't recognise anyone from such a distance and it doesn't differentiate. And then, despairing to see, it oversteps an empty window frame and flies down. The parents woke him, screaming and wet from sweat like a mouse, they were pulled from a ruined bed. Then Mum dried his back, and Dad heated milk mixed in a spoonful of honey. Then he knew exactly what type of pacification to the taste, now all, there was nobody to rub his back, at the war he dreamt a dream almost every night and he continues to dream it since; and there he reached Barcelona and saw it, his own cathedral.

But generally most problems were with his nose, like he forgot everything, everything burned down from itself, and only the nose, only the nose . . .the Achilles heel is the nose. There it smelled of rottenness, so springlike and sweet, or cucumber, or warm blood, and all. In Barcelona it also smelled of rottenness and cucumber and chestnuts. In Barcelona it was his exhibition. He agreed because a mathematician lived there, a second cousin, best friend. And he had been begging him to come for a hundred years.

Alyosha, childhood

A good photograph, the sun, a decorative antique car, green-green and teenage boys, hilarious: One grew up in the summer, bolted ten centimetres and stood, such a tall one, dark haired and swarthy, he is hugging the other one by the shoulders, the second one is the most emaciated and for the time being short, curly and bespectacled. Both are sparkling. With white, in words along a diagonal 'In memory of Palang. 1979.'

When I was born Dad was still happy. He was already happy ten years up to that moment, but later everything changed quickly enough. But he didn't understand this, my unhappy Dad.

And then again, either he found a photograph, or, as I now see the painting, the azure sky, the white steam ship, boys-girls, adults, all in white on the radio, Kumparsita, someone dances on deck and all around is ice cream in creamy tins. Here I take this steamship in two fingers, at it everything is at the bottom in the mire, and I accurately turn over upside down, with all these boys-girls, cream jars in the water, in the depths. And I clean the wet hands with a towel.

We are sitting in our dacha, the weather is terrible, the rain is pouring, pouring all summer, cold, the cotton clothes have been frozen through, heavy, I'm ill, I still hadn't learnt then how not to be ill, Mum, hating the dacha with all her soul, is warming milk on the hob. The little fig languishes in the bucket, everyone is advising, is great from the cough. 'Maybe, all the same we will go to the town?' Mum says calmly, but inside, I know it's a hurricane. 'But what are we already having to go for,' distractedly asks Dad, his thoughts not about that, he is taking some old photographs. 'Summer, dacha, breathing the air . . .great . . .but Alyosha will already not be coughing tomorrow, you wont be?' 'I will be!' I mumble with a nasty voice, this dacha I have seen in the grave. 'It wont be, it wont be!' Dad picks up as if not listening, 'the weather has evened out, I tell you. But we are going to the little river, my Father always caught carp here . . .'

Mum is quiet and rubs figs in the pot.

Later I understand that 'my Father' was Dad's vile welcome, and Mum couldn't do anything any more. Here all my parent's arguments stopped short. 'Here' of course no carp was caught. Where that dacha is with carp, with grapes with spikes, with tightly filled gladioli, the azure sunset, sickening melted sundae in cream jars. . .preference in the evening on the veranda . . .they took Grandfather's dacha, and one dacha was fine. He was already very old. Only only he was waiting for his son. From the front or from wherever else still, to spit, who will tidy up? He so waited for him all through the war and later another year almost. And there he basically calmed down and began to sleep normally at nights and got ready for his pension, because of his age group and his were not as they were and he couldn't operate, they ordered mouldboard in the institute, and there also. The pension, a good pension.

Our present shack, they allocated Mum this allotment at work. Along that rail road. Such a coincidence. Mum wanted to refuse, but Dad howled. There we are sitting around a thin reflector, which hardly hardly warms the room. I'm ill from bugs and I'm coughing heavily. When I don't need to be ill, I'm no longer ill.

'You and I, Lyokha,' Dad all the wearier continues dreamily, 'tomorrow we will plant the gladioli. And on the little river . . .we will not only catch carp on the little river, we will travel there on such a steamer on along it, just look,' he dug in a heap of photographs: the steamer, all in white, the sweet life. 'We will swim, there will be music and we will eat ice cream . . .because this is what I say to you. Truth always finds a little hole . . .(at this moment Mum turns on the hob and tries to go to the porch to smoke.) But don't you lie, don't be in a whirl, don't distort, but still she is where she should climb. They will take it away from you, and they will take it away for a long time! And then it will come back to you, your truth . . .'

My Dad was a very bad writer. Hopelessly bad. Shamelessly bad.

But now I can't even blow up this cunt of a steamer, because it leaves that Dad had unbearable cinematic vulgarity; it's necessary to immerse the hands. It's not too comfortable; the hands in seaweed up to the nails, but the boys-girls and cream jars are revealed between the fingers, the carp is hitting me by the little finger and smells of baked fig milk. But nevertheless.

When Dad published his own work, how happy he was for a while. How radiant he was and whistled, oh, it's not possible to remember better.

Mum was not, Mum in her own eternal malicious misanthropy didn't believe in anything, didn't hope for anything, didn't wait for anything, wasn't disappointed in anything. She knew of course that Dad was a dreadful writer. But not once in life, not in sleep or in spirit, did she give any hint of this to be understood . . . And generally, how she tried for me, to protect . . .

'Alyosha, don't be deluded,' yes, yes exactly this I remember: Mum in front of the mirror, the hair pulled back and tied with a silk scarf, in the face mashed from cucumber skins, therefore speaking not of unclenching lips, trying not to move the facial muscles: Alyosha don't be deluded, with the big finger upwards. 'This promised land does not help you in anything ever, and don't expect goodness from it. Build your own defence, Alyosha. Comply with their rules, pay the receipts. And so, keep yourself at a distance.'

She always said that. When in school there began some rubbish about the fifth point, when they stole a bicycle 'Alyosha don't even think of paying attention, don't even think of being dependant on them. Wierdos don't go anywhere, and you have your own life, a lot of honour to look back at them.'

But in order.

In 1965 Dad published his own camp prose. He had written it a long time ago, ten years previously, he began when Granddad was still alive, then I had been born, he scribbled all the time such at nights and read Mum pieces, she listened very attentively. Later it was brought into a magazine and they published it. I would never have found out about it ever, if it had not been for the story of a drinking bought ten or twelve years later. It was a certain September, little rivers and boats, an Indian summer the mathematician and I were returning from school, Mum took out a goose from somewhere, it was clear that guests were unavoidable. The parents urgently convened an evening of guests. And while Dad fought with the expanding table, Mum quickly got the food ready, Motka and I, languishing in praise, imagining ourselves young geniuses, lounging on the couch, feasted on imported white ripenings from the dacha and brought the stupidest conversations, it shameful to remember. We argued with them then . . .

I took it weakly, to drink a glass of vodka in a single gulp? He doesn't drink. But there I drink. He grinded his lips: 'How do you generally imagine yourself? You honestly fill up in front of Mum?' I say without pity: 'I pour it in the kitchen, from the freezer on the sly.' Motka climbed the wall, he felt very bad for of me: he so loved me, but I wondered all the time about something. 'Perhaps your Mum won't even notice it,' he said nervously and smiled. He always smiled. 'And mine there, for example, notices everything.' I of course, right there with pleasure, called him a coward. I also loved him very much. There were no chances to stop any more. We struck a bargain. In a few hours the guests began to gather, they drove us from the couch, moved the crippled table to him, everyone started to shout, laugh and sit. . .

I had an idea to throw the mathematician out of the kitchen, to quickly pour a glass of water and then in front of him solemnly knock back a single gulp. But in a panic he didn't leave after me, but got up tall at the door and looked at me with despairing eyes, all the while hoping that suddenly I would come to my senses. The lop-eared fool. I then wildly got angry with myself, took vodka from the freezer, poured a glass and gulped it down: that is all, of course, it didn't go in, I choked. But I drank more than half a glass any way. I stood looking at him. And he at me, with his little eyes through his glasses as if it it poison and I was now dying. He blinked in terror.

And suddenly such a despair took hold of me. So sad. I don't know any more how he brought me to the room; and the main thing how to my bed behind the wardrobe, how my parents were, by the way they were all there already adding properly, and Mum and Aunt, of course, understood everything. Mum looked into my corner.

'It's the vodka?'

'Vodka' answered Motka as scared as a mouse.

'Let him sleep. Don't you worry.'

But later I lay in my room behind the wardrobe and as if sleeping. Motya not shaking any more, sat alongside and guarded my dream, constantly applied a wet towel to my forehead, from somewhere he had the idea that as such it would be possible to save me. But I slept as if I didn't sleep. I heard everything everything. And now I hear.

Auntie on the guitar strings, plum plum . . .She and mum sang like that sometimes . . .two voices

Behind the window . . .white with white . . .there is cherry in the garden . . .

But no, they don't allow them to sing. You can't kill conversation anyhow, not kill, Auntie laughs and quietly leaves the guitar in the corner. 'Efim! pronounces one of the guests, one of the institute colleagues. 'Reckon on it.' Mum squints, throws herself onto the armchair. I have a very beautiful mum. 'Reckon on it!' already a little whim. 'How is it there?', Auntie quietly asks. 'Yes almost already. The apples are ready, but the potato is tough . . .' in a tone Mum answers. 'And I take it into account!' Dad in excitement, his eye lights up. Dad is drunk. 'Go on!' 'Get out!' 'But you want to' Dad doesn't know restraint. 'You know what I will reckon on you?!! I'll do such to you! . . .' A hum. Fight. Mum gets up and leaves for the kitchen for the goose.

Epigraph: there were five of us/ we wanted to live/ but they hanged us/we were blackened.

What was it? Where it postponed at the back of my head, not important, not important, next!

I also now, if I strongly squeeze my eyes shut, listen to Dad's voice according to the demands of the wall-eyed guests reading then parts of the first draft of his own prose. They didn't accept it and requested that it be written again. In order that it be in a normal language. Without curses. Without northerness.

Dad then did his prose again, got rid of the obscenities, gave it flourishes. They took the manuscript. But the northerness settled on the shelf and didn't allow Dad to live.

The rascals or the scoundrels, yes, yes, something like that. There were five of them, they had there own order and their own manifesto. So.

'The last chapter. Epigraph: Who aims at the scoundrel, will greet it. Who covers the rascal, supports it.

It was the seventh day from the opening. The sky was clouded by storm clouds. From the morning the political officer read a lecture about the officers' morals. We were the most ordinary prisoners, we lived behind thorny wire, we left he system from the zone to Saman, we dressed in the soldiers bunks, and indeed to there: officers' morals! But he didn't know to know, our corpulent moron the political officer, to whom is he reading his own lecture! He the buffoon! Shabby and tattered, the sick and crooked buffoon yes stays with him.

In the evening we gathered at our place, and again read our poetry Gelli D, our officer with the chemical name.

The daily rigmarole ended,
Again rain. In the heart is disgusting disgusting,
The glorious bed is underneath me,
Over me is the the holy tent.
At times remember a far off house,
Make do on grey days,
Wait for lunch, get wet in the rain
And to curse at horrible words.

We didn't even glance, the link existing between us was a different type: there Tamerlane picked up the rubbish beside his own bunk. Tamplier, ordinarily, listens to poetry attentively. Talerane on the other hand leaves his place and doesn't notice anything around him, Teofrast chews the remains of millet, tosses it into his pocket and in the evening chews; well I get drunk, as usual, but our plan links us, and we think about the same, night. Night. Night. Still two hours until the call, still an hour and a half, still forty minutes. We are careful people as before, but soon it will all change.

I recall the argument in this our last evening: that there is eternity and finality? And what can we understand the sooner? It brought him the commanding officer of he chemical department, but Tamplier supported him. Why does a man need an arse? They meant, indeed of course, the buttocks. 'Why indeed does he sit? Why is there an arse!' Atavism, exclaims Teofrast. Not atavism! Exclaimed the commanding officer. 'The arse appeared on a man earlier than he thought that it's possible to sit on it. Not atavism but simply an absolutely useless invention of mankind! But why the soul? Because if we don't see in directly practically application, it still doesn't mean, that the organ is completely useless to us!'

But I hummed our obscene hymn, of course without words and only the melody, but my associates understood me of course.

Night came and the barracks fell silent. Then we implemented our plan.

Frozen at the threshold, the three of us noticed: Teofrast and Tamerlane approached for an hour a completely synchronised movement, they squeezed the dreamlike artery. They collapsed to the ground by the hours. Then we quietly slipped out. . .

We escaped from captivity, from our intolerable imprisonment, intolerable already in that alone it was carried out by our own.

There were five of us. We wanted to live.

We so wanted to live, this must be understood. We wanted to live with all our strength . . .

(I have failed in my memory here, the compassionate mind deviated drunkenly in the most vulgar and ruined places. The next hogwash I haven't been able to decipher since.)

We built a barricade in the forest (why?), we grew beards, grey, at least my colleagues, but I didn't see myself, because we didn't have any mirrors. We chopped in the forest and dug ditches. We lay in dishevelled haylofts, (where did he get haylofts in a forest?!) and fell asleep that very second, we awoke at the half light and went on. Wasting strength, we fetched our crest and looked at it: crossed bones and an an axe reminded us about the hopelessness of our existence. The axe promised to chop the obstacles on our way, the bone talked: we will all die, but we will die gloriously. But it followed that we had to work a bit. We feasted on stumps and went further. We lost Teofrast, he died from Gangrene of the heart and conscience, and this waste only hardened us. We resurrected him with the strength of our thoughts and hatred. We sang our hymn.

We don't cry under anything ever:
It doesn't help, a cry isn't a cry,
We spit at everything unlucky,
The fuck with us,
We spit at need and nature,
It doesn't lure us from the path of the scatter brain,
With us is truth and the heart of the people,
The fuck with us,
If indeed death overwhelms with waves,
Stream of frost and black,
Dying, we say, fuck with us,
With just the fuck.

We knew: when we turn to the homeland, the scaffold is awaiting us. And only stupid idiots forced us forward and hope for something. Yesterday's convicts and philistines, we lost our reason, instead of it the jowls were left.

'So ended our Alinsky imprisonment.'

My dad was a ffffool.

Alyosha Moscow 2007

And yes still later when this manuscript got out. He had only just flown in from Barcelona.

He came on foot from Paveletsky. The devil could have taken me. The devil could have taken me. Yes, it's my own fault, I myself gave in, but to hell. How painful it is. How painful. He entered the house and ran up to the ninth floor, stood, smoked, stubbed out his cigarette in his palm and knocked on the door.

He knew what would follow: first will be a haze, a yellow scum, a trembling Medusa in front of his eyes and indeed it, the creature, there will be hoarfrost in the throat, it will shiver, the nausea will fly to the edges, and all of this, himself, he will do all this himself, all this he did himself earlier, he is guilty in everything, all done with his hands and correctly, that is better, so good, on the fourth day the ring of the house telephone tore him from the yellow wrath. He wouldn't have paid attention to anything else, but the house telephone had been quiet for a long time; he picked up the receiver.

'Hello' pronounced a clear female voice. 'I need a bookbinder. Have I got the right number?'

Deja vu erupted with a bang in his head. He gulped down the jellyfish, lodged in the Adam's Apple area, and calmly said:

'Yes, I'm a book binder. I'm listening to you.'

(Yes it's indeed not there, the business is in that, once after Barcelona he left any way, to that one's birthday . . .something like that sometime. . .is she a director or a model? The buffet in the gallery or a Lebanese evening in the flat-studio . . .all flew to hell, the first day of the arrival he went for the kettle on the shelf and found dad's manuscript. He read. He laughed angrily. Not good thoughts . . . And went off to the birthday party, knowing that there would be familiar lads from the publishing house. Radically. He handed it over to them. To the little fool. They looked, turned over the page . . .went around by the nose, bristled. And why have you only got Jews here?

A satanic laughter screamed inside him. It was on the second day after his arrival. On the fourth, she rang).

Alyosha Moscow 1985

And here I am returning after the war.

There is nowhere to escape dismissive romantics, she is on my heels. But in the evenings everyone plays music the same way, pum pururum, pum, pum. Italiano vero. I ha-te it.

Don't go out into the streets, because, alas, they so conspired that this music is everywhere, you don't take a step without it. But even if there is no war, no cuckoos, no whirligigs, even if there is simply some lilac fog . . .prum pum pum . . . my love is lilac . . .lilac is my love, let it not be okay, the fog . . . Or also an Italian century, and to me, what do I do? Every time, as on the buds. And it's everywhere, believe me. I have keen hearing.

And there I'm going home and it drifts from everywhere for me, this Italian, I shake my head all the time, like a confused one, so that I had it flying in one ear, going out of the other, but no. But then I still hope, that it will soon pass, as if I had known that it clings for ever, that they would listen to it, and listen and listen . . .the artists. . .The manifestos . . . Partigianni . . . my death. My pain. My sickness.

I go out into my yard, the summer-summer-poplars, everywhere the windows are wide open, and everywhere it's the same, my Italian, there is no saving me here, I go on foot to the ninth floor, I ring and think about myself in order to kill the music, one two three while they don't open, on the ninth they open the door.

(It was nothing of course. There was no one to open the door, that was already certain. He rang at the door of the neighbours, her son came out, he stared questioningly, he didn't recognise him. 'I'm from one hundred and twelve, Elena Nikolaevna should have my keys.' 'Mooooother! Have you got the keys of a hundred and twelve?' 'What is it?' Steps. Alyosha!' In short he took the keys from them, refused tea and coffee, started to smoke with the key in the door, but it wasn't opening. The neighbour was hiding in her place, but, hearing the fuss, thrust herself out into the square quickly again. 'I'm telling you, there there are problems on the lock, come to us, rest, breathe, if you want to take a bath.' 'No, no, thanks. . .' He smiled radiantly and kicked the door with his foot, a cloud of dust threw itself and jumped about the corridor, the neighbour ahhed and moved back; he entered the flat, closed the door, reached the couch and fell forward. He only got up the following day, when they came from Zhek to change the lock.)

And all the time I can't get away from this music, music, music, it's everywhere. You know I have nowhere to fall. My documents are lost, the War Commissariat consider me a deserter, neither warlike nor registered, one introduction from the hospital, there is a tea stain on them; the documents could have been sent to me orally, but in the grave he saw my difficulties; but in general we will be honest once in our lives; the fuck did I give up the documents, where do I go with them?

Oh these sunny streets, these hares. I went there, I went here. The same everywhere. I got disappointed, I spat.

Somehow we will survive. I came home, wanted to drink tea, I got out the tea leaves and suddenly got dreadfully unhappy. What did Mum do with the tea, that it was possible to drink it? In summer blackcurrants leaves, but in the other times? But if only it were just a leaf, where am I to get it through this wearied town? She dried some mint, or what? Or thyme, and yet an unknown herb, which muffled the taste of the broom: a fact, it was possible to drink Mum's tea. How will I live without this tea? Why live without it?

Inside something erupted weakly, and snapped. I sat and breathed. I reached onto the shelf for the tea leaf maker, the kettle, of course, I didn't find it, what to do with it on the shelves, but there is interesting, such a strength indeed entailed in me on the shelf, yes? Amongst the mossy suitcases suddenly I stumbled on a little paper little paper, on Dad's manuscript, on the same unpleasant version in dishevelled binding . . .and finally, on Dad's binding machine. And still later, when I made the tea as it had to be, according to all the rules, but not in a mug, how I did it up to that, I found in the cupboard a little wrinkled brown stick, I put it into the little saucepan, and yet a suspicious packet, on it was written 'oregano', for a minute I doubted, but poured in the oregano, filled with chipata, shut it with the lid, took a cup and said to myself 'well all right. The architect didn't leave me. The teacher didn't, nor the driver . . . They didn't take it anywhere. I have nowhere to go, nothing to do. I will be a book binder.' And I poured myself some tea. The swills weren't so tasty, but tolerable.

(He tells himself, perhaps, so he said, but of course, the bookbinder left him still. He fixed the book binding machine, hung up advertisements in institutes, hoping for people with diplomas. Someone even came up to him, there were orders . . He sat at home and didn't leave, only to the bank. He thought of spitting at these receipts, but something got in his way. Why he bound there, he didn't let in the people with orders into the flat, binding books he left in the box in front of the door, out of which he indeed took, when he didn't forget, the money. He didn't drink, he didn't cut himself, it was all boring. It was something else with him).

. . . And he didn't need any . . .what do you call them? Doping? Oh no, I didn't need them, everything happened the same for me. What sweet dreams I dreamt during the war, what sweet dreams. The dreams repeat themselves, it's the last business, Mum always said: Alyosha this stupid tone. Where do we observe the tone, Mummy? The dream returned to me in Moscow, it returned in reality, and, my God, how it was terrible for me, so shrill . . .

I was a down and out. The alcohol didn't leave me, neither did the drugs, I didn't kill myself . . .I will, it means continue to be a down and out. My down and out, my down and out . . .

(After two months the mathematician rushed to him, simply knocked the door.)

I was a down and out. In truth I was a pile of rags. It lay around near the cleaner, there were clearly visible whisps of wool, from the children's section there; then it came to life and it seemed, with me. And such a spring about it all around, all these sticky leaves, the cold sky, icy, high, and it smells of cucumber, so rarely does it smell of cucumber, but here it means I come to life, but I'm a down and out and a former pile of rags and there is also a beastly smell from me and all this spring I have been choking. People go past me, wincing, quickening their step. It's not that it's nasty to me, it's awkward, that I'm ooooh, and suddenly here I have an insight! Somewhere this was, Mum read to me, that someone out of delicateness doesn't say 'this handkerchief stinks,' but says 'this handkerchief is carrying itself badly,' so there: I'm somewhat clumsy, and I carry myself so badly and that I smell badly. And the main thing, I almost move, it still gets worse.

(The mathematician rushed to search for vodka, which lies in the freezer untouched. He ransacked all the little cupboards, and found some oregano in a packet. 'What did you drink? Did you smell?' then he checked it 'honestly nothing.')

Then I begin carefully step by step, moving somewhere to the side, away from people, I see a high hillside and I think with relief, that now I roll head over heels there from it. And I roll head over heels: some lumps, scraps, fly from me; from my armpits a long-legged flea breaks of huge sizes and carried away in jumps downwards. And over me indeed is all the sky of Austerlitz. And all would be fine, if only I could stop emitting that smell.

For that reason the confusion, a kind of flashes, flare, blackness, and me, that is a huge pile of dirty rags in a fortress. In Versailles. In Oranienbaum, in Plessyburgh. In a wild stylistic mess, amongst outdoor malachite vases. I look around, I hear steps, I pop out, it's terrifying for me, now someone comes and sees in the fort a homeless person, who is turning into rags . . .from the neighbouring hall directly towards me moves my far off long-legged flea, only in a black suit and with a walkie-talkie, I understand that it's an archivist and that it will be a bad look out for me; I want to hide quietly behind the door and here she is and him! the archivist! he sees me! I catch the hem and down the suite of rooms, again I shed some scraps on the golden slippery parquet and I hear the stamping steps of the commanders and I breathe, breathe, I run, all my rags tighten from the approaching terror, I run, run, the turn, I break with a yelp and leave on the corner a velvet bag, I fly to the open door, a bathhouse"! Huge! There is gold and malachite all around. The sink-tulip, from the tap slashes a thick and tight stream, pierces into plums. A huge mirror in petals and curls, a baroque explosion. A bronze bath in claw feet in the centre.

At the side, azure sheets on pegs flag from the light wind from my dreadful breath. The pegs are not simple, all in some stone. The night toilet in Rabelais size, on it a crest overhead, on the crest framed by emerald green leaves a crossed-over bone and little axe. I would have to wash, but is it possible to urinate out a pile of rags? But well how do I do anything? Or do I start to stink even worse?

I turn to the shameless sink, whether it was or not, flap at myself with cool water, I'm at once better, better, my breathing is easier and even the sheets cease to be swelling; I raise my eyes and in the mirror I see my own face, *unspeakably* pleasant.

(The mathematician shook him, shook, no such point. The pupils were normal. There is no smell of fumes. The voice is even, even a little tired, without the smallest affectation. 'I'm homeless, Mot, do you understand? But no, you hardly understand . . .' 'Well take yourself in hand! What are you to me here?!' 'Yes, everything is all right, honestly! Simply here, you understand, as it comes. Some people have a brother who is an engineer, some a mathematician, there as you're to me, but who is a rag. A rag and homeless . . .

An engineer passed from me, an architect didn't . . .' 'When did you last eat?'

'When were you on the streets?' 'On Tuesday I paid for the flat, the receipt is in the cupboard, if you want check it.' This answer, quiet and hard, about the flat definitively killed the mathematician. He checked, the receipts were in place, all paid. Yes and generally . . .Motya saw in his time both alcoholics and addicts and the only one whom he did not see . . .it wasn't like it, not like it. It remained to own up, Alyosha had gone out of his mind.

Then the mathematician threw him out to work in the circus. There they needed working stages.)

Alyosha Sandra. Barcelona, 2007

So there, first the panorama: a huge cathedral, gigantic surrounds, a kind of mockery over all normal architecture, inhuman, wearily huge. For that reason the frame gradually comes closer, quietly, quietly runs on one from the lancet windows in one of the highest towers. The angle changes, there he is, standing, so small, in a windowed doorway. There is no glass. He looks down, form a terrible height, from a terrible height. Down there are people, people, people, he doesn't know anyone, from such a distance no one can tell anyone apart. And then, despairingly seeing, he oversteps an empty window frame and flies down.

. . . He went to Barcelona and saw it, his own cathedral.

There around swarmed certain tourists, humming in different languages, snapped, clattered, having lifted their heads, dropping their caps . . .twice they moved him from his place, he would close his view, they pushed him five times, he could not even be angry with them, he didn't have the strength. These ugly spires, drowned in the clouds, these lumps, scraps, the flaps of torn up hearts and livers! Shamelessly bullied shreds, nude insides! This clinic of lines, what he drank, smelled, what he thought about, the generous builder? How he brought together, how he fitted in his stupid head a fused plastic with hysterical sharpness with jagged dinosaurs? Cocaine user! Fool! Simpleton! And the main thing, the size, of a devilish obsession. To thank, you say?! At this moment someone put her hand on his elbow.

He turned.

A girl. Twenty five years, a girl like any other.

He doesn't remember the moment of their acquaintance, everything was too much by surprise and foggy. It seems the mathematician had befriended her. Or it's not like that, the mathematician knew Latifa and called her to Alyosha's exhibition. She came and dragged Sandra with her. Or is it yet somehow different? Alyosha is angry, he sat tired in the corner of the hall and proceeded with malice. White brick walls, a wooden closure! Tartan and a tartlet, yoooour Mother . . .the conceptual public scurried here and there, pulling nuts. It's your own fault, why did you agree! When Motya shyly asked, whether he wants to . . . here there are a few of his, Motya's, friends. . . Alyosha, not getting up from the bar stool, pecked him at the top of his head: Mathematician, you're going bald. Rub in with cloud berry!' 'Idiot . . .' and just in case he didn't get acquainted with anyone that evening. The exhibition went by luxuriously. Reviews and shit.

Two days later she came to him at the cathedral, just about at that moment one of the fucking spires was just ready to collapse on him. She led an excursion there. She earned her own bilingualism.

Mum is from Leningrad, Dad is half French, half Spanish, the blood is mixed bless you . . .a large part of the family lives in Paris, but they are their whole lives here . . .o, by the way, Aunt, Dad's eldest sister, married a Russian, that was a long time ago! Or has it been? Of course it was, a lot of times, both in Peter and in Moscow, at Aunt and uncle's . . .

'You say what you know,' Sandra asked him 'So I don't have to repeat myself . . .'

He knew everything about him, certainly he came inside, different to all these tourists, he threw himself down, stepping for the frame, there was something for him to tell.

But at that moment he had sensed that something untoward was happening. Something in it, well clavicles there, well all right. Well, yes, Spanish sadness, but this, we'll say, he dreamt everything up himself and read. Or their conversation, a wonderful linguistic compote, started him: she spoke cleanly in Russian, only she would turn out to be sizzling, nearly exaggerated, he certainly heard it from someone . . .but all around tourists crowded, they were asking something, they both in such a strange excursion-like fervour went over to English, back to Russian, but they couldn't tear themselves away from one another, they always returned to each other, this annoyed him terribly. But perhaps it started to madden him, appearing without warning to him the cathedral in his dreams, how many times he saw Sagrada in postcards and pictures, nothing ever moved, there were no thoughts; but here he saw and found out and was furious with himself, so gnashing his teeth. But perhaps all this was beside the point and the business was only in . . .but what had she to do with it? How did she do it, well she clearly didn't want it.

Sanya, that's how he called her. He calls her the same now, burying his head in the glass of the book case, scarcely moving his tongue, pushes through dry lips, San-ya. Why am I here then? But I don't even feel like bargaining.

A pitiful girl. In any other minute he was seriously angry with her, it seems she could balance it. The others, he would understand, to hell she couldn't; she couldn't recognise her own strength herself. Something was in her, thank you to explain, a girl like any other, twenty three, twenty four, eyelashes, bruises under her eyes from tiredness, a wide mouth like a frog. And she smiles suddenly, a happy smile.

And something else, there it's in front of her eyes, easiness. She came into the room, sat on the chair, sat, reached into her bag, took out a block note, started to write, stopped, started thinking, wrinkled her nose, and that's all. On the spot.

He went into her studio: books, discs all around, an understandable set, he had been smirking, all around Eisenstein, Bruno Schultz and Adorno, on blue walls photographs of Latifkin, a solid clock she did herself, from a saucepan, from the fridge with an indelible marker written across: no magnits! On the table Chablis in ice and a huge fire-spitting quiche. Sandra washed the floor and didn't notice how he came in and it was worth him seeing her, all his malice (well clear: Nina Simone, Ayn Rand, Jarmusch!) . . . Yes what malice there, all in hell. He stood and watched: straightening, she began to squeeze a huge cloth in the bucket, she scratched her nose on the shoulder, this was drunken easiness, meanness . . . 'you have come!' He took her hand, the water dripped. 'Wait, dry your hand! Alyosha!' he looked at her, looked: then he pressed his lips with wet fingers. 'My nose is itchy!' laughed Sandra 'Let go! What are you doing? You're drunk on dirty water!'

(. . .Lying face down in the water . . .in the channel and he slurped the water. And around these all crowded at the modulus and they were worried about approaching, the group said in a whisper: leave him now, lads, he received a telegram . . .the mathematician always had an idiotic passion: do you understand, he kept everything under control, everyone tried to do what was necessary. So he screamed, so he was zealous. And what he shouldn't have pushed. He is forced to own up, 'you're too severe with your Father! Yes, it's possible to understand you. But understand yourself: he isn't young, he has endured a lot, and you . . .' don't be trendy, Motenka, the eternally good person. I love him, of course, the mathematician, but sometimes he drives me to madness. It's understandable that only close ones can madden and he is truly a close one, he is a second cousin. He looks at me with puppy eyes and smiles, he always smiles, he mustn't at me, please, look so, what am I, a lame puppy, or what? And he mustn't worry about me, because you, my dear soul mathematician, turn to Aunt quietly. . .pave the way. . .clumsy person. Pay attention by the way, soon you will have a paunch and go bald. And in vain you fucked someone there casually, but in general you, Motenka, are a broody hen. And I advise you very strongly to leave me in peace for ever, forget my name, don't interfere with me, understood, reptilian ass hole. And you mustn't have sent me any telegram. No, I'm nothing, I only lie on my head in the ditch and drink drink drink, I really feel like drinking.)

Sandra went to him and looked with a heavy tender glance. Personally it was everything. What are you doing to me?

The ponies run, the girls are young . . . thousand kisses deep. It resounded and resounded. He looked at her closely and with despair, what are you doing to me, why?

With such a heavy, tender pigs glance. Not coming off. It could not have been that, but he bent down to her and, then tearing himself from her lips, he felt how she unzips the buttons on his shirt, brings with the tongue along sunny texture, higher, lower, higher, his nose is in the clavicle, he exhales 'well at last . . .'

I'm back on Buggle street . . .Moist chords.

At night . . .around five in the morning, when it was already getting bright, we got up, staggering, there was no strength, all the same we couldn't sleep , we sat in the car, went to the port. Something indeed had to be done.

We got out of the car, almost walked past, he sat her on a high parapet and got up alongside, so they were comparable in height. She with ease began to get off to sleep, she spoke sleepily, lazily and complacent.

'I was there then . . .when I saw you at Sagrada . . .I frightened you then.'

'Why this?'

'I don't know . . . You were so miserable . . . And now also . . .'

'And what are you, you're afraid of me now?'

'I'm afraid of course.'

'Idiot . . .' a pause. A cigarette through strength, a pair of puffs. Coffee from a little cardboard cup, it's painful to gulp. Then suddenly something moved him to ask: 'What will you and I do now?'

'But what you say . . .as you say, so I will do. . .' She squints at the raspberry sun, rubs her eyes, then looks at him. And smiles.

Where were you earlier, where were you, where were you?

The fighting began straight away. Otherwise he couldn't do it. Something pursued him, didn't let him stop. So everything was all right, he couldn't prevent this. How was it? There they are arguing until they shout, and later, not having held out, they began to laugh; there the sea thrashes in the eye with glaring stains, there Gaudi gingerbread little houses, palms, mast taps; there she is chewing chestnuts and licks salt with her lips; there she goes up to him from behind, sticks to him with her forehead to the back, between the shoulder blades, shoves her hands into his jeans pockets; there with the last husky exhale suddenly releases a chord inside herself, she falls on him and falls asleep, but he stays himself, and someone (himself, not otherwise) sweetly and despicably talks to him; everything is good, yes? You believed, yes? It all seemed necessary, so that the little girl appeared. And there not a psycho, not an addict, not a terrorist any more. . .how it's all quick for you, how simple!

He frowns from terrible vulgarity, but that's it, generally he isn't powerful in anything he already has yellow sand in front of his eyes.

Ey, poor thing, of course, it left. 'You don't understand, the business isn't in that! You can't understand anything at all! I can drink or not drink, it's all the same to me!' How could he explain to her *that* he definitely *comes*, to tell it was truer than anything, a yellow haze, dune in front of the eye, it's of what, to turn into a pile of rags, to decompose into little rags?! In a pile of rags at the fort, when all around you're mustard maids!!

You can't explain this to a man. She demands; tell me. He began to say something, but quickly shut up, where are you going to understand all of it, a girl from a Catalan school, the outstanding student in the whole university, the favourite one of all her relatives, what am I to tell you? She has white lips from madness: it can all be told! It's possible to explain it all!

He only smiled, he leaned into the fridge, got out a bottle of water. Sandra in a rage ripped it from his hands and flung it out the window, she wasn't picturing anything either, if it's a joke: the third sleepless night, the third day of madness. He seized her by the shoulder, she punched him in the nose with her fist. A terrible cinematic crackle, all around is bloody, such a little girl had enough strength. Well there . . . They didn't hold on, they started to laugh, like abnormal people. It let go. . .the surgeon, the complacent bearded Basque, he set his nose . . .he nodded with understanding. 'Well really, how it fell unluckily . . .on the stairs, ay ay ay. Senorita, rinse the blood, there you have it, on the little bones . . .' Well it would be all right. Then somehow suddenly silly hope dawned, suddenly it turns out? Well suddenly? But no.

A huge flat on the hundredth floor of a skyscraper. Windows to the floor, a blue evening town. Latifa, the girlfriend of Sandra, a full mulatta of improbable beauty, one of the most beautiful girls that he was ever to meet, a cynical intelligent one, a designer, in great demand across the world, now they sat in one of her multiple residences, in the hundredth floor of a skyscraper, windows to the floor, behind them a dark blue town, deep night.

'Listen, Lav,' she said 'permit me to be completely open with you, because in similar situations I want such openness from you,' he looked in the window not opening, Singapore fires, it's thought 'this must be, who would have told me ten years ago; it was so painful for him: why do I need your openness and when, what's the trick! What can I pay you with at all?! Be silent, my darling, be silent. Listen Lav, Sandra is a person who is very kind, she can never tell you herself. You should understand how she grew up,' a long and boring inserted novella about a Catalan childhood (all is total drunken lies), the transfer to university, another hint at that, that without her, Latifa's participation, Sandra would have never become thus, so . . . 'the lies, what lies,' well and so on, he missed out the passage, fires corrode the eyes, but he couldn't tear himself away any way. 'Listen Lav, well simply the business itself is that she is very kind and it isn't always possible to say, what she is in actual fact thinking . . . well let us now simply tell each other honestly, you can . . .you were friends, yes and you will be the best of friends, I'm certain! You acted correctly in leaving, you're completely . . .let only time go by, but . . .' 'Fine,' he said, getting up, 'you're right, you're completely right, let me go now, you understand yourself, that you need time . . .where are you going, sit, I beg you, don't go mad, go to bed, I will tuck you in, or if you want, let us get drunk?' She so forced him to drink some filth, chocolate or sticky, seventy degrees, not less. You killed me with this bigger bit, than with all the conversations, predicting, he said 'What is this?' Listen, Lav, calories, serotonin, alcohol, all that you need now. And feremonas,' he laughed 'don't forget please! This I can ensure you easily! Strumming outrage, she exclaimed. Continuing to laugh, he pulled a corner of the silk scarf with its head to himself, slyly the twisted little turban fell to pieces, her hair gushed, and she with her entire body, greedily and graciously, moved to it, and let go of her eyelashes, like a girl 'Solaris, pure Solaris,' he thought.

So life finished. Though how was it to finish there.

Alyosha Barcelona - Moscow, 2007

How he reached Moscow from Barcelona, he can't remember any more. Which airport, where he flew to there, how he reached it, how the stewardesses shied away from him, how much he rushed about without reason along the Ramblas, along the Ramblas flying at tourists, this by the way beforehand. In Boqueria the fish looked at him intently with hatred and some crab from the counter grabbed him his claws at the side. Gaudi calamari in a trembling batter destroyed prawns, seven hours remained until the aeroplane, it had to be them . . .something had to be done with them. He didn't drink. Nothing else . . .no, there was nothing else also. Then these clocks in the airport, just here it was enough for him, Italian vero from the mobile of some bluish-haired aunt. In Barcelona. On the way home. When the aeroplane took off, he forced himself to open his eyes, in so far as for ages they creaked, and he looked at the town; red rooves, thin lines, a sly idea: and once more the Italian sounded and towards the bluish-haired aunt the stewardesses rushed: Señora straight away, this very minute! The aunt ashamedly shook up the bag a lot.

And you don't get away from the little music. One you mute, as right there something falls on you . . . 'on the Moz-dok, on the Moz-dok . . .' At the entrance to the metro 'Tretyakovskaya', they are standing now with guitars, about Khankala, about Khasavyurt, about Kabul. But this I tell you, all's the same, time goes, but it doesn't fucking change. A drooling disgusting shit head, all one and the same. Whether there is one war or another. Where do they get it from, can someone explain it to me? After so long, all's healthy again. With one and the same words, the same nasty little motive, gut wrenching. But let it, it's not important.

And when I walked from 'Paveletskaya' I breathed in the old Moscow smell, somewhere near Ustinsky bridge it smelled of mud, to hell with me taking it. To hell with me taking it. Yes, it's my fault, I myself gave in, but to hell. How very painful it is. How painful. I went into the house, ran to the ninth floor, stood, smoked, I butted the cigarette in my palm and kicked the door.

Farewell, farewell.

He didn't know what would happen next: first will be the haze, a yellow scum, a trembling Medusa in front of his eyes, and indeed she, the bitch, there will be the horefrost in the throat, will shiver, nausea will flood to the edges and all of this, he himself will do everything, he did it all earlier himself, everything is his own fault, all done by his hands, and correctly, so better, so well, on the fourth day the sound of the house telephone tore him from a yellow wraith. He wouldn't have paid any attention to anything else but the house telephone was silent for many a year; he took the receiver.

'Hello!' Pronounced a clear female voice 'I need a bookbinder. Am I calling the right person?'

Deja vu slammed in is head with an explosion. He gulped the Medusa, lodged in the Adam's Apple area, and calmly pronounced:

'Yes. I'm a bookbinder. I'm listening to you.'

Nadya Moscow 2007

After Gunnar's death, Nadya was so upset that we all started to get worried about her. Her nephew looked after her a lot, Seryozha is a fine boy, so radiant; he took the death of his Father very badly and with the idea of Nadia's efforts he made peace with the labour. He saw that Nadya is tolerable in herself, leaves the house; he knew that as before she is in hot demand, that for whole days the telephone rings and she, giving out and laughing, gives advice to life-long friends; he knew that she organised the repertoire of Marina's grandson and she went every Tuesday to Tonya Blokhina, carried potato pancakes; but he also saw that she overstrains to be happy but unhealthy, but there is no strength and she is ashamed to admit this. Seryozha tried to go to her more often, they were worn out for a long time, she was worried about his institute arrangements, but it was worth her while to start to be suspicious of the attention, she started to grow fierce and urge him home. Once he arrived and she was happy, from the morning for some reason she climbed up to clean in the cupboards and drawers, everything fell in the middle of the room, she was buried in newspapers, photographs, papers, she counted each one . . .old publications, letters, she couldn't tear herself away, her strength left after an hour, she had a tickle in her throat from bitter despair . . .but she had to get rid of the mess. Just here was Seryozha, he understood at once, that he must save her and at once everything worked out: He sat Nadya on the chair, he himself sat on the floor and got up, without rushing, to sort through the junk. Generally, he was not showing her photographs, but he gave her to read the papers randomly, what was shorter, what doesn't irritate. He generally tied up all Gunnar's letters with a string and hid them in a box under the coffee. Business got better. A note from the main editor: 'Respected comrades! Don't serve up unpleasantness of the inactivity of the workers of the pictures, that is you, in the working hours! In this number it concerns Nadya!' His own, of boyhood times, letter from the Crimea: 'Dear Nadya, I'm in good form and you? I'm bathing here and there are hornets and no cutlets. I kiss you.' Nadya was kinder. Here this fat blue folder appeared: Seryozha wanted to postpone it, but Nadya threw herself in with a vulture: well well wait up! This was a manuscript of her book. And so it went. One page, the second, third . . . There Nadya is not answering questions any more, she is already there with the head, frowns, pulls 'Golaus' from her pocket, fumbles, not looking, about the chair, where is the ash tray? She doesn't find it and with a habitual gesture she dumps the cigarettes from the packet onto the table, but ash shakes in the packet. The table is full of cigarettes, from this packet and the previous two. Seryozha so tries to distract her in that way, where to there! 'We'll finish it later, my dear, don't worry, go, go, go . . .' He got upset and left. Well, if he wants to suffer, let him. There is not enough strength any more, honestly.

Nadya read all night, it must be suggested, but in the morning rang home very business like:

'Do you know this book of mine . . . well no one has any copies at all, yea?'

In truth, no one had any copies: on Kirovsky someone took it to read, but didn't return it, and you look in vain. Gunnar, complexly concerned with a reporter's rage towards Nadya, and towards this book, forgot it in some hotel, when he went on a business trip. She herself gave everything away, not even remembering to whom.

'Well there, to buy this book, issued in 1991, isn't possible.'

'Well there I also thought, I want to bind it. So that I would have my own copy. In order that it stood on the shelf. It will be pleasing for me. Maybe somebody will want to read it. The manuscript isn't convenient. . . .'

'It's possible to bind it,' answered Seryozha, gradually getting elated, that it seems nothing . . .a little blood . . .

'There and I thought, you were indeed defending your degree recently, you definitely have a book binder?'

'Yes, now they are not binding my degree, Nad. They are laminating it and such a spring . . .'

'Well, it means that you must take it from Dima,' said Nadya, and he understood that she had already finished the conversation. Such was her manner that she put down the receiver without waiting to hear and he had felt earlier, that . . . 'Dima had, I remember. When he defended it. Well, that's all, bye!'

And the dialling tones. There is madness, a? There were no doubts, that she herself is already ringing Dima.

Dima said: you're not normal, Nad? What book binders? Do you know when I defended it? We'll if you want, hold the line.

Dima had never lost anything.

Alyosha Nadya Moscow 2007

They agreed like old times: the manuscript in the drawer in front of the door, so much money, a period of four days, they swapped numbers. And if she was amazed she didn't show it.

She said her nephew is bringing it, she proposed a part of the money as an advance. The next day he heard a rustling under the door, he waited a little and took the file. The title attracted him, insipid but it attracted him; he pulled out the first page, the second, the third, it was not possible to check anything in it but then he glanced at the middle, later he sat and read from the start to the end; no, this couldn't be, the world around was jerking, like an epileptic, and went to hell.

. . .He rang her and was silent down the receiver. For a long time. He heard the voice, he tried to determine the age, and determined it. A voice like any other, sonorous and pleasant. He was silent for a long time. He decided not to repeat yesterday's untidiness, he had to act quietly here. He was silent silent, took pleasure and then said:

'Well hello Nadya. Let us talk.'

'Well hello,' she answered in a bad humour. 'And why have you called me, tell, please? Why did you frighten me?'

For he had nevertheless intercepted the spirit for a minute, blood tingled in his fingertips.

'Let me tell you,' he answered slowly, feeling as she lets him go, as if his breathing was levelling off, as everything at once was going back to normal. 'I will tell you. I'm your deserter, hello. I'm your book binder, the carrier the replacement . . .I'm one of the Nestroevy, Neustroevy, Nestratovy, of what still? Maxim, Leonid, yes?

Alyosha Kabul 1983

An explosion. Such grey earth! What yellow earth! What, I don't remember! What . . .what glorious earth near the bay of Koktebel. Mum sang, definitely. What grey earth! What grey earth around and in the mouth. The mug covered in dust. Neither spat nor declares. 'Don't take your rucksack!' jokes one of the ones who had been met, the Lieutenant-albino, burned to darkness, his eyebrows white and the eyes too. 'Don't take it, I'll do it myself!'

I didn't understand anything then, I didn't begin to listen to him, I took the strap, he took the other . . .I remember these flashes of anger, it was as if I was ready at every minute then, oh, I was such an idiot, it's terrible to recall. He shouted something at me, the poor thing . . .I tore the rucksack from him, he turned his finger to his temple and rushed to someone else . . .to one of the lads, who flew with me, and took his things.

They are also happy with the replacements, they are just as happy with them, that they are ready to carry their things with them.

Well to fuck with carrying my things! I was such an idiot, now you recall, as much as to distort.

We carried to the heavy goods vehicle . . .nothing was fucking visible, such was all grey and dusty.

I don't remember how she appeared, honestly. My conscious or my sub-concious, how to to say it correctly, replaced her in my memory. I would have wanted to remember but I can't. Now only the imagination draws me how she runs for the car from the helicopter, crouches, yells, coughs . . .the driver sticks out from the cabin and looks at her with happy amazement, where to?! But she waves I suppose some little paper . . .or a crust . . .and then she shakes her head, let us, fuck you, golden fish and she awkwardly, but how still? She climbs into the back and tears the trouser leg on a nail . . .

(. . .she climbs in the back, not one rubbish in the hand did she extend, she extended something in the hands, and she threw the leg ridiculously, disgustingly rolled over the side, but she did not notice the nail and she ripped her good trousers, which she had deliberately sewed for the trip . . .and also the leg, thoroughly to the flesh. Such cunts indeed, what an idiot I am, to hell with me anyway. Why did I come, why? Well it was this conversation: 'Nadya are you certain it's worth your while going? Are you completely certain,' well where to there, when he could convince her? . . .)

How dirty it was there too. It was so dirty there. Totally unlike it is with us. The air is dirty there, you're breathing all the time and you take hold of it with your nose from all your strength, you want to go through the sand somehow to wade and to reach out breathing the air, but no, as for three years he did not breath to the end either, but only wiped his nose. Since it's nearly that, blood comes from his nose.

(What grey earth. Forty recruits on the grey earth. Alyosha was already shattered to the fingertips, but such had the chaps, the nose skewed to one side and was oozing soup. Other lads looked at Alyosha depressedly and with caution. A heavy lorry stood at the block post, they began to load them up to there but here came a 'jeep' lifting the clouds of dust to the heavens and from it they tumbled, crazed from the excitement of the demobee and they began to drag junk up to the recruits. Suddenly a crash: the helicopter. What was the news? But it was at once her . . .at once they brought her and sat her down. An auntie with a rucksack. Dishevelled. I don't remember her completely, even kill me for it . . .only later, this desperate howl, animalistic, it stays in the ears since. And I remember the complete numbness, yes.)

Nadya Alyosha Moscow 2007
The following day she rang herself.
'Hello,' she said very clearly, already very calmly. 'Hello. Forgive me that I put down the phone yesterday. I was very nervous. You scared me very much, I will tell you. Nevertheless

it was very severe (cough). Forgive me. What did you want to talk to me about?'

'I don't really know,' he said lightly 'On the whole I wanted to kill you.'

'It would be difficult for me to help you in that,' she answered drily.

'And yes I don't need your help.'

Oo how it was an amazing feeling too, something like the last section of a distance, when you already know for sure . . .carefully disconnected, and the receiver, as crystal, accurately placed on the table.

He rang again the next day. She, the good person, contained herself.

'You have such strange tactics. You want to kill, so come to me at my home. Nobody kills by the telephone.'

'They don't kill, no,' he agreed 'They explain on the telephone. They explain on the telephone, for what? They warn on the telephone. On the telephone they chat. The black mark, did you hear?'

'I heard. I read. Well go on then, talk . . .as long as you ring. What do you want to kill me for?

'To put it simply, you ruined my life.'

'No harm,' she delayed and exhaled. She got ready: she smoked in advance. But she forgot the ashtray again somewhere, is it in the kitchen or what? Always these ashtrays . . .she began to fumble with her eyes, neither papers nor saucer. The cigarettes are loose on the table.

'Yes. You're from your own passion and thanks to the red word . . .' he sensed suddenly with wonder and annoyance, that the words were the same which had ousted the Medusa and they saved him, now they lodge in the throat with a stake and are strangling. Great! Wonderful! He choked in his own personal sphere. He waited and waited and suffocated. oh ass hole . . .

'You . . . the devil take you and all of you, instead of the captured.'

'Sounds romantic. What is your name even?'

'Aleksei.'

'Go to hell, Alyosha.'

She killed the receiver with a flourish, a bull in a polished counter top: the strength went together, as a toggle switch they turned over. He smiled peacefully and rubbed his nose: it was as if . . .either burned rubber or certain chemical.

'We planted the gladioli! She declared without an introduction. 'on the window. Will they grow do you think?'

'I don't know,' he answered distractedly 'I don't understand anything about flowers . . .'

'No listen to me. I don't understand either. But flowers, this is indeed a house, yes? Life, comfort! I have been an old spinster all my life, I despised life, you don't imagine how much! I hated it. The miller and the Turk, everyone. Not to let anything more into the house, under terror . . .I sorted out the dishes, on purpose. I didn't make the bed, didn't sweep, nothing . . .such God has sent, oy . . .such was my pride. If it would be then . . .are you listening?'

'I'm listening, I'm listening!'

'Well then. If somebody had said something to me then, even a few years ago, that I would plant flowers there . . . Well you understand . . .'

'You would be him,' he slurped the hot tea, not counting and coughing 'You would not have spared him, o yes!'

'Well, spared him or not spared him, this I don't know, but I would have raised laughter, that's for sure. My brother told me . . .I have such a brother, you would not be bored, he is so sarcastic . . it's terrible for me, that you don't know him, you would have joined . . .he told me, there such and such has, like you, and suddenly the whole house accumulates with various crochet patterns, the television stands on knickers all around are handkerchiefs, lights . . .we laughed so much. Are you listening?'

'I'm listening, I'm listening!'

'Yes. My brother . . .And I thought, that the harness . . . do you understand the harness is a terrible joke? They kill an intelligent person, they atrify his brain! Any principle, any barrier, vow . . .I can't understand, do you? . . .'

'And you, it means, decided to plant the gladioli? You have rejected your old ideals?'

'Laugh laugh! If it's pleasant, yes! I thought, why do I curtail my experience? This is narrowness. I, you just listen, drank champagne. They brought it for me, I asked them, 'Veuve Clicquot'. Firstly, secondly, these are bulbs. I truly don't know whether I planted them correctly or not . . .but it inspired me, a new experience! Openness! I saw a film recently 'Broken Flowers,' it absolutely enthralled me . . .do you understand, he lived such a meaningless life only because he didn't tear the harness. And I . . '

'Broken Escapes,' he pronounced wearily.

'What?'

'The film isn't called 'Broken Flowers' but 'Broken Escapes.' Lilian Gish . . .' he was tired of her nevertheless. This talkativeness. . .ostensibly an insight . . .

'Yes, really? . . .She pronounced upsetedly. 'I could have got confused . . .'

'You could have,' he insisted without pity.

'But it's not important, not important,' she livened up. 'Not important. I see that he lived his whole life in a harness. In dusty drapes. In cream drapes (he clenched his teeth; she again fell on her own dutiful witticism, in a calamari carousel). But you don't live your life in cream drapes. You have to tear, tear the drapes. And then I thought, what am I? Not only in books indeed, and ashtrays. I'm wider. Never in my life did I listen to music, I will! I will make lunch! I will lead the cat! Because her whole life she was a a dog person. And there the gladioli . . .as you think, they are growing?'

'I don't think so,' he pronounced with despair. How she got on his nerves with these gladioli Ghiglia!

Nadya's cat also had a history. She of course didn't collect anything specially for the sake of acquiring. A huge samurai kitten had already lived with Seryozha for two years, going somewhere. Seryozha brought in his mother's cat, there were never any problems with it. This time Nadya demanded that they bring her the cat. Why the cat, she asks for two weeks?

'He is living well with me; but your Mum has enough hassle (how such hassle, it's not understood). Well how is it, and there the niece has arrived to her for no apparent reason (well and why the niece, who created no difficulties and only helps Michelle with the economy, she can't live with a cat? The niece had no allergies, this is definite, she is well disposed to cats). I'm telling you, bring me the cat, that will be better! Really isn't simpler to do what I say? I know your Mum better. I will wait for you and the cat tomorrow. And still. . .I wanted to ask you . . .you listen to music: bring me, be good, what is it . . . a minute . . .wait, I will get my glasses, 'Colonel Vasin arrived at the front.' Yes, please. I need it. That's it. I kiss you. Until tomorrow.'

Seryozha gave in and brought the cat over. For three days Nadya carried out a war: the cat showed a temper and refused the food that was offered (Seryozha left a stock of some special cat rubbish in packets, but Nadya judged reasonably that in this pampering of the cat there should be fish). For three days they undertook starvation of each other, Nadya was very nervous, but didn't give in. On the fourth day the cat, with hatred, ate pollock. On the fifth day Nadya rang and with a clear despair pronounced:

'Something terrible has happened.'

'What is it?' Michelle cried with someone else's voice

'Voroshilov! He has probably died. I'm terribly to blame!'

'Who?! What?!'

Everything darkened, she later told me a lot of times this story, in front of Michelle's eyes. Nadya had clearly gone out of her mind.

'Well the cat, the cat. Voroshilov! I didn't follow it and it disappeared!'

Seryozha had indeed called the cat Voroshilov, partly for the syrupy temper and a habit of digging up plastic bags, partly in the strength of a stupid family tradition, but they seldom remembered this, they simply called it cat.

'Wait, wait, how did he die? What happened?'

'I don't know, whether he has died, I didn't see it. But he has disappeared! He is already nowhere for two hours, I looked over the whole flat from top to bottom, he is nowhere.' the voice settled, she started coughing and began to speak mutely 'this is the end . . .I shouldn't have taken him . . .'

'Are you certain that he isn't sleeping somewhere in a corner?'

Nadya was offended, and she was offended little in life. It was as if she was still for the time being in her own mind! Sleep! A great option!

From the stupid confusion (a hundred calls here and there) they rushed towards Nadya from different sides of the town at the same time as Dima, they held him back at work, and he was terribly angry, Michelle his niece and me. The niece looked for the cat for five minutes, all this time he was dozing in a basket of linen. Nadia was happy, in happiness she gave the cat a week's supply of Whiskas, he gorged himself and his stomach ached. The next day Nadia asked: take him!)

At first it's dark. Very dark, somehow depressingly dark, when in general you don't see the outline of objects. Then the projector, the ray, in the ray the clown. We know he is a clown, because we know that we have come to the circus. And so he is in a usual black suit and without make-up, only his eyes shine, black eyes, and he himself isn't young at all, grey, dilapidated, lean. Beautiful. A cockerel is mincing behind him. The clown enters the middle of the arena, takes off his jacket, hangs it on the back of the chair, sits, puts one leg on another and leans back. He leans heavily, the chair rocks, he balances, here and there like on a swing, then suddenly freezes, sits as if nothing had happened, leg on leg, in his mouth an unlit cigarette, but the chair is sitting on its two hind legs. The cockerel looks at the clown sidelong and the clown disapprovingly orders 'matches!' The cockerel cowers in the edge of the arena and brings him matches in his beak. 'Thank you, my dear!' the clown thanks him emotionally. He smokes. Jumping from the chair in one swift movement, he is already on his feet there; he is standing on the chair on his hands: once! And he is already on the back of the chair, also on his hands, he shakes a little, in his teeth is the cigarette, he smiles, winks. Then he stays to stand on one hand and the other one takes the cigarette from his mouth, stubs it out on his sole, with a click casts backstage and lets out a ring of smoke from his mouth, bluish illuminated, it sails sails about the hall and suddenly blows up in a salute, sparks fly around the floor and the cockerel pecks them with machine-gun speed. Here suddenly, once, is a pregnant clown, smeared, the nose overhead, a wig with two yellow locks of hair, in a jumpsuit from scrap. She is flying from a corner, wearing to shreds on the stage with a wheel and hiding herself. 'My colleague,' without pleasure the clown is explaining 'I'm generally without colleagues . . .and today I have very little time. Let us begin!'

Next . . .suddenly a light! A crowd, meaningless trampling, working stages in red overalls, they drag some buckets, huge boxes, sacks with the inscription 'cement,' cinder blocks, bricks: the clown goes between them, screams, manages, somewhere between them the cockerel flickers, they step on him twice and he yells passionately and angrily. Nobody pays him any attention, on the stage is Or, there, the heat: a secret, veer to the left, not there lads! Everyone is busy, someone puts on the bricks, someone is already plastering, smoothly, like a ballet, not looking away for a minute and on the stage a piece of a wall is erected to a person's height. The clown moves backstage, takes hold of a huge pot, with lightening speed pulls out from it plaster from the petals of the buds, rubs glue on it and sits on the stage, once, the whole wall in a ridiculous moulding there is no space. The pregnant clown lets herself down from the cupola on a huge Versailles lampshade, hangs tenderly with her head downwards, catching her foot in a chain, but in her hands she presses a heavy forged frame, inside which is a blue yellow stained glass. 'Where are you going skipping the queue?!!' shout the workers; not listening to anyone, she momentarily gathers a piece of the wall and puts in a window, and then jumps to the other side and sitting atop the stage, catches her lampshade flying past, unscrews one of the hundreds of lights! 'There is no cable there, idiot!' crows the clown, she shows him the big finger, don't be scared, she says! Somewhere there goes around and once! The window lights with a warm light. At that second a little music music begins to erupts from somewhere above, something hardly distinguishable, welcome to the house of fun! Pum, prum, pum prum! . . . a great pum pum !. . .like it isn't there, this music, she seems 'go away, idiot! It hurts!' The workers are mad, the female clown disappears. At this minute the crane rushes to the scene in its beak there is still a piece of wall, the workers stick the cathedral, something tidies up, the clown drags the caryatid having seized it across the stomach, places, fixes and here they hoist her on her head to the little balcony. The other caryatid, the third, the fourth, the pneumatic gymnastic workers go down with them from the upper part, the base of the temple caked now with these dreadful chicks, one with one eye, the other crooked, the third generally with the head of a cockerel; but the genuine cockerel suddenly protrudes from somewhere from the higher window and with happiness screams greetings; from the wall climb three plastic dragon heads and one character, the clown shoves a hand on the elbow in the jaw of the dragon, and whatever the tongue colours at once red and black, and a flame erupts, creepy, welcome to the house of fun! Jugglers go out on the upper balconies and throw each other hot torches, the clown about the stage, with the Charleston, with Gogol, screams: 'Well there go on!,' the crane pulls yet another piece of the stage, still, still still still! A great pum prum pum prum! Spikes, spikes! Lancet windows. These days all workers are on sick leave, they juggle with hammers, they throw each other cupolas and turrets, the clown rolls from somewhere from behind a corner on a gigantic drum, stays, balancing, he starts to paint a piece of the façade. The cathedral grows, grows terribly, it should have been buried already in the dome, but no. He goes on to the stage suddenly, knocking thrown away buckets, the second hoist, the self named crane, obviously someone drunk is managing it; the crane moves as if by touch here and there, the ray of the projector lights the driver's cabin; there is the female clown, the blockhead, with her own belly and pigtail! One lever, the other the crane pulls like a fallen one, 'go to hell!' shouts the clown, yes everyone is shouting. But she doesn't stop, the crane pecks the nose somewhere behind the scenes and gets down, holding a huge ugly spire, ribbed, all serrated, tulips and seashells. Still one! Where to? Nowhere! Not listening to the shouts, the female clown confidently manages the crane to the necessary sides, and there the horrible spire is already slung low somewhere at the highest level. Acrobats are already getting on the hoist and knock the female clown from there, she rolls behind the scenes. They get up to the cabin roof, once, a pyramid! A boy with an axe jumps up on the highest level, he hacks on the cathedral wall a few holes more and someone from that side immediately thrusts in window frames. The music is ever louder louder, flashes of fire, pieces of fire there, amongst the shared jokes the clown and the cockerel go up above. He jumped on the balcony, came on the caryatid on the head, caught the ledge, raised himself, threw a leg, still raising himself, the tightrope walker gave him a hand, once! He jumped on the rope, from there, once! On the window frame, then he orders the worker acrobats 'well there, help!' That once a pyramid, he flies on her, and from her, on the highest tower, and stands his full height in the lancet window 'And well all,' clearly the music overlapping, the clown pronounces 'well that's it, get out of here!' A pause. Confusion. The jugglers obediently drive the torches into the candelabrum. Everyone descends, they unfasten the guarantee and sadly lagging behind by the calusa, when they let the stage go, someone for the last time runs to the side and pulls a huge drum.

The clown stands on his own, with the cockerel in his hands. He stands at the top. The cathedral, the gigantic construction, a mockery over all the norms of architecture, inhuman, wearily big, ridiculous. Welcome to the house of fun! Insinuating whispering in a musical voice.

And the clown does a step and flies down, down, without insurance, from a terrible height, flying terribly, flatways; the same second the pregnant clown swinging on the Versailles lampshade transits past and manages to catch him by the trousers.

A howl in the hall. Thunderously boiling.

Trigger

Sandra, Alyosha Barcelona 2007

Another photograph. CH/B in the frame of tanks T-72 Taman division, the White House. In one of the tanks, two boys, both bald, one in a vest, the other naked to the waist, waves his cap and shouts something in happiness. The little group, a little to the side, contains five people; crampedly huddling, almost hugging. The left one, one of them is a student bomber, skinny, his eye lights up, in his hands scraps of a poster. A woman of middle age, portly, in a sarafan, pushes to her chest a huge thermos and shouts something to the person, who isn't visible, he's behind the frame. The low-lying lad in a skull cap and with a camera, shoots. They all have the same expression on their faces, all are easily amazed and happy. On the pavement alongside the tank sits a dishevelled Alyosha, he looks directly at his objective, terribly tired, but he is smiling, one eye is narrowed, on the cheek is soot or dirt, a sly mug. On the side, Gunnar's nose. Along this nose, oh, peruses a lot. The nose is wrinkled, there behind the frame Gunnar is laughing, flashing his teeth, he is terribly happy, fought, won over all, he knew that he is winning; two months ago a son was born, the third son, late, even late for Michelle and even for him; put simply, Gunnar is happy. A very good photograph, very. Sandra took it from Alyosha and took it with her. On the other side is a date '21/8'.

Because of this photograph also, by the way . . .

'You were not on this world then, I suppose. The devil take me, that I create, that you create . . .'

'Well don't worry about it! I remember everything well, we watched it with my parents, we worried . . .Dad came and said to Mum, in Moscow something terrible is happening . . .she cried . . . Then she began to scream: I rightly left this damned country! This is the first. Then we listened to the radio for three days . . .but then on the other hand she started to regret . . .'

'Yes, you were how many, eight!'

'Six.'

'Six years, my God. Six years, girl, you were, when we all, the ass holes, hoped for the light . . .the light . .. But how old were you when . . .my God, a year! You were a year, when . . .you're simply an idiot, you're a spoilt idiot, why did you then come up to me, what were you to me, what are you now to me, what are you amused, your vanity, your own pride, this monster tamed the scarlet flower?! Who are you to me?! We don't have a common language, nothing, cunt, the language of these State phrases stumbles, it mustn't continue like that, it's a trick, trick; the history of parting shouldn't be long, this is the failure of the system, the clinic, mine, but you're something here, where did you put your hand in, you didn't know where you're sinking it, why did you come up to me, and what, you, are now, doing? . . .'

'I simply want you like, that darkens in the eyes.'

Then Sandra could still quench these flashes.

Gunnar Moscow August 1991.

A few days before that the sister rang and said that the tirage 'of prayer' had arrived, they informed her from the publishing house and would have to take the rights. Usually on such a business they sent boys, but they weren't now in the town, one went with classmates to the hike, the other was at the friends' dacha, therefore Gunnar said that he would go himself and they quarrelled lightly. Putting it short, he left the publishing house on the 18th, he loaded his rucksack with books and gave them to Nadya. In a better view! They drank a little coffee and exhausted themselves about it.

Then Gunnar got ready to go home, he was flying in two days to Prague and it was a pity to waste time and without it he cursed himself, that he didn't change the business trip and it was needed to part with Michelle and the two-month old little one. Nadya reproached him for his manhood a little, then they kissed each other and she lectured him about some original pillow, stuffed with barley, for Michelle some magazine, which she signed on the shelves and fortunately he himself was aware; well and give me my book, encourage the stevedore. It's good that he remembered, it would have been a terrible insult.

But at home closer to evening, Seryozha decided to have the first scandal of his life, for his teeth it was early, the stomach, obviously, or what else could it be, only he screeched sadly and didn't let up. Gunnar quickly took him to the boys' room and all night he lulled. The slyness was that he was not allowed to lie; the baby fell asleep here and began to squeak again, therefore Gunnar looked after him back and forwards half the night, singing the hymn of the Comintern in a whisper and later he collapsed in the armchair and, continuing to shake the young one with one arm, began to judiciously search with his eyes what to read, in order not to fall asleep. The idiot, he didn't imagine, but here now in the most boyish den, it seems that discovery, the magazine 'Fire' is lying around on the table, is it not good? And here in his pocket his sister's book is moving. Yeah. Well at the end of it all it's the same when he would be forced to familiarise himself with it. Gunnar carefully pulled it from his pocket. A soft binding, badly straightened up, very comfortable: terribly uncomfortable, you don't put it anywhere, you must put one hand on the weight, and so you definitely don't fall asleep. He began to read and then it disappeared into the rubbish. Such a seamy side, but not the seamy side . . .something was not right, something not good, can't spell it out . . .a sea of typos. My poor little fool.

In the morning they and the young one fell asleep as ground hogs on the lower floor of a two-tiered bed, and at half twelve a scared Michelle shook him; Gunnar get up, something terrible has happened! I don't understand anything on the television!

Business trips, what kind of business trip there when such happens. Everyone was sent to the devil.

All scattered, they went to fight like Rostropovich.

It was not very humane from his point of view, we say directly. In the evening Nadya appeared without warning at Michelle and said: take the young one, get ready and come to Kirovsky, we are all there. Together it's somehow, you know . . .

They on the whole didn't get very friendly.

'Afghan prayer,' a fragment
Yesterday we buried two radio operators. There was a raid in Mezhozeri, from where they don't return. Beside me stood Dima Tikhonov, the gunner operator, ordinary, a secretary of the Komsomol office, candidate for membership of the Communist party, I heard that suddenly, that he under the nose displays 'saintly God, saintly strong one. . .' I shuddered, started to listen in. No, it's revenging itself. Must write to mother. How many such letters have I written, how many bought.

After a few months I return to Moscow and travel to Naro-Fominsk, to chat with the mother of one of the dead, Starchenkov. Olga Timofeeyevna will talk mutely, ironing with the ribs the palms the folds on the table cloth, she will show me the school photographs of Igor. He didn't study badly, but it didn't interest him, he dreamt of going quickly to serve. Father is now drinking. 'But I . . . I began to drink but this doesn't happen for me. I thought of finishing myself. It didn't work out.'

In Barnaul, I'm not going to the mother of the other radio operator, also Igor Sergeenko. She is refusing to talk to me on the telephone. I will think, all the same I must go. But here a crying woman calls me back, the Aunt of Igor. 'I beg you, not not come. Don't torment us.' I'm not going.

But this will be later.

. . . The same boys stood a while at some distance from the grave. I almost didn't know them then, I only glanced from the side, they reminded me of their similar surnames: Nestroev, Nesterov, Aleksei, Maxim, Leonid. They were always together. Then for some reason our interpreter Rahim clung to them, he would stand there having hung his head and mumbled something under his nose. But still the Leningrad correspondent arrived to make a report. I thought how ridiculous we look at the background of war. He had a summer jacket with a strap. These three boys were all the same together and apart from all the others. Why do I call them boys? Youths. But there was a certain high note of boyhood in them, domestic brotherhood, brotherhood of the front. All three are Muscovites. I knew little about them. But they attracted attention. And how it later explained itself, not in vain.

They became firm friends from their first day at war. They educated their own command. Their own clique, their own band, their own secret company, conglomerate and order. This happened involuntarily, irresponsibly, they didn't think of such a union. But they all called them so, were are those three? And they tried not to be apart.

In that terrible day the news came to us in the morning that in province L, an oil cistern was blown up. Someone from Dushman wanted to destroy our big division, he thought that he was blocking the exit to the tunnel and our servicemen appear to be his captives, but his plan didn't come to fruition. In amazement the commanding service worked clearly, they managed to unblock the exit. In my memory, the first time that operativeness. If I had known, than all changes for us . . .

In the day time the lads should have moved closer to the mountain pass. We already knew that soon they are landing four thousand people of personal team of VDV, and therefore feel a certain confidence. I write 'we', as if their feeling transferred to me. It's not possible to be there and feel otherwise.

Two heavy goods vehicles arrived, but there was no UAZ. They loaded everything, only a few State people remained, Rahim, the Leningrader, me, and one of the boys, Maxim. There wasn't enough space for him on the heavy goods vehicle. His comrades didn't want to go without him, but really could they keep everyone waiting? We stood and waited. Finally far away the UAZ appeared, it raced towards us, raising clouds of dust. It wasn't our driver at the wheel, but a local, but the car was definitely ours. . .They told us, there will be a different transporter, sit. Us. The four remaining got inside . . .

They ask me often, what is most terrifying, when they take you captive. There is no answer to this question. The terrible everydayness of what is happening. The busyness of the terrorist. The terrible your own readiness to obey: I'm indeed tied to the hands of Rahim, the Leningrader and the boy Maxim when the driver puts the muzzle to my neck. Then he began to say something, but Rahim pulled his Adam's Apple a couple of times, he tried to say something but couldn't at once say anything. Then he raised an eye to us:

'This is a capture.'

As if we didn't understand it ourselves.

'He will demand a ransom. He knows that you're citizens. He says that he has already understood for soldiers he does not get any kind of ransom. But perhaps the Soviet Union pleads for its own journalists.'

A naive idiot, this soul, what was he hoping for? He is clearly not in himself, it shakes him, they shake his hands, and this I feel, because he is holding me by the shoulders and puts the barrel to my neck. Probably, he has been smoking. His first morning attack finished with failure. Now he has decided for some reason that he can get something for citizens. Behind the window of the 'UAZ' there are blue mountains and brown dusty country.

It's difficult for me to work out how much time went by. Maybe twenty minutes. It seemed to us an eternity. The Dushman all the time mumbles under his nose to himself and even Rahim isn't translating any more. It's clear that there is no point. We are quiet, stupidly and hopelessly. By then Rahim suddenly starts to answer something, we don't understand a word, but we feel that the pressure is growing. And suddenly Maxim, with hands tied behind his back, throws himself forward and his head, in the dark, he hits the Dushman in the face with terrible strength. That one doesn't manage to ward off the blow, leaks blood and the flames fall back. At that moment I, with wonder, snatch his pistol, I use it, so that my hands aren't tied.

That's it. The second attack also failed ignominiously. We are lucky this is of course not a real hostage taker, but an idiot from the hash mountain dwellers. Had a genuine spiritual fanatic been in his place, we wouldn't have survived.

We tie our terrorist with the very same ropes, which had only just tied our hands. We swaddle him from from fright for the sake of faith, like a little baby, he just clenches his teeth. Rahim sits at the wheel, he is trembling so, that it's difficult to drive the car. We return to our previous base, it's clear that we are not to reach the crossing.

Having arrived, we fall out of the car and fall directly on the dusty and crumpled grass.

'Thank you, Maxim.'

'Don't worry about it.'

We arrived. How did we get here? With wonder. The UAZ stopped, we fell out directly to the ground. Yes it was like that. We breathed heavily as if we had run from the enemy. Although on the whole we drove in the car. But the tied-up enemy is falling in that same car. And he isn't breathing. I furtively drink valakardin, it's funny, furtively, from whom is it hiding, I live on my own, but just just in case she hid the vial of valakardin and the records of Validol in a box in the office, so that it was not lying around and just there no one unknowingly gets into it; and it would be similar to stupidity, just imagine; I'm ready to drink other medicines in full view of others and why hide it, but these, it isn't possible. Validol for old womeness? No. But there, it's as if he is breathing evenly. And only this Eastern boy . . . But be quiet, you're ok.

There are three boys. They're always together. One is definitely tow-haired with a charred nose. The other two have merged, you cannot tell them apart any more, the high cheekbones, yes, the skin . . .olive skin . . .olive heat, fatigue. And Rahim is with them, our interpreter, from Tadzhik stock, but Rahim, this is definitely not that, Rahim is stooping so bleak, long nosed . . .How old are you, I say, and he me: twenty seven. I look young.

There was such a moment: I enter with the module in the tent, the module isn't offered to him. He rubs the bowl with his skin, but the sun is low, heavy, the tent is moon-lit, the little bowl shines. And his mug shines from the sweat, the hair is dirty, sticks up, as there is a wet sparrow, and these collarbones . . .the shirt unbuttoned from the heat and the collarbones. My Great-Grandmother, he says, always cleaned so after plof. Oho, Great-Grandmother! Yes. I lived all my life with Granddad, Grandmother and Great-Grandmother. And I heard all my life. How Granddad gave out to Granny; how much will your mother teach me?! Laughter, yes? And the parents? He answers severely, the parents have died and I was small. They hurt themselves badly. They went in a car on their journey. They thought far away, but they didn't reach Dushanbe. Mother's parents indeed took me in, they were young then, what is it to them. 'And where did you live?' In Chkalovska. It's far to Dushanbe, even further to Moscow. Therefore there is Uranus there, have you heard? Though it was indeed not on the map . . .well there. I lived my whole life there. Well, Mum's family. Father was from there. 'How from there?' But so. The family is from there. How do I know the language? I know a lot of languages. From childhood Yiddish, my old people hid it from me. Later I knew German well. An inheritance from father. Oho! I'm thinking of myself: so he is a defector, perhaps?

The tent fills with sunlight even more, and the sky is so blue and releases releases on us, and we are all around the grass, but I see, he is lying with his head in a puddle, I want to go up to him, but the parents have died, who stops me, hods me by the elbow. He has just got a telegram. Gonchar came, the old driver of the BTP.

He lifts his head, I see, this is it, not him, not the Eastern boy, not my Eastern boy, not the transporter, not those cheekbones, but this is Rahim, our interpreter, gloomy, dark, long-nosed, and where else then?

There will be a telephone call for her. Gelena cries down the receiver: Nadya why are you not coming to us? Why are you sitting there? Why should I go to you? you're what, you don't know? You're what, sleeping there?!

She goes to the window and looks at everything in her alley, a tank got stuck in the arch. It tried to get passed but couldn't, the entrance blocked. Two soldiers are sitting on the curb and are eating ice cream. Do you know, my dears it's too early for insanity for me. Perhaps it's too early for insanity. Someone is wanking inside, it's the very time for hallucinations.

Gunnar, Alyosha. Moscow August 1991

Gunnar knew that when he draws himself a left eye, behind the window they turn the bushes inside out and the trees fall into line. When the right one, at home not that they are budging, but are losing severe geometry and they are changing into the Big and Little Bear dippers. When he rubs his cheeks, he begins to play Kum-par-sita. Well that's all, he is ready for the off. He doesn't need either a wig or a nose. He generally thinks make-up isn't necessary, it's not about that and she makes herself up only thanks to this ritual. In order to disturb the world around. In order to excite. In order to ir-rit-ate. He also knows, he understands well, that this is all inner quotes, eternal belle and idiotic delusion. But he willingly allows himself this small prank, no one will ever find out about it.

But today he is sitting in front of the mirror without reason. Why he decided to enter here, God knows. The summer, dust, emptiness, all went on business trips. Business trips, yeeees . . .good that he managed to change the business trip. He would still have been happy, if he had flown to Prague, and here

Michelle with the little one and the older boys, the sister and such they do. As he would have scrambled back, no my God is happy of course. But why did I come here, I wasn't at all prepared to come here? To collect something. An old momento, a stub! I dreamt of a trick on my own, and something doesn't fit well with him for the meantime, but I didn't appear here because of a trick. What could I need here? Really to make myself up in front of the entrance . . .and there it's. . . In order that the world stirred? I have already gone crazy, the maniac ballooned. And all powerful. A total idiot.

Then he goes to his telephone and picks the number.

'Alyosha? Do you know, yes?

He was not hoping for anything in particular: now there was no work, they didn't speak for a month and a half, and maybe Alyosha is in his most difficult phase. But then he answers unexpectedly sober and kindly:

'Yes of course

'And what do you think? We will go?' Oh hardly this. Hardly, Alyosha is going somewhere, he explains rather that he is thinking about it all. He has seen all of this in a zinc coffin, with such a weak liver he has all of this . . .And I'm calling him in vain, of course, it doesn't weary the lad, to him it's little already, perhaps. But less likely, that he will explain anything to me, simply . . .

But Alyosha answers:

'Yes'

And they agree to a meeting on Krasnopresensky.

He leaves and he sticks in the doors and can't exit, for the umpteenth time he casts a glance to the dressing room. Why is he indeed stuck here, he has to leave and here he overshadows it: yes there it is. A cupboard, well well. There is an ideal tidiness in the drawers of the cupboard, maybe only remember, where exactly I stuffed it. We had dreamt up such a way: when the bear Vonnegut was shooting at me from the bow and the pistol, with single bullets and I pictured Saint Sebastian and Alexander Matrosov, there we needed it, aaaa there he is! In a polyethelyne packet, an accurately laid vest. Well although I understood, why I rushed about.

He locks the cupboard, a bag of vanities under his armpits and leaves. How much they wearied with this bear, he and the trainers, and it turned out to be a wonderfully dumb animal: he didn't picture anything or want to learn, he just demanded to feast all the time. But he is kind. Now he has been acquired by the zoo.

The circus. Yeah. A full circus.

Somewhere around five in the evening.

'Did you take the vest? I took it. The one which remained from the bear.

Well now he certainly sends me somewhere further. But let him. Here there is such a heap, as it is, I didn't even expect, in the uniform, a lot of decorations. A lot are clearly in vests. I look at him so, so that he doesn't notice, how is he going to react to everything? Why generally was I dragged here? The devil take me, this is certain. And then I ask, as they say, generally I couldn't care less, I'm simply curious. I'm cold and waiting. Now he is soooo to me . . .But Alyosha answers me completely calmly:

'Yes. It's worn under the shirt.'

And he narrows his eyes at the feeble sun.

Warm, glorious, mud oozes from the river, rain, that means it's not, well. Tanks, BTR and BMP, ruined on the banks. The soldiers chew at a sundae. To the people, I can't count, a lot a lot (but the meaning doesn't remain: a handful!), all as if concentrated, like ants, they scurry, pull something somewhere; but the faces, honest mother, what faces. Yes I have the same on my mug, all the same; to hell I don't understand, the excited ferret, he didn't say goodbye to his children, but what the dog fuck he put his hand to the head. And tricks don't give me peace, as if all took shape, but later, no the idiot leaves.

Little music from somewhere. This disgustingness.

. . . But the stars fall under the Kandahar in rays of dawn.

Only don't tell mum that I'm in Afghanistan . . .

Then suddenly our circus people appear, they were at first in the Kremlin, then here they somehow forced their way through. Three workers and three trainers, with thermoses. They scream and reach in to hug. They greet Alyosha accurately, as if they are afraid of him when he came to work for us (terrible animal, ill animal, roars so! The buffet girls says), so since and . . . And to say that there is something to say.

'Gunnar Grigorievich! Coffee! Alyosha! Help yourselves! Come everyone.

They drink down their coffee in turn; two other thermoses in the throng went at once in agreement.

A little music. One cuckoo, the second a third. One slobbering over the other, you don't understand which is worse. Alyosha makes a wry face but puts up with it. Suddenly in the crowd there is such a lad in a square glasses and with a microphone, behind him, an operator with a camera.

'You're what indeed . . .what are you thinking, they will allow you on the airwaves?

'They won't fucking let me on,' smiling, the lad speaks 'not the slightest chance.'

He queries the soldiers and the men. The soldiers are embarrassed, the men willingly mutter something in reply.

Later Nadya in a moment, oh is unintelligent! Runs! The little bag on wheels rides after her!

'What are you! How did you find me?!

'I brought sandwiches! You don't ring, you disappeared!. . .'

'You ring here.'

The newspaper spreads on the asphalt, unloads bundles, bundles, packets.

'There is madness.'

He hails the guys, each of them by the hand. Alyosha isn't there at that moment, he left for somewhere.

'Eat, please!'

With the friend of Oleg, that he returned I hold the steam You only don't tell mum that I'm in Afghanistan. . .

'Your ones are all ok, we are sitting in Kirovsky! We are worried, of course. Now I'm going to them. We will watch television.'

Nervous laughter.

Alyosha left in order to inhale a little of this tune.

And if she asks about what I write, well what about it, lie.

You just don't tell mum that I'm in Afghanistan . . .

There it's not possible to get rid of something, some doughnuts all around, doughnuts, doughnuts, recruits, bayan players confusion Mothers . . .the howling mathematician on the platform. Alyooooosha!

Mathematician Moscow 1983

There was nothing worse for Moti in life than that summer.

What worse to remember than all . . .the serenity of his donkey. Before that all happened. Since, well many years have gone by, as you remember as you throw into the heat and stuffiness and it's not possible to think about it all. As much as it's impossible, that the allergic reaction begins, a cough.

Checked a hundred times. Therefore he can hardly talk about that period at all.

At first everything was very good. No, that is also a lie; it was not good, simply he was an idiot. It was still April, wonderful, warm, the end of the first year, and he went to Alyosha's dacha, there shouldn't have been any Alyosha there, he didn't like the dacha for a long time, but Motya from the inertia of childhood love named everything after Alyosha; visiting Alyosha , to Alyosha's dacha. So was his rainbow mood, the hysterics of the university entrant and clinic history with an action that was not only behind him, but he had just finished a period of withdrawal symptoms, it became clear that after the session nobody would be thrown out, the more so that he studied no worse than anyone on the course and already understood this moist feeling . . .in school he with all problems was a capable, but strange boy and here were a few good boys, with whom it was possible to talk, they began the special seminary . . .and there he is travelling on the suburban train, he wrinkles his nose to the sun, smiles, he is good: upcoming sessions only made him happy, there is one riddle, which occupies his thoughts already for a month and a half and he is steadily approaching it stealthily and it's a girl. It's possible to tell Auntie about this, she always asks about everything and worries for him, and in any case it was not possible to talk to Alyosha, one doesn't provoke: Alyosha does not own up to the category of 'one girl' on the whole. Uncle didn't blunder once: any of Alyosha's new girls he accepts and why say it; how did you get home last night, without incident? And that you left home so late . . .Alyosha maddened, there is a new girl every day, and where's yesterday's girl! Uncle in terror hits himself on the lips, it was him by accident, he is blindly and kindly soulful . . .Yes, Alyosha will of course be mad, but on the other hand, let him be mad. Motya has been used to this for along time and only laughs. But the fuck you drag Alyosha to the dacha, he sits in town, uses his parents' absence. . .

As Motya thought of something, while he was on the train, while he bought newspapers in the station, while he ran through the forest . . .he got caught out in warm rain and got wet. He flew to the terrace wet and dishevelled and Auntie got up from her patience to hug him, sent him off to change into dry clothes, started to drink tea and in all this he didn't notice anything, didn't notice, the fool . . .and only later when they judged him in institute business, over washed the bones of all the friends, she smiled weakly and said; here is something else, Motya . . .and he suddenly saw how white and unhappy she was.

The information fell in lumps and tufts, terror came; he never saw his Aunt ironic, 'self composure,' as Lyoshka and they called her . . .she spoke quietly, sparkly, 'well you understand . . .', and for one didn't understand anything! She invited him to the dacha deliberately! She was afraid to talk in the town, where there is a telephone. She smoked one after another, she exhaled the end of the phrase with smoke, bitter, exile, letter, judgement, they requested Uncle . . . 'I asked him; you don't need this career height!' Motya saw the boar with a boar, she would explain, as to a little one . . .He frowned, trying to understand, which such honourable conscience about everything, and then she stubbed out her cigarette and pronounced, circling with her fingers squares on the oil cloth: 'They told him if he doesn't write, they will throw Lyoshka out of the institute and send him to the army.'

Sugary peace with riddles and girls staggered and settled. Motya suddenly felt that he wants to drink terribly and insatiably from despair, but he couldn't get up; everyone looked at her with dry, over dry eyes; why indeed was everything so ruined? But she turned over the match box, looking at the table. Motya shook his head, got up like a drunkard, went to the stove, poured water from the kettle, and here she was held like a current, why had she called him, why did she tell him all of this? And he limped the idiot! Here he had to decide something and it was clear what, to spit at all! He threw away the pot holder and went up to her, sat squat and said terribly tenderly and persistently: 'Auntie! Let him sign! Spit at everything!'

She looked at him sadly and laughed 'it's not about that . . . he hasn't signed yet. Already refused. You don't move him he is stubborn. . . and a fool. It's not the time!' Oh if you knew . . . I said to him then: I will divorce you. But how would I divorce him?! He has the second heart attack in the nose. Motya, I'm another . . . I have a request for you. You can hardly fulfil it . . .looking at things realistically, you can't, of course. But I don't know what else to do . . .' So beautiful, dark eyed. So, even on the dacha, elegant, how does she manages this? She wears a huge dacha sweater, male with holes in the elbows and it looks on her like a fashionable . . .this . . .. how is it? Motya was not strong in this. How unhappy she was . . .already if she was in a panic, if she turned to him for help, and they both knew, that he couldn't help her in anything . . .she asked about one thing: when Alyosha shoves out, she begs him to sit on though in the dacha, though anywhere, to hide and wait. It was clear to both of them, that this wouldn't happen. She didn't sleep the whole night before, she sat in the kitchen, endlessly, helplessly putting out the patience, there was no way out, none none. Suddenly it dawned on her, similar happened a couple of times in her life, that Motka managed to reason with Alyosha. Literally a couple of times, when she already couldn't do anything herself. Yes, yes, an occurrence, when he was about to jump with a parachute. He was ten, they took him for twelve; he of course was about to lie. Motya then wrinkled his nose suddenly and announced: I also want to jump, but I'm not ab-out to lie to the State! Unexpectedly for everyone Alyosha agreed to wait a little.

But the last time so totally was recently, a year and a half ago, when Alyosha announced suddenly that he was going to Mohammed. Together with Motya, Motya had clean form, by a complicated road, you don't tell it in two words. But Alyosha dreamt of becoming an architect from childhood, he drew wonderfully, painted, got ready all year for Markhi, and suddenly here he leapt. 'I will go with Motka. How is it they don't take us? Yes if you study so that they don't find fault, let them try not to take us! . . . Yes how much is it possible to go on occasion?! And I won't enrol I'm going to the army!' She tried to say something then: it's not allowed to tear up talent, you're an architect from God, you indeed wanted that . . . all was for nothing. Then Motya in despair suddenly blurted out: you're behaving like a pompous ass hole!'

He made a proviso, he didn't even think to joke. But here the devil was clearly telling fortunes on him. Something acted, caught. Alyosha neighed like a stallion. Mohammed was postponed, he entered Markhi easily, playing and also he studied the first year. Yes you don't change talent.

But now . . .the chances were there, but destroyed.

Uncle woke up, went out onto the terrace, wrapped in a blanket, we sat at dinner, later portrayed a bullet, Motya arranged everyone without pity. Then it was still possible to hope.

Later still there was Lyoshka's call, after a month and a half. 'Hello! I have two pieces of news, one is crappy, the other is assy, which one to begin with? With the crappy. Father's in hospital, it's not a heart attack, it was a fit, the cardiogram, they say, so so. I think indeed about such heat. He is in Yausa on the 23rd, they transferred him to intensive care, I was there now, but if you find time, go. But tell your . . .tell you the second piece of news? I failed my English, What about it? All right, I'll do it again, a full fuck, they were fucking around with the heat. That's it, Motik, I've already gone, I've a meeting.'

That personally speaking is it.

A month after Lyoshkin's . . . .after they accompanied Lyoshka . . . The mathematician lay on the bed in his room with his mug to the wall, melting from the heat. He lay like that all the time now, he got up only for exams. He did them well by the way, although he fucking didn't prepare for them. After every exam he went to honour the occasion with the lads. He drank and joked. Then he would return home and lie down. One time he didn't get up for the exam: his mother said 'Matvei, get your act together, help your Aunt and Uncle!' They released Uncle from the hospital, he felt like going to the dacha, but it was not possible to go on the suburban train, he must get the car ready. He did everything, he took them, he returned to town on the last train and lay down . . .he would lie, lie, he circled a pattern with his finger on the carpet on the wall. And later, after a couple of days, the telephone. Mum's steps in the corridor. And Mum's shout.

The gas cylinder in the dacha blew up. She rang the neighbour.

He wrote Alyosha a telegram.

That's definitely all.

Nadya Moscow August 1991

Nadya gave a sandwich to Gunnar and went towards the metro, slowly, unwillingly; She would have stayed here, but on Kirovsky they are going mad, they swear with her that she adjusts her dress in an hour, Gelena shouted: what are you, the honey is spread, again to hell, what are you! Michelle threatens that the milk is spoiling. Yes we had to go there, but she bought a little wafer glass, and the boy journalist in the square glasses, so glorious, again fell into her eye line. The heavy operator went to him, he dragged the camera on his shoulders and greedily examined it. The boy suddenly, as if decided on something, ran up to the group of people and thrusted the microphone on them.

'What do you think will you be here the whole night?'

'Well and how? Of course . . .we have bread . . .yes we can go without bread . . .(different voices).'

'How do you know about everything? How to build barricades, this is all?

'There was experience,' the shaggy man in a windcheater answers squinting. 'Vilnius taught me . . .'

'We are already shot,' picks someone on the crowd, people part, ahead, under the camera an elderly man reaches, breathing with asthma, his mug and neck are crimson, his jacket with medals. 'we are shot yes . . .we are already beaten sheep, bless you . . .no meeting Senya!' Somebody pulls him from behind, that one shrugs, you don't hit him that easily. 'Our experience will come in handy now. Are we in vain, perhaps? On our own skin! Like they taught us then, we'll do that! Do you know how they taught us?'

Nadya understands what he just said. Her first movement is to rush, to run, not to hear it. But for some reason she stands, her feet are stuck to the ground, you don't move from the place you have nowhere to go, feet, boots, skirt, belt, gymnast, in sweaty hands a sweaty handkerchief, the sun of squeezed ages and suddenly a clap of the bayan, 'the apple' shouts angrily and pitifully into the microphone.

'Did they teach us in vain not a step backwards?!

The bayan somewhere at the river cuts open, knocking the agreement and 'the Farewell of the Slavs' bursts out, warm plombir drops drip on the pavement, on her bag and shoes.

Gunnar Alyosha Moscow August 1991

The time stuck, black evening. Little bones. Who the devil brought them here to this damned tunnel, there was a reason, but yes there in the corner was the single working public telephone. The lads said: they don't work anywhere but there in the corner of the ring at Kirovsky there is one which isn't broken at the moment. Gunnar thought that if he indeed doesn't ring Kirovsky today, Michelle will simply go mad. Who had known indeed . . .

The screams of the chicks, the dark wrenching foul language, where is this unbearable screeching from, I will never forget it? They pulled out one, the second the third. The dark haired chap popping up in the midst, holding the weight in his bloody hand, laughs, entering, bending in a harlequinesque breaking; Alyosha before hitting his leg, manages to lightly rub his mug.

So stuffy, that not a thought is thought of to the end, so all weak despicableness and there is a carousel in front of the eyes and in the throat; but the thoughts lie somehow, about the children, about Michelle, that would be ok, but then suddenly, 'chemists write letters', where is this from, what's this? And this unthought of trick turns everything in the head, wearing me out totally; later suddenly, that the postponed business trip will have to be fulfilled, but how, when? The season begins, wwwwhat season is there, what is going on in the head . . .Gunnar pulls from his pocket 'Yava' but it's impossible to smoke. Alyosha somehow will be etched from the crowd, goes up to him, the mug perhaps dirty, perhaps sooty, the lips are crooked.

Blood and plombir in blots on the asphalt.

And later to say directly is funny, comes grey and a colourful day of victory.

And then a tank comes straight towards us, as it is, a tank comes towards us, T-72 tank division, the hatch swings open, and from there like a devil from a box, the soldier pops up, light, round eyed, some kind of exophalmic , poor guy. Shines! He shouts : 'Comrade clown! Comrade clown!' this one is shouting at me! I stand, I look at him with a wild glance. 'Comrade clown, I recognised you! I was at your presentation! You flew with a cockerel under the cupolas! You did tricks!' A round there is hysterical laughter.

The sun does a freak somersault and whoops on the parabola to somewhere down to me along the spine, and soars again upwards. I'm getting ready with a tough effort; must joke in something, but here I see with a sideline view, that Alyosha is becoming bluish and sits on the pavement.

(. . . Alyosha got rid of the annoying little sister, at the wall, as if all is nothing, only there . . .the dear sun . . .)

He clearly remembers the tears: not a day am I remaining, damn it all, where is the helicopter?! Where is the helicopter, the devil take everything, cunts, scum bags!! He clearly remembers his own numbness: the chick screams. It's a pity, she's an idiot. The battle beats drum-like webs, better if she could be put somewhere further away, because she's in hysterics, now she will squeal for a long time. Around her bustles the little sister. The other little sister hits him on the cheeks: well go on my dear, well go on, wake up. 'Yes I'm all right, all right, I'm not in shock. I'm simply tired of you, with all the talking.' he pinched the little sister by the side, that one stared with her eyes 'Comrade Demin!' screams the company 'The helicopter will come in a day! Nooooo!' A howl, he swallowed. Demin wrinkled: should have been earlier, young man! You see yourself what to do . . .N'oooooooo! Where did you get ready for all,' with a quiet clearness the company speaks.

. . .To hell with him . . .. Sunshine . . .he shut his eyes.

Through a yellow jelly, a little red sun. The bedlam of a picture from a child's album. Motya remembers, he never drew without yellow, eternally some kind of tear-eye-rays or a pear on the dish. And there please, again yellow haze around. Yellow-maned lions around the corner, on the flews they have such glares, I blink blink, but all the same it's painful. Exhaustion at the block post at the last stadium, there it flares up. Around are caterpillars in lace trousers, first tanks, it's stuffy. The yellowness is eating at my liver, as a Prometheus eagle, I really feel that. Perhaps the point is that this sad terrorist rubbed me on the trousers, in the stomach? But no, where there. it's I who hit him, hit hit hit . . .

There it's that hurts me, it's definitely the liver, it's on the right. And I have a reel on the right. And the kidneys don't come into it. I have read this literature. And I have listened to Mum's girlfriends, oh they have repulsed it in the army! . . . Oh I returned such and such! . . .

Mum's girlfriends . . . 'girls' she always called them. We will go for a walk with the girls along Gogolevsky. I don't want to cause any worry, it will only be the girls. The girls were my Aunt, Mum's sister and some others from school and the institute . . .

By the way, we wont talk about it now, right? No one has written to me, no one has advised, there was no tel-egr-am. No tank approached me, the hatch didn't swing open and this one didn't get out of there, how is he? He didn't say my surname, didn't hold out a telegram. Wild words, I sympathise . . . double burial . . .

But I will tell you all one thing, my girlfriends, girls, institute girls, hellish little girls, let them be mine, yes, in order that they didn't think about me too much. If they warded me off and I returned not like that, he is himself an idiot and an axolotl. An his brain is axolotlish and the soul.

To safeguard the kidneys and the soul is a technical business. There won't be a problem with your kidneys and your soul if you're a person and a man, and put in even a little . . .

The nose, the ears and the eyes, there that you don't save. An axilotish nose! And the eyes. I will pass on this. Because again; a yellow kissel pulls with a bitter little smoke, it eats away at the nostrils and from somewhere far away a little music hatches, a nasty shake shake pum pi du di dum dum. Shake shake! Pum di du di dum. I raise the clumsy heaviness for ages and I see how nearby our module, on the little square, on the yellow scorched earth, amongst thrown away bowls and basins, the old woman in the red dress and white gloves, the curly-headed old woman with the smoked cheeks, a savings bank weasel, rat faced witch, the devilish Grandmother, terrible, in one word, an old woman.

It dances
This
Neck
Neck neck
You don't do anything any time with him.)

At that moment they open the hatch of the tank, from where comes a woozy soldier and Gunnar yells: 'Oy, I recognised you, comrade clown! You do tricks! Show me a trick! . . .' Gunnar bares his teeth, all around is a regatta, not so happy, so wild, shameful relief, relaxation . . .

Alyosha suddenly stops feeling his fingers. What the hell, there are no fingers and that's it. So it seems to him? He tries to undo his buttons on his shirt, in order to stretch them, but they are not listening, completely cotton. He is sitting on the pavement with terrible strength swallows the Medusa, lodged in the Adam's Apple area, and hears clearly, how the vulgar voice inside with poisonous piece of cake says to him: 'Trigger, yes? Trigger!' or the other whispers something to him, this inner scum bag?

(Many years later Sandra and the others will be sitting in Barcelona, in the port. There will be peace, he doesn't exasperate himself for long and her, there will be the sea breeze, he is trying to tell her something and she answers him; this is called a trigger, Alyosha. We read a lecture about it. Some kind, you know, a morsel of experience, a scream of the brakes, a cry of the child, a knife in blood or something of that kind of detail . . .)

Gunnar understood between them, that there was no way out as long as there was a circus, such a total circus, well they don't get rid of it, already all totally brainless. But to hell with everything! The lad at the tank demanded a cloth cap, that one gave it, laughing, and he turned out to be completely bald like his friend. 'Take off your shirt too!' The cap in the shirt, he folded the envelope, rolled a tight tube, took his knife out of his pocket, cut the salami in slices, he started to divide it all around. A howl laughter: 'salami! The real stuff! Doktorsky! AAAAAAAA!' People come up, the flock strays, they shout, laugh! They chew salami! Some lad, on his look a student bomber, completely not in himself, but glorious, yells: 'This is Doomsday! Doomsday! A great moment!' The aunt in sarafan places the whole thermos 'drink up my dears! don't eat dry food without liquids!' Gunnar tries to swing, but he easily turns and sits on the pavement beside Alyosha. The bald little guy in the tank, sitting, shouts. 'And the cap, the cap, comrade clown?! Did the cap fall?' 'Look in the tank! That one dives inside and after a few seconds emerges, swinging the cap and almost crying from happiness.

Alyosha's breathing at once is even. All as if nothing, nothing . . .only he's tired. The low person in the skullcap brings the camera and clicks, clicks, clicks.

The binding

It's time! The capsule was set on the spatula, one. The removable map case curved inwards lightly to the grooves, so he didn't come, that's two. The low flying attack aircraft hooked on to it, three! The buttonhole was added to the trigger, four! The barrel was screwed on but from the top of it's the rifle scope, five, six! He checked the trigger for endurance, seven! He twisted the drum, pulled the shutter, eight, nine! All! Eleven seconds. A record.

He sighed, woke up. He passed over with his tongue along dry lips. Again these words, again heresy . . .

Nadya, Moscow, the 60s

Sometime, the 60s perhaps, Nadya opened 'Neva' and, let's say, a monthly prescription, all valuable stuff was read there, over read, issued to the day, one piece only remained unread, she as before didn't set out to read it because she suspected rubbish, the unknown author, title, something about the author . . .or about captivity, prose about war, speaking shortly.

There was nothing new in hand, Leskov, always helpful, somehow didn't leave, she started to leaf through the pages of the magazine and she retracted in the same 'medal-captivity-flight' it was certainly rubbish. But one page, the other, the intrigue flew around and somehow stupidly it delayed her, as if there was nothing to read, but she didn't want to throw it out. She very quickly gulped down empty chapters, in general, later she started to pass big passages, later she started to leaf through and glance ahead and somewhere closer to the end the eye snatched the upper sentence: 'This was Gelii D, head of the chemical department with a chemical name . . .'

The finger, holding the page, jumped, the magazine closed, she rushed to leaf through it, and there it's, there it's yes indeed, Gelii D, head of the chemical department! On went his poetry! That which she heard a lot. He was some certain episodical personage, a fellow camp inmate, a big romantic, that which you do it out with the friend of the main hero.

She rang Kirovsky, said that there was business to discuss 'well come' said Alya 'what are you ringing for? But I need Gelik to also be there. Gelik I don't know, he writes now. No I certainly need him to be! Fine I will try,' muttered Alya 'I will try.'

They again turned off the light in Kirovsky. The preference players took the kerosene lamp. They found a candle but there was little coming from it; Gelik meanwhile took it to the kitchen, sprinkled the velvet jacket with Stearin. Who thought of wearing a velvet jacket at home every day? Stupidity. Gelena straining her eyes, led a studious plan, these conversations annoyed her so, there was no strength. She took out of the wardrobe a winter hat and would wear it, so though it would be less heard. And it had to be, that to hell they turned off the light, and you don't leave them now for another room, because you have to deal with this hellish plan, but they hum and hum, they have great things to do there. The tap in the kitchen has again dripped and from it kap kap kap unbearably, go out of your mind, who knows why the cat miaows, it's certainly not hungry, it has a harmful character. Filled with smoke again wondrously, they smoke one after another. Alya sits straight, a leg on a leg, the back straight, the very elegantness, as usual; but Gelik, it's obvious, is embarrassed, upset, fucked. Nadya triumphs but contains herself badly and feels as if she is the landlady of the situation, says to Gelena 'don't hunch!'

'But perhaps it's not me?'

'Not you? Head of the chemical department with a chemical name? But with your poetry? Well what are you generally?'

'Yyyes.'

Gelik didn't like it all, but why, it's possible to explain, but sickeningly and unwillingly. But is Nadya really simply getting off so?

'Listen, I don't even feel like talking about it . . .'

'But why? it's possible and necessary to speak!'

Well how was it possible to talk about this, yes still with Nadya, the feisty fool? He became ill still on these first pages, when the heroes (then there were not the five of them, but only two, and thank you to remember their cretin nickname, Telemachus, telegraph) in Austria they saw looters, bandits in Soviet uniform. Next went a glorious moderate macabre, in moderation the phantasmagoria is allowed on the background of cleaned realism, not a pinch of symbolism, nor a grain of futurism, and perhaps it would have been nothing, but already despair despair, despair, despair. Changed dress it means . . . .Well, well! And later this end . . .At the end the heroes are given medals. Medals! This had to have been understood. The knight order of ass holes won acknowledgement in view of medals for valour. And the truth, slandered before, celebrated, strong as the sun, which can't be hidden . . .and the old faith, which they killed, returned to the heroes as a new faith. Flourish, maestro! March! Uproar! Something like that. In that there was a way out from a weak not marquis standard, the last pages were written already with an entirely simple peredvizhniki language, without a plagiarised substrate, without the shadow of a swagger. These very final pages where there was a happy interchange. Gelik didn't read any more, but leafed through it, he hoped all along not to immerse in this shit with his head, but where to? The devil take Nadya with her meticulousness. They themselves, of course, glanced at this wastrel in the last edition, whoever would start to read: a war writer, called 'my order,' the author is a debutant on the fifth tenth, a front-man. Hurt by an Aksenov syllable but decorating himself. But still also the camp prose, you all think. We know what the so genuine camp prose is.

So he understood this hellish little mood, this shy pitiful shuddering, little hope and well as the truth, is it *possible? Possible* yes? Well I write to you, I also something somewhere . . .I grease in the corner, I shadow, darken, shut over, and so you and I agree well and . . . I took a mouthful here. Yes what to say there, you almost wrote so, it was an idea. Therefore he sits now, tears a fragment from the table and scratches off the Stearin from his jacket, not raising an eye to Nadya.

'Listen, you tell me anyway. But there, did he lie about everything? You didn't have such people there? You didn't have ties with them? You didn't read them poetry? But hold on, the poems are yours, how does he know about them! Or he somehow describes your reality?'

They didn't remember so much of it all later, as this their conversation was interrupted, nothing was allowed to recover properly. Some unhappiness happened, according to the version of Gelena, a fire started at the neighbours, because a candle got caught in the curtain; Alya recalled that Zhenka was brought by the lads from the street with a sprained leg; Nadya claimed that Mikhdikh's heart was bad and they were forced to call an ambulance and that it turned out to be the first of his two heart attacks; well Gelik said that the cat got caught up in the couch. Only Nadya was not right; Mikhdikh by that time had already died, and she confuses the activities of the previous year, but can you really convince her? Indeed three other events happened in that mad year, but what so exactly from them interrupted their chat, just try and check. So or otherwise, they all sprang from their places and rushed, Gelena in a hat, as she was. A genuine fire engine arrived and they put out the fire quickly enough, set Zhenka's leg, breaking away from the preference, Tolya who had some medical help, the cat got caught in the jammed drawer of the couch, they pulled him in turn, the cat drank, Alya was worried that they would break his paws, at the end if it all Viktor ripped the lid of the drawer and removed the fool. Such or otherwise, so that it would not happen on that day exactly, Gelik used the events and changed the subject; next, obviously, he took himself to work, was hired and in Nadya's further efforts to explain how she so killed his idiotic prose, he answered one: why judge such mediocrity, when it was possible to talk about Bely? What was the terror, woe and madness, this author, that there was nothing to talk about.

And you don't force your way through.

In a letter to the author Gelik, of course, began to sketch, 'dear Efim, I doubt whether you remember me, as far as one writes to your personage . . .' however the matter didn't go further, yes he didn't have ideas of sending the letter. The magazine 'with my medal' he hid for some reason in the attic. Woe and madness, yyes . ..

Nadya Moscow 2007

In one of those April days Nadya bumped into Dima at the entrance to his house, she had just returned from the shop, and he caught up with her with a greasy packet of doughnuts in his hands, cursed, that she again pulls along useless sacks with conserves, he took it all, but handed her the doughnuts, a terrible rarity, in car oil, such as was needed! He had an hour and a half of free time and he decided to run to Nadya, he hadn't been there for a long time. She gave out that he didn't warn her and they went to the entrance. At that moment, while Nadya shook up her bag, searching for the key, she always took it out earlier on the first floor, in their footsteps came a a round and moustached major in the police (a security point took up position these days at the entrance). Or such and such nonsense. The major squeezed to the side between them, a blocked journey, they made way . . . and here Nadya suddenly started to shout at the back of him. 'Comrade Policeman! Dima stared with his eyes, 'what are you doing?!' Nadya brushed him aside 'I have to, as they say, don't interfere.' The major turned around and gazed and them questioningly 'or mister policeman, I don't know which is right,' continued Nadya 'you know, I have a question for you which will take up literally two or three minutes of your time. If it's not convenient for you to talk now, so I will come another time . . .' 'Speak' the major graciously ordered.

Next . . .Dima didn't know what to think at all. Heaven knows Nadya put up with them terrorising her with calls, that this carries on not one day, that she already recorded one call on the dictaphone . . .She hadn't said anything to anyone! Now this painful conversation! Calmly, like a tortoise, the major listened to her very attentively and asked: 'well and why did you need me?' 'What is that?' exclaimed Nadya. 'I'm turning to you as a representative of the State. . .' she stopped for a second, but right there she caught the meaning . . . 'Security of order. And I wait from you safety and security.'

Continue? When they went into the flat and Dima was ready to hiss at her, the cop, it seems, went after them, he rang at the door, and withdrew to the side. 'But tell me, there your Mum . . .or who is she to you . . . a relative . . . she lives there on her own . . .it's not good . . .you see yourself . . .'

In a word, worry.

'Nad, what are you creating? Do you generally imagine it? You . . .'

'Don't hang your head in this generally, this is all my affair, sit! Right now five minutes, there will be coffee. So that is your deputy, you say?'

And you don't move her. Well and Allah be with her, let it create what you want, let him have fun. He plopped down on the crooked little couch, he pulled his nose, Batumsky coffee, he closed his eyes. He was tired. They annoyed him. Nadya put the cups on the table, sat at the stool and they passed two hours well, they drank their fill. About all his business, about the mess with his deputies; somehow she proposed business, if to gather them all, but not for a meeting, but for a little sturm und drang, they then felt in command. They spoke very well. And they ate the terrible doughnuts.

'You know you're already worse than bitter radish. You frightened me terribly at first. Later we kind of agreed on something. Now you are again . . .I'm your target, well there kill me, I don't understand . . .'

'So this is indeed my target.'

'What exactly?'

'Yes there . . .a bitter radish. The bitter radish is my aim.'

'It means you simply decided to annoy me strongly? Drive me to psychosis? Enough, enough . . .'

'I decided to prove to you, that you should answer for your words. That for any crime there follows a payment.'

'Oh there is already a crime! How you throw about words!'

'No my dear. I'm not the one throwing words. You're the one who throws around words. You're flinging your lies and you sit hiding in your own nice shit and you believe that it's not possible to find you. That everything comes out of your hands. You didn't think of anything, apart for your personal whims, not about anything other than yourself. You only thought about how to present yourselves as heroes. So it turned out beautifully.'

'Wait Alyosha . . .but what is beautiful indeed. . .'

'Quiet! Exactly that is beautiful! Beautiful but with flaws! Heroism with cowardice in necessary proportions, pseudo-honesty, her Mother! You decided that's as they gage you so to survive . . .and if you crawled away then later, although the grass didn't grow. Anything is possible! It's possible to cure your nervous wounds with any abilities! it's possible to lie, lissssten, you all have indeed a mania! You can't say a word without lying. you're simply psychos. But we, your unhappy descendants, psycho descendants! . . .'

'Yes, it's our fault,' she pronounced obviously 'we are very guilty, but how to exist with it?' She dragged the time obviously, holding her voice under the necessary cello strings: in continuous calm 'I think it's necessary to forgive . . .simply be stronger and more sufficient and forgive . . .'

'You couldn't explain to me anyway, thanks to what . . .why did it attract you so there?' Here it was as if he had given in. He asked so deceitfully and tenderly. Exuding false sincerity 'I wanted to ask for so long.'

'I can't understand you,' she answered also obviously.

'Not to understand you, no . . .'

'And why are you asking then?'

He wanted to answer, but didn't succeed; she suddenly spoke up, at once changing the tone, kindly and quickly: 'You don't understand, don't understand, meaningless one, there is what is most interesting, the most freezing. There! Exactly freezing! This is such a magnet . . .everything on the planet has a meaning, I'm a chemist, there was a time when I saw the link between things, substances. But there, she isn't there! That war, the second, the third . . .when the troops called, I . . .me . . . I have such a . . .wait! (Aha, she has reached for cigarettes) there is no sense!. Well I had . . . I didn't decide to leave at once, nevertheless I was already . . .how much? Well not little, not a reporter's age. I mainly simply chatted with them, with the first returned ones. And it flooded directly with this spit: a turntable. AKM, mamani, mamani, AKM . . .I told them 'yes you wait to sing, let's talk,' but no. I interviewed thirty people, but no. No and no. I must say, and I was a fool of course, all to the heart of it and so on. Then I decided to leave. I thought: there's the meaning. He was in it and not in that.'

'But, so you're for meaning! He was hellishly surprised 'and for the smell of the Taiga! Under the rumble of Russian drums! The bullets dum dum and tsepelin!'

(He was not allowed to explain anything. She is twenty or twenty one, she goes across a wet forest and drags her body, wet, heavy, disgusting. Drunk. The body is trying to sing, pulls a thin voice 'Little Luchina.' It spews vile words. It lets her spit at the gymnast. It seizes her helplessly by the sleeves, she wrinkles, compresses the teeth: heavy, scum, and around the heavy April, such a twilight, oh brothers. Fleur! Fleur! What to do, what is going on; only just well, still in March, he looked with his own eyes, some poetry, one was, the second, and there please, if you want to be happy: Little Luchina, Little Luchina! Dragging him to vomit in multi-coloured glades, she would discard him to others, there who is so, who is a corpse and who tries to sit. One on the log, our man on the airwaves, scratched mug, the tuft of hair ripped out, he caught the mouse, clutched in his fist, the unhappy mouse clogged clogged and froze. The man on the airwaves brings his fist to his nose and whispers to the mouse through a hiccup: do you hear, apodemis uralensis! I'm of victory! . . . of the matter! He unclenches his fist and holding the other hand, holds the mouse by the hind paw on the scales, it wriggles, tries to bite the torturer by the finger. 'I will do you want tear off your paw? I will tea . . . ar off your paw!' She comes closer and says 'Enough! Enough, well!' The man on the airwaves focuses with difficulty on her glance, winks and tries to take her to the side. And she, breathing deeply, hits backhand, it falls not on the cheek, but evenly on the nose: the guy on the airwaves, losing his cool, didn't sit so strongly, falls from the little branch from above with his little brakes and cries from pain: he has a painful shoulder. The mouse, flying off, flops into the puddle and from there headlong, once and he is no more. And she understands that life is over but instead of it the victory has begun, and from now on they will get drunk and tear the paws off mice, and that . . .)

'Call it as you want,' she said angrily. 'I'm trying to explain to you, but instead of that . . .well pick an argument, pick an argument, if it itches.'

'Forgive,' he repented. Temporarily. The kettle whistled, he lowered the flame. 'I . . . to put it briefly, carry on.'

'Well I've decided . . .well let this be funny, yes, but I thought: what if I suddenly understand something? But what if there is some aim there? (There was such coquettishness, such lies, but what could she do? She certainly couldn't tell him the truth, why she called it here, and named it here for one thing only: to understand, but there, in this war, whether it's there, yes what to say, all the same no one will understand. We'll continue then our beautiful version). There is another people, other nerves, another structure of blood, who could come to terms with it, as if no one, yes, but suddenly if someone could, suddenly some one needs us for some reason . . .

'Us!' he interrupted voluptuously, only he was waiting for that 'us! Oy you're my close one, my golden one! Us! Under the sound of the Russian drums, you think . . .your Mother, but . . .what indeed are you saying, what are you bringing . . .(she tried to argue something, she tried, but where to there.) It tried to taste the meanings of you, to touch life! It happened! To touch the Dushmans, explore villages . . .And drugs, but how indeed, drugs! Conquerers . . .developers . . .bastards . . .(again it blows, well cunt, well what indeed is it, well there were indeed such words, and must be the words. Well to where there). A passionate Tsitsianov!

He threw the receiver out the window. The twilight poured into the room, the bulb rattled in the cartridge, the kettle went into hysterics. Ten-nine-eight-seven. You're an ass hole yourself, who are you proving it to? Climbed on the shelf: there there was an old telephone, a disc one.

As if there wasn't anything:

'Listen, what did you tell me there yesterday about Cincinatti? I didn't get lazy, I took it out and read it, you know. I solved you! Your secret, As if you're speaking evenly there.'

'Me.'

'Yes, yes, yes! You're so even there, all with such a little pun, some rhythms . . .or what do you call it, when the words are the similar, shorten it, shortener . . .a secreter . . .the federation, Efferalgan. . .or what was there . . .'

'Listen, but that is simply laughable!' He was outraged 'this is how you talk, this is your being . . .'

'Yes God be with you, where would you be from? I'm from the old school, where to take me. But you, yes I noticed. At once there I began to read and I found out, it's all yours. Such there is an allegory, all this is a joke, all with rhymes. And I understood your parcel to me, you didn't camouflage it slyly. About Cincinatti. The invitation is to an execution, what indeed is there here not to understand. I invite you to the execution! Very gracefully. Because you're a coward. One time I said: I want to kill but where are you? Well go on! Come! Find out the address! Enjoy! Break the lock! Have your court! No! you're not coming. It struck you only once speaking directly, but next you run up hastily. How did you say it, a mercantile awareness, reptilish? Slender. How is this all about you! Reptilish coward! Ah how you have broken us! Ah how you have brought us to a sacrifice. Yes the devil would take you. There are no innocent sacrifices, you are your own procurator. And all your little songs, about the train, there it played this with you! Self gratification! The nurturing of your cowardice, no more than that. You will talk with your own teeth, because you are, oh, not a fool! Because as soon as you shut up even for a minute, you will yourself understand; click on an era to blame, if your mug is crooked. But yours is crooked. (Just here you don't say anything, it has fallen to the ground. It didn't hold on. It was shameful and all was not what it seemed, but there was not enough strength any more. He was ashamed of her, ashamed, all these days, he mocked, she took everything humbly, she repented, but how much is possible! The strength came, already tormenting me enough, we are alone or what, guilty for you and . . .) There are no guilty ones for you, my dear! But if you're worthless, that . . .(it unexpectedly crashed somewhere in her room and the shattered glass began to clatter) but wait up . . .(a pause) . . .To hell! To hell! The window is broken . . .'

'How is it broken?' he asked. 'you're on what floor?'

'On the second,' she answered nervously 'oj the second they are not putting in the gratings any more.'

'Well there, you will be busy with something. For the meantime!' (It was time to end this farce with the calls, time, time. These daily conversations already filled his throat. Himself an ass hole, he was forced to own up but nothing came from me that came from anything, the terrorist didn't come out of the telephone. That's it, it's good that the fool is wearisome.)

(It happened that on the same day that I came to Nadya, we had agreed that I would bring her a fresh edition of her magazine. 'I had wanted to change you,' Nadya angrily said to me. Letting me into the flat; a draught, Nadya didn't hold the door, and it slammed with a noise, we both shuddered, 'yes . . . I wanted to change it, but I didn't succeed. I have here an emergency. . .' the devil created something in the room; splinters along every floor, the wind is walking, it dispersed some little papers on the table, a football. I was dumbfounded. 'Little boys!' Nadya angrily explained the same. 'Just like in the films: little boys played football in the yard. They found there an idiot of remarkable strength . . .they are not putting up the grating on the second floor. The first time I have such here . . .but I'm not throwing them back the ball, let them not hope. So they have angered me, well what is it? You have to have some reason. Let us go to the kitchen, here it's impossible . . .yes, they are coming, they are coming, I already called them. But you don't understand when they are coming, wait during the day, yes they still tear through money out of urgency, for what in this very day . . .so well sit, I don't need anything here and so it's cramped, I'm now everything . . .' she went around the kitchen, knocked the cups, everything scattered from her hands 'sit there on the couch. Where is the business of the coffee grinder, my Goooood, well what is it?'

. . .that wasn't with her, that wasn't. She finally reached for a spoon, she pinched her hand by the box, she winced, sat on the stool, threw back her head, shut her eyes. 'What's with the day today, a? And well he isn't ringing, you think. But I'll ring, he isn't picking up the phone. He hasn't picked it up for four hours. Why?'

So I found everything out too.)

Gunnar's letter to Michelle

4th August 1985

Mishka my dear!

I've missed you terribly, there is no strength. The devil guessed to release you in this idiotic holiday! Only pampering and stupidity. No more separate holidays and generally I'm not letting you away from me any more. You there I suppose are conducting yourself pigly and conducting chickens all around, you're not looking after yourself, you've forgotten about me, and you've forgotten the children. Outrageous! Zhenka is also to me like wind in the head! I'm coming by and by, the old threatening husband. Cut out the faire la cour, don't touch the chicken, don't be angry with me.

Seriously Mishka, I've despaired terribly. I hope very much that you're resting there properly, sun bathing and over eating. A person rang wearisomely yesterday along the international city, rang, rang, so he didn't connect I thought, suddenly one of yours? Just in case today I hurried to ring, the first time they connected me, it seemed no, it wasn't them yesterday, they are all amazing, your Mummy is healthy, sends you greetings, it it hot in Paris, they are preparing their whole family to go to the north to rest.

It is as if nothing is going on with the little boys, they both swear they will write to you. I played chess with Dimka on Sunday, both times with hellish pressure it was a draw and seven days of rain. It grew on my head!

And generally I'm working a lot, ha ha. There you're surprised probably? But now, my dearest one, who to curse at all for my working nights now? You're not around! My little sister is lecturing me on morals, but boringly she doesn't have enough of your enthusiasm. But recently I've also understood, that what I took hold of, I woke up naturally at 11 in the morning on the stage on a folding bed! The head buzzes, Kliment Effemich walks around, important and sad, nibbles at the splinters. Our workers sleep in the audience hall, having sat previously on the armchair covered with newspapers! This we thought up on the eve one little piece and installed something . . .I wanted to tell you that, a wonderful success happened to me there. One lad works for us, he a looong time has summoned my interest. They are nervous of him in our place, he's as gloomy as the devil, not that he is unfriendly, o no! Simply at other distances, where there are no categories; friendliness and greetingness. All sorts of legends are going about him, that he is mad, that he hit someone . . . or killed, that he is a bandit or an Afghan. I don't know anything about him, but I don't believe that rubbish! Bogatyr settlements, all the heavy work, which we usually both do, he does on his own. He can't tolerate partners. A huge lad, black, shaggy, such a jaw. Oho. Somehow even handsome! You would like him. Definite, accurate, he does it in the time limit, not once did he disappoint. But listen further, as work is ready and they begin the rehearsal, he sits in the corner, he attracts the devil somehow, but he reads. I checked, Viyon in the original. How do you like such a turn around, my dear? I already thought whether he is your compatriot, but you don't understand he has clean pronunciation.

And there it means, what am I to all of this. . .this wearisome idea entered my head, I needed a fountain on the stage. But there I can't, I can't sleep, can't eat, I have already thought of all, seen, presented, like Kliment Effemich picturing a drunkard, it will jump out from here with mangy feathers, still there it complicates matters somewhat unnecessarily, in short beauty! And what do you think? I have everything in one voice, no one is building a fountain on the stage. You need a specialist! Where to get it? Yes how much will he cost? Well, the boring person went! I was upset, and it's a pity to spit! It's a pity to spit, what an idea! And here this our Alyosha rises, Alenka's little flower, and says this through the teeth. I will make a fountain for you on the stage, for free.

That is how?! But how!

And what do you think? He did it.

How, I say, are you creating this? He grins; I, he says, am self-taught, from childhood I have been keen on architecture, and this and that . . .and hydro-technics there is easy . . .I pressed him here; let him show what he draws there on the sly. He rested, no he says and that's it. There he shut himself back, unwound and left. Then, what do you think, on the next day while he hung under the cupola and mounted the trapeze, I reached for his little papers. I took it directly and started to climb, I sense that this isn't a simple boy! I look, all is sketches, sketches, and the mugs are occasional, but so good! Great mugs, with character! With similarity! Somewhere suddenly, the flower, so light and so he feels the flower . . .Mishka, I declare to you responsibly, this is a talented boy. Very. A rarity. But why so fierce? Why didn't he go to study, on what great talent? Riddle, just riddles. And the making of them, how to approach him, well he kills, not winces.

I'm not going to give up so easily! I have already understood, that he keeps himself apart from me so simply. He'll be with me also as a hydro-technic and a decorator and a pyrotechnic, and a landscaper, and generally Leonardo in his Milan period, when he worked under the patronage of Ludovico Sforza (Sforza, this I must understand.)

The next day I went up to him and asked him to build on stage a wooden hut . . . certainly for nothing do I love superfluity on stage, but here there is such a business . . . I thought up even under this hut a few preparations . . .with Kliment Efremich and a few cats and a good number upstairs, as if it would be on the shelf. He, this Alyosha, stared at me: they say, why did all of you dream this up? I make an impassive mug and say: I ask you to carry out my request, but you've already decided that you don't want to build it.

He made the decorations excellently. Mish, I'm telling you, luxuriously simply, there it is, personally, we arranged late there and I rehearsed a little, it was already night . . .I couldn't hold on, everything had happened very well. And later also I napped on the folding bed and awoke all worried. I'm deliberately telling you, my close one, in order that you began to give out and curse, I miss you so Mishka if only you knew.

I filled up a lot of pages of some rubbish. In actual fact, I already wait and wait up for you to talk, to tell you everything, that I have thought up . . .I keep for you a few good little books and little magazines. Your pupils irrepressibly broke the telephone, for nothing is it the holidays! And still the director of studies from school rang, about the timetable for the coming year, but it isn't urgent. I asked her not to put you on the first lessons! But I saw your director at the bus stop with a string bag of shrimps. We bowed to each other. Nevertheless she has seven chins and don't argue even I counted them. This rubbish

I write! And all because it's hard to say goodbye, Mishenka. My happiness. My happiness How I'm waiting for you.

Your Gunnar

Michelle's letter to her nearest and dearest

14th March 2007 (In French)

My darlings, dear Gi, Lizochka and Sandra! Don't worry about me. Do you understand, Gunnar's strength seemed more than his life. It's difficult for me to explain. A year has gone by already and even more after his death. Of course, I cry. Of course, it's very difficult without him. Of course I can't pull myself together and I walk since about our house and around his things and I'm always waiting, that he rings now and shouts down the receiver as usual: warm up sooner, I'm coming, we are all coming famished and he comes and brings with him ten people and they will tell me how the presentation went today. Yes I feel all the time, as if he's on a working trip and so indeed all recalls me terribly, that he is no more. What am I to do in the New Year noise with this inner rhythm . . .(this phrase in Russian) and next, all the time I repeat myself. But not once have I said, that I don't want to live any more. The business isn't in that, that the children, the Grandchildren, the family, students and the feeling of duty ahead of them . . .This is only his merit. He infected me terribly with his ease. Now even my grief doesn't break in two, Gunnar poured in my blood some strong antidote against him. I would be happy to despair, but the memory of him doesn't allow it. I see this in my boys.

I'm getting ready to go to Paris in the autumn, on holidays, it won't happen earlier. Perhaps, I will take the young ones, if Dima and Alyona don't mind. How I would have been happy if you had also come! Perhaps if you all can't, so Sandra can even come on her own? I haven't seen you for a long time, my dear girl! Perhaps you will take a break from your studies? Seryozha, on the other hand, can totally, he comes soon in your area, he is getting ready first to go to Madrid for a couple of days and then he and his friends plan to go to Barcelona. Well, this he will write to you himself, Sandra, he wanted very much to meet. But there I wanted to tell you; in a week you will open an exhibition, to which I recommend very much that you go. This student of Gunnar's, is a wonderful decorator. Gunnar 'opened' him, they got acquainted a hundred years ago, when this boy had only just returned from the army, totally unhappy, he was working on the stage in the circus, but Gunnar saw in him a huge talent, and now there he is a well known theatre and circus artist. Come, my dear, come all together, he has indeed very strong work.

I dream of seeing you. If you can't come already to Paris, then whatever happens I will try to come to you at New Year. There are already other holidays starting.

I kiss you strongly strongly

Your darling sister and Aunt.

Alyosha Barcelona 2007

It poured in Barcelona, for the fifth day it poured. We were forcing our way to the exhibition in the first days, as since, Motya glistened, all of it wasn't in vain for him, not in vain, not in vain, and release all, everything hurts and he returns to the circles, you will see there, Alyosha only expressed annoyance. He hid Sandra from everyone carefully, Motya, of course, knew everything, but he didn't let on: he wants conspiracy, but would not carry on. On the fifth day of rain Alyosha announced himself in the morning, found the soaked Motya who had only just escorted his son to the kindergarden and now with pleasure warmed himself with tea, demanded tea also for himself and asked poignantly: well are you going to be quiet like that? Motya very calmly said; that I will. And nothing interests you, you don't want to ask anything? I don't want anything . . ? Motya answered carefully. 'What I need I see and am satisfied . . .will I give you bread? 'You think, what indifference! But a long time it seems . . ? 'What?' 'Are you so delicate for so long? As if he never differed. . . (this was piggery). If he didn't differ indeed,' Motya threaded slowly through his tea, 'I ask for forgiveness, I was not right. Although to say honestly I don't know why you pay me occasional visits. . ? Alyosha thoughtfully plastered his toast with butter, plastered plastered, brought even layers, then suddenly with the end of the knife he drew Motya's profile in the butter. 'Do you know what? He said suddenly with a human voice. 'Do you know what Mot? Invite me and her to visit.

The mathematician sat so.

I shouldn't have been this. Maybe not in this matter.

It was a wonderful evening. Laura, Motya's wife, she could do this. Without candles and deafening music and the other labuda, without buffet confusion. They simply sat in the big dining room, having thrown open the balcony doors in the armchairs behind a low table, Alyosha with wonder recognised a couple or three of Mum's and Aunts' favourite dishes, either mathematician wised up to Laura or she herself guessed something. Some drank vodka, some white wine, they blathered lazily, kindly; the dog slowly walked around the couches, the elder girls spent time on the young one, Laura didn't pay them any attention, absorbed conversation, the mathematician sat down, throwing himself onto the armchair and squinted peacefully at the light of the floor lamp, Latifah began to passionately admire some picture of Alyosha's on the wall, yes and on the whole, a talent! Strength! My sudden Russian friend and at once a genius! but her ecstasy so much didn't coincide with the general quiet and kind soulness, that she herself somehow understood all at once, calmed down, softened and turned into an impatient conversation. In the general rhythm of laziness Dietmar went around in self circles, the German director, Alyosha somehow once formed his spectacle 'Emilia Galotti', that was a rare occurrence when he was almost satisfied without reservations and part of your work came to the exhibition in Barcelona. Motka's classmate Tikhonov, remembering Alyosha from Moscow, sat in the corner, smiled quietly and stroked the dog: there it somehow came out, but; the lad had such a tragic fate and some turns, yes and he himself, Tikhonov finished Mehmat, here and there and there already a professor's place in a small Catalan town and it was possible to meet his friends as if nothing had happened in Barcelona, and such wonderful friends! Sandra chewed the cookie monster and quietly exchanged remarks with the mathematician about something, then they summoned her to the experts, something they didn't share about Latin quotes, and she smiling, judged the argument; and speaking further of this argument about her uncertainty, she put her hand on Alyosha's forearm, and there it started again. Everything was fine. Everything was very good. Everything was so good that he couldn't present it any better.

If the devil is on me, this is me, that I will come to terms. But the devil is the devil, I'm worried, don't equal me, I haven't got enough of the imagination for all this eclectic heresy, that it exasperates me. Let the yellow haze be mine. But this castle is a baroque wailing, these Gothic sandy spires, these antique little gargoyles, hurling sound bites at me on the surface of blood-stained kidneys, oh no it's not me. This is my devil. In one word I ask for an exact and hard answer, perhaps the person, which was a pile of rags, be normal, in whole and completely normal? All thought to go mad, so hoped, but he couldn't. Or?

It poured and poured, he got up and went out onto the balcony 'Alyosh, it's so wet!' shouted Laura. So he was the devil or what? Was he? He didn't become an alcoholic because of me, didn't become an addict, but that psycho it seems . . .loved life on the brink, so it was comfortable, so it lay in his heart well, well and about some talent and dust in her eyes, it works particularly gloriously; they say he is a wonderful artist, but only, you know with a strangeness, well and not wisely . . .

He returned to the room and shutting out the general noise, proclaimed: 'Lorochka, get the tea perhaps?' Laura started and was boiling, a kind of bustle started around dirty dishes, the nephew, escaping the captivity of his elder sisters, creeped up to him, got up on his knees and pulled demandingly by his trousers. Taking hold of his hands, Alyosha went passed the dining room, humming something and threw a glance at his picture on the wall . . .the same, which Latifah began to foolishly admire . . .this picture . . .

He had only just return from the war and Motka blew dust from him as he could, and he endured a lot. In a moment, wishing to bring Alyosha to the feeling, brutalising from his antics, he screamed; well draw now! Poignantly and sweetly smiling Alyosha took the ball point pen and pages, for ten minutes he sketched the hellish picture, a terrorist holds the woman, hugging from behind by the neck, putting a pistol to her temples, at that very moment a couple still aim at him. The devil would take him, Alyosha: clean nonsense and speculation, but how he drew, the scum bag, what faces the four of them had, what despair, passion, hatred, how the Adam's Apple went at the terrorist, who understands that with the second shot everything finishes, all this ball point pen for ten minutes!

Motya with clarity tore the drawing in scraps: 'You're a real vulgar one! You've despaired me with your terror!' then he regretted terribly, but Alyosha picked an argument over him ('you've missed mathematician, you destroyed the work with your own hands!') But well here draw something good! Draw a still life! But he threw it in his jar with gouache, as now he remembers: drops on both of them remained.

And then Alyosha threw about these little Dutch people on a little sketch: the table, an open fresh table cloth, a carafe with pomegranate juice, lemon on the little plate, and sandpaper spiral hangs from the table, but from the side, a skeleton with Motya's mug sits at the table, with one hand he hangs his sad head, with the other picks half a washed pomegranate. And the signature, nature-Motya . . .Motya thought, to be nasty or to laugh, he couldn't hold on, he neighed and collected the picture for himself.

It wasn't done badly, although he didn't have a completely sure hand then and a certain proportion was ruined, but this too healthy skeletal gentleness, clinging to the pomegranate, even well, if you please, it looks, intentionally. Yes he never dreamt of being an artist, so everything is post-modern, the little toys . . .what is it so with me, who can explain it to me?

But they somehow argued so about him there, it was a stupid conversation, the funniest, and there about this picture, by the way indeed . . .

'There is no possibility to endure in our time! There this jokishness more simple, but the truth indeed, it's possible, this Laura, half-turned, from the kitchen, cutting the cake, having lifted the knife towards the ceiling, didn't spread jam, 'well there, in that there is a meaning,' sang Dietmar 'what decoration! Peripheral! And through that all the strength! It's difficult for me to say it in Russian!' 'Yes yes the decorator,' the mathematician came in 'he is fulfilling his order. It would seem, formally, he is free from his own will, but it's all of course an illusion.' The conversation again went to the Russian jungle, Sandra hastily translated some with flapping eyes to Latifah, that one interrupted. 'My friends!' It was already well loaded with white 'what are we talking about generally! Here is an example! There is no decoration! Chic! How it's done my dears! What plastic! Such pain! Irony! Bitterness!'

The jokishness is simpler, oh . . .a curiosity . . .

'I think,' Sandra said quietly, 'that an artist always carries his own personal truth. Fiction . . .' she picked the word 'refraction of reality . . .from it it's not allowed to demand the truth, reliability . . .'

There is the idiot.

The evening sank smoothly until full darkness, they lit the light, chased the children to bed, Latifah aimed at Dietmar and was planning a separate proposition; Tikhonov grabbed some shut eye with the dog heating himself under the floor lamp. All began to subtly separate to their homes.

They went on to the street and wandered. The rain stopped suddenly, the wet Ramblas, all in street lamps and sticky sweets, exuded stupid happiness, all around laughed and pushed, the green-faced woman with the beak and powdered wig pulled from her bag an endless garland of false asters, the clockwork taxis came with a bark. And yes, there was a farce, the vagabond circus. The acrobats were out on the rampage, an equilibrist lounged around on the ground and with his legs knocked a barrel of beer, the Lilliput fire-breather devoured the Bengal fire with his eyes, and a full enough gentleman in a cylinder loudly broadcast something crackling, people around laughed loudly 'lets go!' Sandra pulled him away, but he remained standing out of spite and looked with easy contempt; all this was not even possible to compare with Gunnar's circus. 'Alyosha, we'll go!' And he remained standing and standing, and he waited; at first the break started to shout from afar, for that reason the laughing crowd parted and let in the demonic car driver, a colourful parrot. The car driver, wobbling with the wheels on the turns, dashingly drove off to the square and stopped; the hatch suddenly opened in the yellow roof and from there a shout of salud! The clown thrust himself forward around the waist, so spreading, red-haired, with the most usual nose, In his hand a whistle.

At that moment Alyosha catches her eye. All would be nothing, if it would not be her glance, momentarily her glance at him, full terror and sympathy. All would be nothing, if it were not her glance. And there you mustn't look at me so, girl. You mustn't look at me so.

Well generally he was already ready.

Farewell, my lovely. My wonder.

And there he left for ever, simply escorted her to the home and left for good.

Nadya, Alyosha Moscow 2007

Nadya rang on her own birthday, with a somewhat dry voice, very quickly and nervy, he even took fright.

'Hello can you speak?

'I will go in an hour, but for the meantime I can . . .' he pronounced carefully, wondering along the way, is it worth him congratulating, he knew about her birthday and he even had a certain plan and agreement, is it worth it early? Not to congratulate at the first moment, and it seems, for the better, she was very on edge.

'An hour is totally enough for me. Listen you were completely right. I mean when you rang me. And I don't have any pretence to you, I want you to know.'

'Nadya,' frowning, he began 'You and I are already twenty times . . .'

'Don't interrupt me, don't interrupt!' she was almost screaming, and this was completely unpleasant and even terrifying, what is it with her? It was always now terrifying because of her. 'Don't interrupt, I ask you, I beg! Let me say it, this is important! If you had the bravery then to ring me, have the bravery also to speak further.' This was clean stupidity and idiocy, but he was silent. 'So there. You blamed me in lies. You terrified me, you decided, that you can in such a way take revenge on me. Your will. But I want you to know. Let me be guilty in everything. I was lying all the time, I took fright indeed at the first trumpery danger, I didn't the days . . . I . . .' cough 'I was . . . such a loose idiot, soft bodied sub-fibral bitch I was . . .' he wanted to ask; are you composing again? But she bethought herself: 'Simply, I'm not saying that. I was a nervous idiot. You understand, there are such things in life, which will never leave you. Some single plot and all repeats itself and repeats itself and repeats itself and you think all, now I overcome it! Now I tackle it. This terrible delusion, it seems, well you know I'm still hoping.'

'Then how have I judged? My war, and that is how I wanted it. I come. And what? All isn't that. There isn't that feeling, I can't explain. I search, catch, not anywhere! Ok, I think. I'm a reporter, it's my job. I will examine. And here the story is almost not the first day. And who knew that this would happen to me? Tell me, I was not alone there. Well ok for you, but because Rahim too, and this, how do you call it, well a journalist! Well such, the cape with a strap, I don't remember.

And because nobody, nobody . .. But understandably here is stress, but really could I wait for such from you? What I so shamefully chicken out so monstrously . . .'

(Yes, it's true, she had such a strange reaction, disproportionate, and all right Rahim, and this memory the stooge journalist hung on better, he even didn't manage to take fright really, everything happened so quickly; but she, not everything was all right for her, so she was, she demanded this helicopter herself quickly, now even . . .) He doesn't begin to say any of this to her, of course.

'And what am I to do, tell me? I came back and didn't day anything to anyone. I didn't announce myself in the publishing house, yes what there (why?). I didn't ring my brother, I didn't ring Kirovsky, no one anywhere . . .They thought all the time, that I'm still there. I didn't generally leave the house for two months to go anywhere, I sat at the table, I buried my forehead against the window and sit. I didn't do anything, in truth, there I watched the news, listened to the radio. And so I sit and sit . . .And do you know, I think of something. But two months have gone by, I ring the main editor; I have returned. O, he says, great, but so what?! Well how?! I will write. Well we are waiting, we are waiting!

They gave so much time. All the conditions. They proposed to change the machine, although the old one printed prettily. Generally, the regime is favoured. I spend another two weeks with my forehead to the window, I told my own to everyone, that all is in work and so that they don't touch. But after two weeks I sat and began to write, all as it is. (Alyosha couldn't contain himself and obviously too noisily drew breath, because she pounced on it there.) Yes, yes I know what you want to say! I'm about something else! I started to write things as they are, about this hopeless badness, about the bosses, about the conditions in which we lived! I wrote about the terrorists, so that everyone knew, how the Soviet leadership acts for its own . . . how it spits at us, how it takes us for scum bags, even worse than scum bags! Understand! What do you say, it's not true?! Because it's true?! And I wrote . . . I had one aim, one salvation, I knew that they were not publishing. In 83' in the yard, whether it's a joke! Also only that I hoped. I finished writing, took it off. Another three days with my forehead to the window, while they are reading it. What was it, a ring! The boss demanded I come urgently, but I had already heard on the telephone how he sizzles. I'm coming. He tears, shouts curses with a whisper, you have gone out of your mind! You were simply crazy, you overheated there! He called me a crazy chick, I listened . . .all right. We agreed that no one had seen my manuscript, no one had heard anything about it, but I as they say, continue to work on the book. He very well relates to me although he held on to the foolishness with ease, that is for sure. But he was so kind, with a conscience . . .

(Should he have asked her about a certain something? He didn't know. But she couldn't stop herself any more.)

Well and yes . . .time went by. You believe I generally didn't touch this manuscript. My own asked me everything. I tell them honestly; they didn't allow it to be published, I came up against conflict. I didn't give it to anyone to read. And later, in 90', he rings, my current main editor. The publishing house isn't breathing all right any more, but he laughed, he tried all the time to think of something. He rings, Nadya, you see yourself, what's happening, let us publish your book. Agree with your Mothers, perhaps, read over it once more, correct what you like, and give it. At first I said no. Categorically no. Then I think, seven years have gone by. Let people know the truth.

(And there he didn't hold on all the same. But in vain.)

'The truth, Nadya? Which truth?

A cough. A long pause.

'Wait, I will take a cigarette.' The oft clicking of the lighter, I'm clearly idle. 'I will say to you, which truth. Yes I was a fool.'

And my God she begins to talk sparkly and her tongue falters a little and the words don't come out distinctly, but he is a fool he doesn't hold on and because he wants indeed to pacify her somehow and doesn't like her getting nervous, but doesn't hold on, o the idiot, softly, tenderly he interrupts:

'I understand you. You sought a fleur but you came and saw a black slaughterhouse . . .'

'Fleur?! Sighing, she questions 'you're daring me about fleur? You know what they did with us? You dare to compare!' And not holding on, she screams helplessly: 'The order 'not a step backwards,' maybe you heard it sometime?!'

And choking with a scream, she despairingly cries and puts down the receiver. Crying, she delays for the last time and stubs out, breaking off an unfinished cigarette. Crying she sits, shutting her face with her palms, she listens as the telephone peels; crying she goes to the cloak room, takes a hanger with trousers and a sweater; crying, she goes to the bathroom, washes, gets dressed, strokes her dishevelled hair. Crying, she returns to the room and, already calming down, she lights up and smokes three deep puffs. It's time: without the fourth, but she has to go in half an hour, forty minutes. She takes her bag, checks for the keys, checks the gas and water, puts on her shoes; on the street, they said, it's plus eighteen, but in the evening it will be colder, she throws on her coat and, not paying attention to the telephone noise, she turns off the light, leaves the flat and slams the door after her.

The photograph, always, as much as I remember stood in the wardrobe in Kirovsky, behind glass, simply so, without a frame. In it is Alya and Mitya. Mitya stands, akimbo, one hand is hugging Alya, happy, a glance straight at the photograph , have I seen such? No, have you seen it?! Alya happened to be a little in the shade, its harder to see her, she's in profile, looks at Mitya, she looks maliciously, raising her eyebrows; she's hardly breathing from tenderness. The photograph isn't framed, it's always standing in one and the same place on the bookshelf, behind the glass. Up from it on the glass with a diamond is cut a little letter hybrid M, which has the right little half crossed with a horizontal dash. The photograph always stood just in this place, when you wipe the dust, they always follow that to then put it back under the monogram.

In the celebration of Nadya's 85th people gathered, well I don't know thirty? Somehow it didn't enter my head to count. We were late, therefore we didn't see the preparations for the surprise, how they laid out the table and they dragged from the kitchen an additional one, as Dima, worrying terribly, seated everyone, ('Uncle Vitya, go further, you're very tall . . .the children at the little table . . .oh my God, where is mother! Sergei, ring her, please!'), as Gelena for the last time wiped the silver forks, but Alya gave out that the table cloth was stained, as Gelik prepared his speech, as they tried to get rid of the dogs to another room and he sobbed bitterly there, as Michelle arrived with a huge fire-breathing quiche, only from the oven! as she rushed to open the door, when already as if everyone had gathered: 'That is for me! My niece! I also called her,' as all sat, having concealed the breath, they waited for the appearance of the person whose name day it is. We didn't see the the most important, Nadya's desperate delightful surprise: she's already step by step coming to, there she already realised all the beauty of the drawing, there she already looked at everyone, ahhed and over kissed everyone, laughed, nearly cried but resisted, calmed herself down, and here a ring at the door, 'What, still more guests?!' And Dima, following the persuasion, says to her Nad it's certainly for you, open it yourself already! She smiles at his cheek and runs to the kitchen, there entrance door, she opens it and asks surprisingly and happily: 'Are you for me? If you let me in,' tenderly answers Alyosha. 'You let me in . . .to hell, I don't understand, are we at the familiar you or the formal you . . .happy birthday, Nadya.'

The toasts were ceasing, and no one else was singing. They were ringing with tea spoons and they rustled sweet wrappers. Everyone was tired. We were all tired from coincidences, from hassle, from expectations and from all thwarted expectations of events. Let to a terribly exhausting happy ending. But for some reason it seems to me, that that is correct . . .That all is correct.

('I was terribly angry at myself, when I thought of all this. Yes, it was intolerable to look at Nadya and I felt though that to dream something up, and yes, Nadya helped me so many times, all of us, threw herself on help, selflessly. . . generally to poke my nose into strange business stuck in my throat so much, and I was very angry at myself, when slyly wrote Alyosha's number for Nadya, when I advised her close ones. Dima of course objected. ('Yes we're all worried and don't want to see anything. But we must see! . . .) But Seryozha supported me. Michelle said: Dad would have definitely been for . . I got terribly angry at myself, when I rang Alyosha all the same, when I begged him to meet me, when this meeting happened. Yes and at the time of the meeting . . so my demiurges got on my nerves, but annoyingly arrogant, but in any case he didn't understand why I came. Putting it shortly, I cursed all on this earth for this half hour. But all the same, for some reason it seems to me that it's correct.)

I slyly get up from the table, I go out to the dark front room and along the winding little corridor I sneak into Alya and Vitya's room. Aunt Alya and Uncle Vitya, as I called them all my life. There they always smoked. The long couch, at the corner Viktor and Gelik always sat. The vanity with two little caskets, the brush and the flakon of perfume. In front of the vanity always sits Nadya firstly, not yet lighting up, grabbing some one else's comb and stroking her hair: she was always that dishevelled. The others sit anywhere and smoke smoke. . .now the room is empty, the air in it is bluish, for nothing that at this moment no one is smoking and the vent is closed. On the side chest beside are Vitya's glasses in a gold frame. In the armchair where usually Alya is, sleeps a red cat. On the shelf nearby are photographs; there all the company in 1960 something in the Pushkin Hills, there the Grandchildren together, the youngest in a wrapping cloth lies on the table, only just from the maternity hospital, the oldest is six years, hanging over the basket, propped his cheeks by his fists and looks at the camera with sly eyes, there is Zhenya . . .very nice . . .on the table lies a pile of letters in a dull celophane packet, this is for me. Gelina told me: I put them there for you, take them.

I sit on the couch, bury my nose in its back and breathe deeply deeply, yet as deep as I can. What does it smell of, not only nicotine, almost burned sugar, almost Stearin. Well what, I take this pile of old old letters. Let them be here in the form of an epilogue.

Translator's notes
about Anna Nemzer and her
book, her style, the Russian
vernacular and why to read it

At first glance upon picking up the novel 'Prisoner' we see a tale about war and the trials and tribulations that conflict can visit not just on the people who take part in it but also on their families and friends who are left behind at home. War is portrayed as being harsh and unforgiving, led by people who are themselves harsh and unforgiving.

On further and more detailed perusal of the book, we see that the characters are not just prisoners in a war zone or just captives of the consequences that war brings, but are captives of the Communist Gulag system, and of the totalitarian regime under Josef Stalin and are confined by race and circumstance as they attempt to build their lives in an invisible straight jacket.

It is because of Anna Nemzer's journalistic background that she is very inquisitive about the world around her and that she is interested in the way that people live. The heroes of the story, a group of friends and acquaintances, are put under a metaphorical microscope and we examine how they react to life's challenges and how they cope with obstacles put in their way.

Notable in the style that Anna Nemzer uses in her book, 'Prisoner,' is her use of repetition as a means of getting her point across. When the attention in the story turns to the action in Afghanistan she repeats the words 'that day' a few times and at the end of the sentence amalgamates them into one word: 'thatday.'

A lot of authors use repetition it to stress their point and to hammer their idea home to the readers. In writing 'that day' so many times in the one paragraph Nemzer is emphasising the monotony of the situation in hand and intonating that it dragged on for the characters mercilessly and that it was a memorable day for them at least in its weariness.

Nemzer's story of 'Prisoner' is in many places very abstract in its composition and it leaves the reader to imagine for himself the situation at hand. She makes use of the abstract as a mode of writing in such a way as not to make the continuation of the plot too obvious to the readers. It is written in a very subtle style with a light touch.

For example, she refers to one of her characters as having hit on hard times and intimates that he was a down and out. She says of the character that he was a 'former pile of rags,' and she writes of how people reacted to him. This is done again with a light touch of her pen and in an off beat way of speaking.

Nemzer seems to write 'Prisoner' in a dual way. She writes her book in a manner that is lyrical and prosaic in places, but in other passages which are downright rough and coarse. She seems to be aiming the novel at readers who are attracted to well composed books but who might themselves not have a wide grasp of their own Russian language.

The book is littered, especially in the first part, with curse words or a lot of swearing. Sometimes the swear words that are used in the original Russian are not possible to translate literally into English. An example of this could be the word 'cunt' which is used far more widely in Russian than it is in the

English speaking world and is less offensive in Russia than it is elsewhere.

In my translation of the book, I have left the word in the original Russian sense rather than think up a different word to replace it. I did this in order to maintain the original aura of the Russian vernacular speech and so as not to lose the essence of the average down-to-earth Russian citizen, about whom Nemzer writes.

Why is Nemzer using curse words in the story you might ask? I think she is using such words as a way of saying that her characters are normal people, people who could have been plucked from any walk of life in any Russian flat complex and she is also appealing to readers from similar areas and backgrounds to read the story. This is a story of your average group of Russian friends.

'Prisoner' is not classical literature in the sense, style and manner of Dostoevsky's 'Crime and Punishment' or Tolstoy's 'War and Peace,' in the way that the author writes in a style which is vernacular and is the normal language of the streets, rather than in the style befitting the salons of the eighteenth century Russian Empire. The use of slang and dialect places the book on the bookshelves of not just average Russian readers but also in the living rooms of westerners who may not necessarily be Russophiles.

Jewish words and the Jewish identity as a whole are dealt with subtly in the book, but are written about as if by the way. Nemzer uses the word 'meshugena' in the book, which means *crazy*. Characters in the story are ostracised or left out of events and society because they are of Jewish origin, but the author refuses to indulge in pity or weeping and wailing, but takes a step back and allows the reader to decide how they feel.

The author deals with 'not a step backwards' rule of the Soviet army in a subtle way without being pathetic about it. The rule was in place in the military of the time to warn soldiers who may have been scared and thinking of running off from the rear and hiding that the would be shot if they did so. In actual fact, it just led to more carnage on the battle front because soldiers stayed in untenable positions, but Nemzer writes about the diktat in a light touch and without pathos and judgement.

Why would someone pick up the book? Immediately think of a westerner interested in modern Russians viewpoint on the past and the Soviet military.

The book is also very ground breaking in so far as it is a tale that is normally written by men aimed at the sole readership of men. The tale's importance lies very carefully in that the story of war and how it affects people can also touch very heavily on women and have a greater impact on the them than the men whom books about war are normally aimed at.

The word *prisoner* is not just to be taken as a prisoner in a war situation but also as a captive of a system and way of life, as a way of portraying the group of friends as being part of a system which did not allow freedom of speech or thought. It can be taken to mean that the friends were trapped in war, trapped in Soviet society and ultimately trapped in who they were as people.

'Prisoner' as a story may appeal to historians, amateur or professional, of the Soviet Union and people interested in how the ordinary people survived at the time of communism and in the aftermath of the fall of the system. It will attract readers keen on the Second World War and the Afghanistan War of the 1980s and will entice a readership which is used to the Western view of the Soviet Union and allow them a new perspective.

Nemzer writes about war and how it affects people in 'Prisoner,' but she treats the subject as if it were brutal and unromantic. She doesn't try to glorify the fact of the Soviet Union's ultimate victory in the second World War for example, but rather focuses on the carnage, on the uselessness and futility and the lives lost within the group of friends which make up the novel. The number of pals is depleted along the way, the commanding officers are foul mouthed and brutal, and the subordinates are treated with disdain.

Ronan Quinn

Glagoslav Publications Catalogue

- *The Time of Women* by Elena Chizhova
- *Sin* by Zakhar Prilepin
- *Hardly Ever Otherwise* by Maria Matios
- *Khatyn* by Ales Adamovich
- *Christened with Crosses* by Eduard Kochergin
- *The Vital Needs of the Dead* by Igor Sakhnovsky
- *A Poet and Bin Laden* by Hamid Ismailov
- *Kobzar* by Taras Shevchenko
- *White Shanghai* by Elvira Baryakina
- *The Stone Bridge* by Alexander Terekhov
- *King Stakh's Wild Hunt* by Uladzimir Karatkevich
- *Depeche Mode* by Serhii Zhadan
- *Herstories*, An Anthology of New Ukrainian Women Prose Writers
- *The Battle of the Sexes Russian Style* by Nadezhda Ptushkina
- *A Book Without Photographs* by Sergey Shargunov
- *Sankya* by Zakhar Prilepin
- *Wolf Messing – The True Story of Russia`s Greatest Psychic*
  by Tatiana Lungin
- *Good Stalin* by Victor Erofeyev
- *Solar Plexus* by Rustam Ibragimbekov
- *Don't Call me a Victim!* by Dina Yafasova
- *A History of Belarus* by Lubov Bazan
- *Children's Fashion of the Russian Empire* by Alexander Vasiliev
- *Empire of Corruption – The Russian National Pastime*
  by Vladimir Soloviev
- *Heroes of the 90s – People and Money. The Modern History of Russian Capitalism*
- *Boris Yeltsin – The Decade that Shook the World* by Boris Minaev
- *A Man Of Change – A study of the political life of Boris Yeltsin*
- *Gnedich* by Maria Rybakova
- *Marina Tsvetaeva – The Essential Poetry*
- *Multiple Personalities* by Tatyana Shcherbina
- *The Investigator* by Margarita Khemlin
- *Leo Tolstoy – Flight from paradise* by Pavel Basinsky
- *Moscow in the 1930* by Natalia Gromova

  More coming soon...